Omah

Copyright © 2019 by Randall Lane
All rights reserved. No part of this book may be reproduced, scanned, or distributed in any printed or electronic form without permission.
First Edition: July 2019
Printed in the United States of America

RANDALL LANE

Omah

by

Randall Lane

Omah

"But ask the animals, and they will teach you, or the birds in the sky, and they will tell you; or speak to the earth, and it will teach you, or let the fish in the sea inform you.
Which of all these does not know that the hand of the LORD has done this?
In his hand is the life of every creature and the breath of all mankind."

-JOB 12:7-10

"The hairy men among the Giant Cedars of old, are to be honored and feared, for they are not only charged with guarding us in our walk among the earth, but they take no issue in spreading the prideful among us as dried weed in a passing breeze. Stay humble and never challenge such authority."

-Kosumi Windburn
Elder of the Yurok Tribe

 OMAH

Foreword

This is a story that came to life while I had the privilege of visiting the beautiful country of Northern California back in the winter of 2016. I was completely awestruck at the beauty of the landscape. From the breathtaking forest of Redwoods and jagged mountains to the vast Pacific Ocean, Northern California truly is a special place. Not to mention, it is right in the center of Bigfoot Country. Having been a Bigfoot enthusiast for most of my life, I instantly felt right at home. The pictures you see are of the time I had there with my family. It was with my experience in Northern California that I was inspired to write my first story. I had never written anything before and simply dove off the deep end in hopes of learning to swim.

The original story titled, "The Legend of Omah", was just a simple short story written by a true beginner of the craft. Over the following years, I wrestled with the nudge to re-write the story and expand it into a full-length novel. It wasn't until February of 2019 that I began just that. For the next 10 weeks, I was up most every morning, seated at my desk no later than 6 *o'clock*, hammering away upon the keyboard. By the second week of April, I had the first draft of "Omah", complete. Which as of today, is my third novel among a half dozen or so short stories.

While the characters are mostly fictional, the towns are actual places you can visit in Northern California. With the chase scene in chapter eight being a true story that happened to my mother (Rhonda) and her friend in rural South Carolina during the 1970's. The scene that takes place in the beginning of chapter 31 is loosely based off what happened to my Mom's dad, her brother, and two neighbors, just weeks before her encounter.

I didn't want this to be another cheesy Sasquatch story filled with blood, guts, and people screaming aimlessly through the woods (though it does have its share of creepy scenes, just without all the gore). But I wanted it to be different. Different in a good way. In a way that I hope will deeply connect with the readers as they find themselves engrossed and drawn into the authenticity of the story and its characters. The story is not out to prove one way or another that bigfoot does or doesn't exist, it just simply asks the question...what if he does?

This a story about hope, family, nature, and our connection to the Earth and its Creator. One in which takes a moment to stop and gaze with wonder at the beauty set before us in nature's majestic display. With hopes of bringing about a new appreciation for nature, family, and all that makes life worth living. And it also goes to show, that you should never judge a book by its cover. No pun intended.

Told with real-life encounters and filled with Native American wisdom. This story has been an absolute blast to write and I am ecstatic to be able to finally share it with everyone!

—Randall Lane
June 25th, 2019

 Оман

1

The light died hours earlier as the darkness now creeps deeper into the night. A crescent moon peeks out behind wispy clouds. The air brisk and chill enough for breath to steam. Towering Redwoods continue their thousand-year journey to reach the heavens. They stand on each side of the meandering road which snakes around the hills and mountains like a river in the Amazon.

A light mist had begun to fall after a good rain. The strong and refreshing scent of leaves and earth filled the cab of the Ford pick-up truck. A low-lying fog crawls across the road which is narrower than most. A sharp decline to the left and the high rock wall on the right seemed to eat away at the asphalt the farther the truck continued down the mountain. With a tight grip and a balmy palm, the leather wheel cover was like trying to grip a wet bar of soap.

In the back of the black truck, under a blue tarp, lay two poached deer, which the brothers had taken while spot lighting on the way home from work. A long day with the logging crew could always be made better with a truck bed full of meat. Even though they'd both already reached their bag limits for the season, Travis and Dave Hodges never paid it much mind. They knew where the Wardens weren't, and they took full advantage of that fact.

The tires roared as they rubbed away their tread against the damp asphalt. The stereo struggled to find a signal as it skipped through most of a Brad Paisley song before Travis decided to shut it off.

His brother Dave checked his phone while riding shotgun.

"Huh...one bar. Figures," Dave said with a smirk.

Travis looked over to him, "Yeah...probably won't pick up till we get back to Klamath."

Angling around a sharp bend, the headlamps poked into a thin patch of fog coming down the mountain and inching to the ravine below. It reminded Travis of a passing freight train while waiting at a railroad crossing.

A sudden flash of a darkened silhouette got Travis's attention. Before he could even turn his head, it'd done streaked in front of the truckin efforts to cross the road. Travis slammed the brakes, tires screeching and skidding around the curve. Heart in his throat and glutes pinching the seat cover.

A costly misjudgment sent the large figure slamming into the front passenger side of the truck. Crinkling the metal and busting out the headlight. It jolted atop the hood and smacked the windshield before rolling off and thudding onto the cool and steaming asphalt.

Travis and Dave stopped in a ditch about thirty yards away, after Travis skimmed the side of the mountain.

Steam billowed from the engine with a hiss. The dash was lit up like a Christmas tree. The interior lights flashed, the radio squawked, time blinking its green digital numbers, 1:21

An irritating ding continued until Travis unbuckled from his seat belt. His vision blurry, his mind foggy, he

Omah

blinked in rhythm with the dings enough times to clear his sight. He tried to turn on his caution lights, but the truck seemed to forget what they were. Dang it. The truck was more confused than he was.

His brother Dave moaned and clinched his forehead with both palms. A red flow snaked down his fingers and wrists.

Travis scrounged and found an old shirt wadded under his seat and tossed it to his brother.

Travis winced and grabbed the side of his head after he did so. His left ear and temple felt like they'd taken a cheap shot from Tyson as a hot pain seared across his flesh. A throbbing welt wasn't far behind.

Travis blinked again and flexed his jaw; he felt the side of his head with his right fingers. He stole a glance out the side mirror to the big man lying in the road behind them. The man squirmed and grunted in effort to get to his feet. Must be homeless or something.

Travis grasped the door handle. The door popped open with another ding. Feeling like he was trying to gain his balance in a raft upon a troubled sea, Travis found the pavement and steadied himself against the door of the truck.

"You okay man?" Travis beckoned with another wince.

The man grunted and snorted out a long breath that looked like steam from a coal train.

Limping to the back of the truck, his hand gripping the bed rail, Travis asked, "Man, are you all right?"

More huffing, more steam rising to the night sky. Finally, the man sat up and formed an L.

In that instant…the world stopped. Travis felt like a rat stuck in a glue trap. His heart knocked against his ribs, his veins thumping in his neck like a subwoofer. He felt his spirit fly to that crescent moon behind the clouds, leaving him there to fend for himself.

The moon high in the background shone its light around the man sitting on the pavement. His long hair waved in the passing breeze. The stench of rotten eggs and soured socks ripped the air. Travis gagged and was forced to hide all but his eyes beneath the neck of his shirt.

Travis' blood had turned to a cool slush as a douse of it trailed up his spine.

"Dave-Dave-Dave!!!"

The size of the man in the road was twice that of any Travis had ever met.

Travis' whole body began to quiver.

"Dave-Dave!!"

Hearing his voice, the hairy silhouette snapped its head toward him like an owl.

Travis' breath caught in his chest as it couldn't pass the lump that'd formed in his throat. His heart struggled to pump blood fast enough for his pulse.

The passenger door opens. Two feet land on the pavement. Dave hobbles along the side of the truck, one hand pressing the reddening shirt to his face, the other sliding along the bed rail.

The hairy silhouette pushed off the pavement and stood on wobbly feet, hunched at the spine, but still towering any man standing six feet or more. This guy was massive. At least seven foot.

Dave coughed out his question, "What?"

"Loo—"

Travis' voice was cut off by the bone rattling howl that had emitted from the hairy man's lungs which must've been the size of two propane tanks judging by how long and baritone it was.

Omah

    A glimmer of light peaked around the bend behind the hairy man. His head jerked to it. Within two seconds, he'd jolted to the guard rail, tossing itself over and down the ravine. It sounded like a tank had been rolled off the cliff. Trees snapped as if they were toothpicks. The crunching of leaves and logs continued until they were drowned out by the tires and blaring radio of the approaching SUV.

    The brakes squealed as the tires crunched over loose pebble. The red front bumper was held in place by duct tape. The passenger window struggled to lower. The true definition of a clunker.

    What in the world do you say after something like this? Would anyone ever believe such a story? Did he and his brother really just see that? Should they even tell anyone?

    "You guys all right?" a younger fella with a face full of acne and eyes redder than his square bodied Jeep Cherokee, asked as he lowered his head and peered across the center console at Travis and Dave.

    Travis struggled for the words. His breath huffing out faster than he could think.

    "Can you get us an ambulance? My brother's cut pretty good. And we should probably call the game warden too," Travis manages to get out in between breaths.

    Travis felt the look from his brother and heard him clear a phlegm. Right.

    "Uh...well...wait about the game warden...we'll call them tomorrow," Travis said stealing a glance into the bed of the truck at the tarp covering the two deer. His eyes were then drawn to the guard rail where the creature had disappeared.

RANDALL LANE

Thursday   October 20th, 2018

HUMBOLDT TIMES

Brothers claim to have hit large and hairy bipedal creature while travelling along logging road in Bluff Creek

Travis Hodges and his brother Dave, both who work for Aldridge Log and Tree service, encountered something on Tuesday night, that neither of them can explain.

According to the brothers, as they were traveling from Bluff Creek on the way home from work to their hometown of Klamath, a large, bipedal creature stepped out onto the roadway, leaving the driver, Travis with no time to react.

The impact caused the man to lose control of his pickup truck, sending the men into a ditch. The brothers say they witnessed the creature limp off into the darkened forest as it disappeared through the thick fog.

Game wardens were called to the scene along with highway patrol to investigate. According to Warden Jimmy Connors, the damage to the truck was so severe, it must have been due to a large Bear or Elk.

"That was a lot of damage for that truck to take and for whatever they hit to not be laying in that road. Hard to believe something could make it off into the woods after that. I know them Elk and Bear are strong, but I never would thought they could've made it through that."

When asked about the brothers claims of the creature being bi-pedal, Connors said it was likely just their imagination getting the best of them along with the poor visibility due to the dense fog at the time.

-Continued on Page 4B

OMAH

Thursday

October 20th, 2018

HUMBOLDT TIMES

Page 4B

Another Possible Bigfoot Sighting in Bluff Creek

As Brothers Travis and Dave Hodges retell of their encounter with what they can only explain as the legendary "*Bigfoot*", the two claim they are now firm believers in one of the Nation's biggest mysteries.

"Oh no doubt...it had to be a Sasquatch. I mean this thing was massive...heck just look at what it did to my truck," said Travis Hodges.

"I remember Grandma and Grandpa telling us stories about the hairy men of the mountains, back when we were kids, but I mean we always just figured it to be old folklore stuff, you know. But not anymore...I know what I saw and the only answer I can give is...Bigfoot," answered Dave Hodges when asked about the encounter.

"Yeah I mean, there's no telling what lives out in these woods,

as dense and secluded as this part of the area is, it'd be easy for something to tuck itself away up here," added Dave.

Game wardens combed the area for any sign of Bear or Elk, but had no luck in locating the injured animal.

"Just be careful out there...I mean if one of these things wanted to make a quick meal out of you, well I'm sure it'd be easy to do," said Travis

If you have ever seen the all allusive "Bigfoot", give us a call

Senior Editor:
Bobby Thatcher

2

Tossing the last of the luggage into the back of the family's 4-door black Jeep Wrangler, Randy Jacobs lowered the hatch, turned toward their beach themed two-story home and called for his wife, "Bev...you bout ready?"

"Yeah...coming."

He stole a glance at his watch, 9:34, not too bad, could be worse. Traffic should be light as long as they made it on the road by ten. Not that it would make much difference, for it would still take a good five days to reach the Pacific Coast. Carolina Shores to Myers Flatt, California to be more precise. A trip this distance had taken a lot of planning, but Randy enjoyed every second of it. He knew down to the minute when they'd reach each state and city as long as they stuck to their plan.

With Bev's help, the two already had the whole trip planned out as to where to go and what to do once they reached the Golden State. And he'd even prepared for any potential delays or emergencies which he'd learned to do over the years while travelling with three kids and a wife. A delay in the schedule was inevitable, but he was prepared for it.

The lyrics to Otis Redding's *Sittin on the dock of the bay*, "Left my home in Georgia, headed for the Frisco Bay,"

kept playing in his head. He couldn't help but whistle the tune. Though it wasn't Georgia they were
leaving, it was close enough. The North Carolina Coast is a fine place to live and Randy wouldn't change a thing, but he and Bev had always wanted to take the kids on a cross country road trip. So, when the stars
finally aligned for it to happen, they couldn't load the motorhome any faster.

    To avoid the unnecessary mileage and wear and tear on the Jeep, Randy opted for a car hauler rather than a dolly or simple tow behind set-up. Randy checked the yellow straps spread across the tires which held the Jeep in place atop the trailer. Much like the ones U-Haul offers. Tight and secure. He then began checking the brake lights and turn signals of the trailer with his daughter's help. Jennifer sitting in the driver seat of the thirty-two-foot 2005 Fleetwood Tioga C-class motorhome, as she obeyed directions from her dad.

    "Tap the brakes," his voice carried from the tail end of the train.

    She gave a few soft taps.

    Two blips of red emitted from the trailer's brake lights. Check.

    "All right. Do ya left turn signal."

    Two years from being eligible for her driver's permit, Jennifer was still learning all the gadgets. It took her a second to figure out what the left turn signal was, but she did and bumped it down.

    Tick-tick-tick-tick

    "All right, do the right one."

    Jennifer bumped it up.

    As Randy was busy checking the connections for the brake lights and such, the sound of the front door to their house shutting was followed by the dead bolt sliding home.

Randy, with hands on his hips, a blue and white flannel rolled to his elbows above khaki pants, turned to see his sweetheart since middle school, the former miss Beverley Wilmore, now known as Bev Jacobs pattering down the steps.

Dressed in blue jeans and a cute black jacket with brown fur around the neck, it accentuated her long black hair quite nicely. She toted a small handbag and a lanyard set of keys. The soft breeze brought her hair to life as it fluttered about her face.

"Here you go. Everybody ready?" Bev asked.

A beat.

Even after all these years, she still had a way of stalling Randy's heart and breath. He was fortunate to have someone as special as Bev. To those that say soul mates don't exist, well he and Bev have plenty of proof to counter.

"Uh...yeah-yeah...just checking everything before we hit the road," Randy smiled.

"Okay...well I checked each room to be sure we weren't leaving anything. All the doors and windows are locked. Ted's supposed to check on things in a few days, right?"

"Yeah..." Randy said with a grunt as he hoisted himself up to the Jeep's driver door, checking to be sure the radio was off. Last thing he wanted was a dead battery, "...yeah Ted's coming by Thursday to check the mail. Said he'd keep an eye on the place," Randy shut the door and hopped onto the pebble and shells.

"Can you lock it for me?"

Bev found the key from the lanyard; the Jeep gave its reassuring double beep.

"All right...we ready?" asked Randy.

"I think so. The kids are already in I guess?"

"Yeah, they're inside."

"Okay, well let's hit the road."

They gave each other a peck then disappeared as they walked along the motorhome on opposite ends. Randy climbed in from the driver door as Bev passed through the side entry next to the sink.

Tyler and Andrew were busy watching YouTube videos on Andrew's phone, while Jennifer was busy texting on hers.

Randy turned the ignition.

The engine roared.

Bev grabbed two bottles of water from the fridge and angled toward the front.

"What are you watching?" she questioned Tyler and Andrew.

"It's a documentary about all of the bigfoot encounters where we're going," said Andrew their nine-year-old son, never breaking his gaze from the phone's screen.

"Yeah...it's crazy," said Tyler with a slur and toothy grin. Typical for a six-year-old.

Bev smiled. Passing Jennifer, she asked, "Who are you texting?"

"Sarah. She was asking when we'd be back," she said as her thumbs resembled the flipper bats of a pinball machine.

The RV lurched forward as Randy shifted the gear stick to drive.

"You tell her it'll be a while?" Bev said with a chuckle as she steadied herself with a hand to the top bunk bed over the driver's cab.

"Yeah she knows."

Bev patted Jennifer on the shoulder as she bent to take her place in the passenger seat opposite of Randy.

He busied himself as he searched for the right playlist on his phone. He found it and turned the knob of the radio.

Willy Nelson's familiar twang filled the air as he sang *On the Road Again.*

Randy pulled the seat belt over his shoulder, clicked it, then looked to Bev with a grin and gave her a pat on the leg.
She smiled back and placed her hand on his, "I'm so glad we're doing this honey."
Randy kissed her hand and said, "Me too."
He eased his foot off the brake, sending the RV into a slow roll over pebbles and shells, before resting his foot on the gas.
"California here we come," Randy said, adding a few taps of the horn. Bev gave a cheerful whoop-whoop. Tyler clapped, Andrew whistled, and Jennifer added Morse code with the tap of each letter on her phone.
Singing along to ole Willy, they began the first step of a 3,073-mile journey.
Here come the Jacobs. California better brace itself.

SATURDAY at sunrise, deep in the wilderness of Northern California, birds began their songs as squirrels rummaged about the floor of the forest, with deer rising in search of another acorn or stream. A cool breeze swept through the trees, bringing with it a dense fog that crawled its way passed fern, service berry and Giant Sequoias.
The scent of fresh soil and pine filled the air along with the thudding of flat feet against the damp earth. A hush filled the forest as every creature went silent at the arrival of such a presence.
A glimmer of a sun ray cut through the dense canopy of limbs and branches as it meandered its way around a red Sequoia. The stark odor of a wet dog mixed with manure and rotten eggs sliced through the air. Causing the deer to

snarl their nostrils at such a stench. The sun's ray ended atop a patch of reddish-brown hair the size of a mattress, leaving the hair dancing in the sun's spotlight with the breeze. The creature had massive shoulders, a rounded head, and two eyes the color and size of a billiards eight ball.

The creature locked its gaze on a lifeless and hairy body curled in a fetal position next to the Giant Sequoia.

The creature gave it a few nudges with its leathery foot that'd dwarf that of any man.

The body didn't move.

Its left leg looked broken as it was twisted at an awkward angle. Dried blood was caked around the knee and shin in large flakes. Oozing from the nostrils down to the mouth and chest was more dried, flaky blood. Its eyes were already glazed and distant with death, its spirit was no longer here Was this the one that'd been screaming into the dark night and sounding in such anguish?

Light crawled over the towering creature gazing at the body and shone on the stiff ape like figure lying on the ground. Its dark purple Gorilla looking fingers and hands tucked to its burly chest as if withered from a ruthless disease. Its big feet—ravaged with cuts and scars from years of rough living—poked beneath hair covered tree trunks for legs.

The creature standing over the body, jerked its head to the heavens and bellowed out a howl that carried an O to Ahh sound before ending in a gut twisting shriek.

It caught its breath, then proceeded to repeat the same howl twice more.

A tear rolled off the creature's cheek as it breathed out a deep sigh, bent down and took the hairy body by a black foot with only four toes.

The creature drug the body until a hollowed-out Redwood was suffice. It was here, it'd be laid to rest. Ashes to ashes, dust to dust.
    The hairy creature closed its eyes and wagged its massive head. Its lips twisted in a grimace, it snorted and huffed then beat upon its chest. It knew something wasn't right, this wasn't a natural death. It knew the spirit of the Omah would have trouble resting. The creature tucked its top lip tight against its gum and let out a soft tea kettle like whistle. Another tear fell to the earth. In the distance, tucked deep within the forest of Giant Redwoods, another whistle responded. The message had been sent and all of the forest was silent as it dreaded what was to come.

3

Twigs snapped, leaves crunched, and bony branches got their fair share of sucker punches across the stubbled face of Jimmy Davis as his eye darted side to side, in a careful scan of the forest. With his heart pounding, his balmy hands struggled to grip the Winchester rifle.

Only minutes from the blind, he was still wearing his orange vest. The hair on his arms and neck had stood at attention the instant he heard the howl. It was just the third time in his life he could recall hearing such a hair-raising thing. It'd been at least a decade since he last heard it. And before that, it was over five decades, the first time he heard it, while he was only a youngster helping his grandpop till the garden.

Much like the other two times, it stopped him dead in his tracks, cementing his feet to the ground. It was as if nature and all its occupants had paused to acknowledge such authority.

His grandpop said it must've been an alpha wolf or big cat. But Jimmy Davis, even at the young age of nine or ten, knew better than to think it was a wolf or cat and by the look in grandpop's eye and the crack in his voice, he didn't seem to think so either.

The second time Jimmy heard the howl, he was fishing the Klamath River around dusty dark and after about fifty or so last cast, the world went still at the sound of that lonely, eerie howl. It started out as a deep guttural tone before rising like a woman in distress then falling once again to mimic a baritone bluegrass singer. The howl was loud and close enough to drown out the ripple of the river, and that took a lot to do.

Jimmy reached the blind, allowing his heart to return to its normal beat. Although knowing the flimsy polyester wouldn't keep out the source of a such a howl, it was the thought of being inside a barrier that gave him comfort.

He plops down in a fold away chair he'd stationed in the center, rifle still squeezed with his greasy palms, finger only inches from the trigger.

It was five after seven, Saturday morning, October 22nd. The Sun had unleashed its rays as the forest and back side of the mountain to his left came into view.

If he was lucky enough, he might hear a Marbeled Murrelet let out its "keer-keer" call to start its day. Having become an endangered bird over the last few years, he'd have to consider himself quite special to hear it, let alone see it. Much like the creator of the mysterious howl, you were unique to hear it, but you were even more unique to see its source.

Although, those two brothers' in the papers claim they'd saw the source, Jimmy would have to see it for himself to be sure.

Until that happens, it'd remain a mystery. Like the wind, it was there, but from where it began, who could tell?

TWO DAYS into their journey, the Jacobs found themselves travelling along I-10, leaving Louisiana for Texas.

"Dad, can you stop somewhere so I can use the bathroom?" asked Andrew with a twisted face.

Randy looked to the rearview mirror shining toward the back, "Huh? What do you mean, why can't you go now?" he asked.

"I can't go while we're moving."

"Boy. All right. Hang on just a minute, I'll get off on the next exit."

"Hurry up, I got to go."

A mile down I-10, a square green sign showed exit twenty-seven. Randy eased over a tad more than he should've and the rumble strip vibrated the entire RV. Andrew's gut grumbled a growl to match the rumble.

Randy found a Pilot gas station and pulled to the side. Stealing glances out the side mirrors, he was careful not to block any truckers.

Feet thudded toward the back, the bathroom door flung open, then slammed with a jolt.

Randy took a breath and sighed it out, flexing his arm to unkink a cramp. He yawned and craned his neck.

"So, where are we?" asked Jennifer from the couch next to Tyler.

"Beaumont, Texas," said Bev with a playful southern drawl.

"How long before we make it to California?" Jennifer asked gently, as if not wanting to hear the answer.

Randy snuffed out a chuckle and looked to his wife.

"Oh, about two days."

"*Two* days?"

"Yup."

A sudden windstorm seemed to emit from the back. Andrew sprayed down the waste as the toilet screamed in agony.

The door opened.

"Whew," he said wagging his head and wiping his brow. "My gosh boy, you got to spray something,"

Randy said as he ducked his nose beneath the neck of his shirt and quickly fumbled for the button to lower the windows.

"Look under the sink, there should be some Lysol," Bev said between coughs.

"Eeewww," said Tyler as he ran up front to mama.

"I think I'm going to be sick," Jennifer in a half heave as she buried her face into the couch pillows.

Speeeeeshhh

Andrew coughing and choking while emptying out the Lysol can, Bev began to yell, "That's enough. That's enough!"

The spraying stopped, the door opened, Andrew stepped out, short of breath, looking as if he'd just defeated Goliath.

Fresh lemon pine chased out the stench.

Aww...only two more weeks of RV living.

NESTLED IN a cozy forest, surrounded by rivers, mountains, redwoods, and only a four-hour drive north of San Francisco, Garberville makes for a nice place to get away from the hustle and bustle of life. A place where you can breathe again and connect with nature.

Having lived in Northern California for most of their lives, Adam and Brenda Lightfoot wouldn't change a thing. They own and operate a tourist shop known as *Legends and Tales*. Keeping it stocked with art and carvings from local artist and craftsman, along with souvenirs and gag gifts they'd collect from online wholesalers to sell at a reasonable margin.

"No, now scoot that one over and bring the bear carving more to the front," said Brenda.

OMAH

"This one?" Adam asked in a grunt as he stretched to reach the top shelf.

"Yeah. Bring it closer to the front. Like the ones over there," Brenda said as she turned and pointed to the Bigfoot carvings above the door. That's when her eye caught a car door open in the parking lot. Looked like campers perhaps, judging by their attire and the cargo mounted atop their sliver Ford Bronco. A bearded man wearing a brown flannel shirt and jeans with a black beanie stepped out, while a lady with a red flannel and jeans and a brown beanie atop sandy blonde hair angled around the front of the Bronco.

"We got customers. Just uh...yeah...right there. That's perfect."

A bell tinged above the door as the young couple stepped in.

"Howdy folks. Welcome to Legend and Tales. If you have any questions just give us a holler," said Adam coming down the ladder.

The place had everything one might imagine could be carved from the remnants of a Redwood tree. From walking sticks, rocking chairs, bowls, spoons, forks, and plates. But over towards the back under the big hand carved sign which read *Sasquatch*, stood numerous Bigfoots carved from Redwood.

The couple thanked Adam and Brenda for the greeting and was then drawn like a moth to a flame toward the back. An area Adam and Brenda had done their best at making like bigfoot heaven. Books, bumper stickers, t-shirts, stuffed bigfoots, movies, you name it, the place had it all.

In a large glass display, rested casted feet double the size of any man and pinned along the wall was countless newspaper clippings and posters. One such poster was a picture of large, hairy, dome headed biped with an odd gait and lanky arms striding across a creek bed, head twisted like an owl toward the camera in mid stride. A still shot from one of the most famous films ever captured of the creature.

The couple gawked and gasped as they pointed from artifact to poster, to cast, and back again.

Hearing their chatter, Adam grinned and headed toward the back.

"Bigfoot piques your interest I gather?" he asked as he'd made it within ten feet of them, without them even knowing. His last name wasn't given for nothing.

The two spun around. Wide eyed with wonder.

Brenda strode to her husband's side.

"That's why we're here. We've heard so many stories, just had to come check it out ourselves," said the man.

"I see. Where you from?"

"San Diego," said the woman.

Brenda rose her brows and nodded, "Oh wow, my brother lives there. He was based in San Diego for seven years while he was in the Navy and after he got out, he decided that's where he wanted to be. He loves it there."

"That's awesome. Yeah, we love it too. Just not much of the place to catch a squatch."

The four chuckled.

"Well...I'm Adam Lightfoot by the way and this is my wife Brenda," he said extending his hand.

"Nice to meet you, I'm Les Conrad and this is my wife Sam."

They acquaint themselves with smiles and nods.

"So, where are you staying?" asked Adam.

"Up around the Willow Creek area."

"*Oh*...you trying to catch a peak of the old fella? Huh?" Adam smiled and gave Les a playful slap on the shoulder.

"It'd be nice. Be one way of knowing for sure he's really out there, you know?"

"Oh, I know all right and believe me...*he's out there.*"

Les cocked his head, Sam cut her eyes to her husband.

"So, you've seen him before?" asked Les.

Adam looked him in the eye and gave a reassuring nod. Straight faced, no fooling around.

"Well tell us...what did you see? I mean if you don't mind."

"Oh, I don't. It helps to tell my story to people, especially to those who actually want to hear it. Most just wipe you off as some whacky nut job," Adam said as he rubbed the back of his neck and glanced at the stack of books to his left. Most were titled something about "Bigfoot" or "Sasquatch", but his eyes seemed to be trained on one stack, with the title reading, *Missing people of America's National Parks: What happened to them?*

Les followed his gaze, Adam noticed and diverted the attention by beginning a story, "Well...being a Native as you've probably gathered, I've heard stories from the elders all my life. My grandpa and grandma have told me so many stories about these things, that it'd take me days to tell you, so I guess I'll tell you of my own personal encounters to save time,"

Adam cleared his throat. "I've seen him twice now. Once when I was just a kid and another time about five years ago. The first time was when I was playing with my older brother down by the South Fork Eel River. I couldn't have been any older than about seven or eight, which would make my brother eleven or twelve I guess," he said with scrunched brows and eyes turned toward the ceiling. "Anyhow, the whole time we were fishing and goofing off— you know skipping rocks and what have you—I kept getting this eerie feeling that I was being watched. I turned to look behind me, I don't know how many times. Jack felt it too, but he wouldn't admit it. Whether he was just trying to be tough or didn't want me getting scared, I don't know."

Adam drew a breath and rubbed his brow.

Sam moved in front of Les where he could drape his arms around her for comfort.

"We started hearing big splashes in the river upstream from us. Like someone was chunking rocks or something. Jack played it off trying to say it was
Salmon jumping, but I didn't believe him. It wasn't long before we started smelling this horrible odor, I can't even give it justice trying to describe it. My best offer...imagine a skunk, a wet dog, and a cow patty all rolled into a soured rug and left out in the Sun to dry."

"Oh gah," said Les as he and Sam snarled their noses and snickered.

"Yeah. It was that bad. Sickening. Well after a few minutes of this, we had about all we could take, so we started gathering our stuff. That's when something crashed up the mountain across the river. Sounded like a tree fell. But as soon as it hit the ground, branches and limbs started snapping like a logging crew had taken to work. Jack stumbled backward with his arm stretched in front of me, protecting his little brother. He went to holler, but before he could even start, this heart stopping, spine chilling howl ripped through the air, as loud as a train. I remember covering my ears it was so bad."

"What'd it sound like," asked Sam.

"Like someone dying. It started out real deep and almost with a growl, then rose to a shriek like that of a weeping woman," Adam tried to shake the gooseflesh, but it'd already set in, "Man...still gives me the willies even some thirty years later."

Omah

    Adam suppressed the memory and continued telling of the encounter. Les and Sam giving their full attention. Brenda gripping Adam's arm to show her support.
    "As if that wasn't enough, this thing leaped from the wood line and splashed into the river about twenty yards upstream from us. I caught glimpse of something dark and the second I locked eyes with it…the world stopped. Seconds felt like hours. This guy was a giant, big thick neck, barrel chest, with arms the size of my legs, and legs the size of my body," Adam said as he talked with his hands.
    "His face was so leathery, I almost thought it was a mask. His eyes were like two black baseballs. His lips flinched into a snarl, revealing humongous human like teeth, all yellow and grungy looking. His nose was flat and wide, almost like the nostrils stretched under each eyeball. He sniffed the air and made an awful face, much the way I did when I first smelled him. But within what couldn't have been more than five seconds, the yank on my arm felt like it popped it out of socket. Jack was dragging me backwards. I kicked and fumbled to grab a footing. That's when I saw the thing throw its head back and let out another howl. I didn't watch him finish. I twisted around and trailed Jack up the river bank as we raced toward our old rusty three-wheeler, that only crunk when it felt like it. Luckily it was in the mood that day. Jack about kicked the starter off, before it grumbled and crawled its way out of the valley. The whole time I was afraid to turn around, I just knew that thing was right on our heels."
    A breath.
    "The only people me and my brother ever told was our family. With everything they'd experienced and heard through the years, they knew we were telling the truth."
    "Man…that's crazy," Les said wagging his head.

"Now that was my first encounter. The second time I saw one, was about five years ago when I was out Elk hunting up near the Oregon border, just above Happy Camp. I'd been tracking this monster Elk for about two weeks and I knew I was closing in on him. I made my way to a steep ridge line overlooking a valley where Crow Creek flowed south from the Tanner Lakes in Oregon. He stood out like an Elephant among a herd of donkeys. I mean this joker was massive. I put him in my crosshairs and waited for him to turn broad side. He shifted, I eased my finger around the trigger," Adam cradled an invisible gun as he aimed it at the wall, "Then he flinched and jerked his head toward the wood line. Within seconds he and the heard went roaring into the woods opposite the wood line that caught his attention. I scanned the area for a minute but didn't see anything. I huffed out a breath and was just about to lay my rifle down to gather my things, when that tall dark bush next to a towering pine shifted to the other side. My heart sank. It was one of the hairy men. His hands rested upon the bark with his body hugged
tightly to it as he leaned his head around to pear into the valley. His red hair camouflaged against the pine bark. This was the first time I ever got to really take a good look at one from a safe distance."

Adam sucked in a roomful of air and sighed it out.

"All I can say is, I know what I've saw, and I know what I've heard from my family through the years. You can take it or leave it...they're out there. And one thing for certain, I try not to stay long when they're around."

SO FAR Jimmy Davis was having an uneventful morning and if it continued, he'd likely be packing up in an hour or two.

Omah

The passing cold front must've had the deer feeling lazy.
Crunch. Snap. Thud.
Jimmy's heart palpitated. The first real excitement of the day. Visions of a two hundred-pound, twelve pointer filled his mind.
Crunch. Snap. Thud.
Wait.
Something doesn't sound right.
It's not the normal flitter and scuffle of a four-legged deer. It sounds more upright.
Thump!
Jimmy flinched in his seat and tightened his grip on the rifle. A quick vibration seemed to rattle his feet from such a thud.
What in the world? Did someone fall out of a dang tree stand or something?
More snapping, crunching, and thumping upon the dirty green carpet floor, covered with pine and bark from dying trees.
There was more than one now.
Who the heck? Jimmy opened his mouth to yell out to the pesky trespasser but was stopped short as a foul odor wafted against his nostrils. His gut turned at such a stench. He smacked his lips in effort to rid the taste of soured milk blended with rotten eggs.
He thought he was going to lose his egg and cheese biscuit right there on the blind floor.
He dried his right palm against his camo pants and clung tighter to the rifle. It was coming. He waited to hear the wailing woman let out her spine-tingling shriek.
It would come. It would surely come.

4

As much as Jimmy prepared himself for that blood chilling howl, he still wasn't ready when it blasted through the air.

Every hair on his body straightened when his veins turned to ice. His heart began to knock and vibrate his entire rib cage.

The deep guttural howl emitting from a slimy throat straight from hell continued with no promise of ending. It rose in pitch to that of a banshee in distress over a lost loved one. The piercing tone stung Jimmy's ears. It continued for a good thirty seconds before the origin's lungs were void of air. The cry of the banshee had finally ebbed away.

Thud! Crunch! Snap!

Heavy feet pounded closer, just on the other of a thick patch of brush. The smell of soured roadkill still kissed Jimmy's nostrils. Gripping the rifle with balmy and quaking hands he steadies his aim at the wood line, less than thirty yards to his 2 o'clock.

Bushes quaked and rustled as two pines swayed to give way to the beast. Surely hell was releasing its largest demon. Its hot breath seemed to enter the blind as Jimmy struggled to catch his to breath from the sudden lack of oxygen.

Omah

Silence.

Rifle squeezed with trembling hands; Jimmy craned his neck to peer into the scope.

He scanned the wood line. Nothing but bark and browning leaves stared back. Stop. What was that?

As Jimmy busied himself with retracing the track of his scope, a husky gruff roared from the bushes as they trembled while concealing the beast.

Jimmy's heart crashed to his feet. Time stopped as did his pulse and thinking.

About two foot off the ground, resting upon broad and square shoulders about the size of baby grand piano was a domed head with inky black eyes glaring into his soul. Yellow stained teeth bared by stretched rubbery lips in a tight snarl. Brows furrowed and intent with fury.

As beastly as this thing seemed, something about it struck Jimmy as having an uncanny resemblance to a human. Like a cross between a Gorilla and a pre-historic man. Is this what those brothers saw on their way home the other night? Is this what people have been calling bigfoot? Had to be right? But was it an animal or man?

How could he ever live with himself if this thing turned out to be more man than beast? Even if it wasn't a man, it looked too much like a Gorilla to want to shoot. He'd have to know his life was in jeopardy to be able to pull the trigger. And right now, by the look in this things eye, that might just be the case.

Jimmy's breath in short gasps and huffs as he had the origin of the howl in his cross hairs.

The creature growled deep from its gut, its hot breath steaming into the chill air in a steady release.

Quicker than Jimmy could blink, the creature hopped out of the bush and gave a reverberating grumble that chilled Jimmy's spine as every inch of flesh was now covered in tiny bumps.

The creature was crouched low like a cat and crawling toward him at a slow steady pace. Long, hairy legs as thick as telephone poles glided across the forest carpet of fern and pine. Its crawl reminded Jimmy of a big spider. So awkward and unnatural.

It stopped after crawling about two yards and tilted its head, sniffing with a scrunched nose. At Jimmy's scent it tossed its cone head to the sky and let out that haunting, screechy, devilish howl.

Jimmy's bones quaked as a wave of fear crashed over him like a tsunami. The rifle's aim jarred so much he could barely keep the scope trained to the beast.

As the seconds of the creatures howl crawled past like a spider mystically weaving its web, the black-eyed beast lowered its gaze and in a quick gallop, gained five yards in a quick dash across the soft earth.

Jimmy squeezed the trigger. The shot rang out, his body jolted backward from the kick. The creature roared, now less than twenty yards from the blind, it stood to two legs and pounded closer.

The smell of gun powder filled the blind along with the strong odor from Jimmy's fear glands secreting into beads of sweat that trickled into his right eye. He wiped the burn away and hurried to chamber another round. The pounding of those heavy flat feet gaining ground with each passing millisecond which felt like hours. His pulse racing, his heart knocking, the rifle clicked and clattered, the round was in. His finger found the trigger. The barrel aimed to the beast's chest.

Boom!

The creature let out a hellish scream and barged onward, unfazed by the blast. It raced near on the brink

OMAH

of being within arm's length with only another second. Mouth wide, teeth dripping with saliva. Gaining yards quicker than the Jimmy's heart could keep up. His eyes glued to the rifle cradled in his grips, Jimmy chambered a round and hurried to fire another shot.

Nothing.

Silence.

His eyes darting side to side in frantic sweeps, his heart pulsating faster and harder, his breath escaping in short gasps. His heart and mind falling deeper into the black hole of fear and hopelessness. Not knowing where this thing was, was worse than seeing it gallop towards him. At least then he wasn't left questioning which flank to cover.

Above him and to his 9 o'clock somewhere along the slant of the woodsy mountain, a long mellow whistle cut the air. Before Jimmy could twist to peer up the mountain, a hiss filled growl permeated his soul as the clatter and thrash of the polyester blind crashed and twisted, tearing away like wrapping paper, before a set of sharp bony fingers ripped at his back, cutting through his vest, flannel and flesh. Hot pain seared across his flesh. He collapsed to the floor of the blind with a thump, his breath escaping him as his lungs screamed for mercy.

Up on the mountain and edging closer, a loud gravelly screech resounded. Rocks tumbled southward as heavy footfalls hammered against the slope. Have mercy, another one is coming!

The thing shrieked again, sounding as if it was right on top of him.

Jimmy wheezed and coughed, his lungs begging for air. He pushed himself to his feet and stumbled from the tangled mess of the shredded blind.

Gripping his gut, he hobbled through the thicket of pines and Redwoods. Sticks snapping beneath his feet, limbs like bony fingers slapping across his whiskered face that hadn't seen a razor in days.

The beast roared again, but this time it seemed stationary. No heavy feet slapped against the earth in pursuit. Maybe it was all just to prove its authority. Protecting its territory, that sort of thing.

Wheezing and gasping, a burning pain spread along his back like three fresh paper cuts, only these seemed to be from a sheet of paper the size of a bookshelf. Droplets of blood along his skin, soaking his clothes before falling to the earth.

His heart ached, his lungs crying out for mercy. But he had to press on, he had to create distance. He couldn't stop now. Must keep moving.

STANDING HIGH above the battered and shredded blind, were two muscled beast that'd dwarf even Arnold Schwarzenegger. One covered in flowing reddish hair that glistened with the sun, the other a darker brown with a little gray sprinkled here and there.

The darker one wore greying whiskers that draped past its neck, growing toward the navel. It was by and large the bigger of the two. It snarled its nose and sniffed the passing breeze.

The smaller and reddish one crouched low and toyed with a piece of torn camo polyester.

The big dark one marched a few yards away and grasped a pine log the size of a violin. Its eyes scanning the wood line until they rested upon a lively red pine.

The hairy creature angled over with the log in hand and thrust it against the tree.

Wood on wood.

The knock travelled for miles. Again, it thudded.

Again.

Omah

The creature rested and glared up the mountain. Less than five seconds passed before three knocks separated by a brief still, resounding in the distance.

The reddish creature tilted its head, pursed its lips and bellowed out a warbled whistle. It continued until emptying its lungs. The creature dipped its head then disappeared into the thicket.

The other one dropped the log and followed.

5

After having buzzed his phone at least a dozen times since 2 o'clock, Jimmy's wife Suzanne paced the floors of their home, hand to her brow and phone to her ear. Feeling discomfort in her gut as she knew something wasn't right.

He never stayed in the woods longer than noon and he's always apt to answer his phone. Something didn't feel right. When the clock showed three thirty-four, she made the call down to the DNR.

It was just under an hour later when she received the call that two fishermen had found her husband two miles northeast of Hoopa, about half a mile from his blind.

Apparently, he'd crossed paths with a bear, as his back now wore large stripes as if he'd been flogged by a pack of angry Roman soldiers.

The fisherman had rushed Jimmy to Six Rivers Medical Clinic. Only about a half hour drive from his and Suzanne's home in Del Loma.

The moment Suzanne learned her husband was at Six River's, she grabbed her purse and bolted out the door. Still learning details from the Game Warden, she turned the ignition and roared out the driveway.

She'd done told Jimmy a hundred times how he was too old to be out hunting in these woods. He's not young like he used to be. If only he'd have listened

Omah

instead of being so hardheaded, he wouldn't have ended up at Six Rivers.

Suzanne sighed, ended the call with the Warden and sped to the medical clinic, only breaking the speed limit when no one was looking. Which as deserted as route 299 is, it meant most of the way to Six Rivers Medical. Her little white impala getting a workout as her foot grew heavier and heavier upon the pedal.

SEVEN O'CLOCK Monday evening, the Jacobs found themselves just outside Fort Stockton about four hours east of the New Mexico border.

In passing a green sign which reads,

Van Horn 120

El Paso 241

Tucson 558

Bev sighs and says, "My goodness, are we ever going to make it out of Texas?"

"I know. It takes forever. It's just about nine hundred miles end to end. We've got it now though, we're around three quarters of the way across," Randy said looking to the green numbers on the dash, "It's seven o'five now, you want to go until about ten? That'd put us an hour outside of El Paso."

Bev nodded and said, "Yeah, that's fine, as long as you don't get tired."

Tyler and Andrew giggled and laughed with their eyes fixed to an iPad. Jennifer had dozed off on the bed above the driver's cab.

"I'm good. If I get tired, we'll stop sooner. It'd be good if we could make it near the California boarder by tomorrow night. We did that, then by the time we swing through LA, we could be in the Bay area by Wednesday night. Check out San Francisco Thursday morning and be in Myers Flat by that evening."

Randy, no doubt the planner of the family. Details are to him like oxygen is to fire. Important and necessary for existence.

Of course, being a college baseball player had a lot to do with his obsession. Having an eye for details and being able to follow a strategic plan meant either spending most of your college career with your feet on the field, or butt on the bench.

Fortunately for Randy he spent the majority of his three years at Coastal Carolina with his feet in the grass patrolling centerfield. The Rangers, Giants and Red Sox all had plans to draft him his Junior year, until two months into the season, he shattered his ankle attempting to bring back a homer. The crash with the wall still plagues him to this day, as he can't take a step without a limp, let alone attempt to sprint after a liner in the gap.

Randy's playing days ended before his pro career ever began. It wasn't supposed to be that way. He was primed to be another Lenny Dykstra according to the scouts. No doubt, he would have a long career ahead of him. Hard to do with a bad ankle though.

After a few years, the bitterness and pity parties began to fade. Still there but tucked deep with only half its power.

So, Randy tried his hand at a handful of different things.

His major was in Entrepreneurial Management, and he'd finished it two years after he crashed in the outfield wall. But with a degree like that, unless you had money or good enough credit to start your own business, there really wasn't a whole lot to be done with it.

Shockingly, Randy had failed to create a solid backup plan, being led to believe he'd spend the next decade or so in the big show, making the big bucks. But of course, that didn't happen.

So now with a talent that couldn't perform and a degree that wouldn't satisfy, he ended up at Proline Marine Manufacturers outside of Grissettown, about a fifteen-minute drive from their home in Carolina Shores. His job? Applying details to the boats. The fancy stained wood, the chrome touches, anything to spice things up. Basically, he's an interior designer, but for center consoles and sailboats.

Nice job with a good paycheck and benefits.

"Oh, will you look at that. That's awesome," said Bev as she hurried and thumbed through her phone before the sinking sun disappeared next to a line of iron framed cowboys on horseback next to a large sign that read, *Fort Stockton*.

Bev's phone clicked and shuttered as she extended her hands to the purple and orange glow behind the metal men.

Tyler chuckled in the back, "Mama you look like Rafiki holding Simba."

Randy slapped his knee and belted out a belly laugh.

"Oh, hush it. I ain't no baboon," Bev said with a cut of her eyes and playful grin over her shoulder.

"That was a good one buddy, just be careful saying your mama reminds you of a baboon," said Randy with a grin as he glanced in the rearview mirror.

Andrew puffed out a nosey laugh and wagged his head, swiping the iPad with a finger to find another game.

"Can we play some music?" asked Tyler.

"Yeah...what you want?"

"Mmm...how about the baseball song?"

"Centerfield?"

"Yeah-yeah, that one."

Randy passed his phone to Bev, she scrolled and found the playlist titled Fogerty, then with a mash of her thumb, *Centerfield* crackled out the speakers.

Tyler bounded between Bev and Randy's seats and said, "Turn it up-turn it up!"

"Here sit down," Bev said as she pulled him closer and sat him in her lap.

Jennifer rolled to her side and pressed a pillow to her ear.

Only another four hours of driving before they'd reach the outskirts of El Paso, and Mr. Fogerty would help get them there.

JUST AFTER ten o'clock West Coast time, and Jimmy Davis was resting on his side, as his back was too slashed to lie on. IV bags ran intravenous lines into his wrist and elbow crease.

Suzanne sat in a chair beside him gripping his hand as he grimaced at the burning gashes across his back. Her attention was pulled to the set of knuckle raps thudding against the door.

"Hi, I'm Doctor Thedford," the man said as he extended a gentle hand to Suzanne. He was dark skinned and wore a flat top haircut. His skin was smooth and cared for, no wrinkles or acne scars, he looked to be around forty something. He had facial hair like Lionel Richie.

Thedford nodded and gave Jimmy a soft pat on his left shoulder.

"How are you feeling?"

"Hurtin," Jimmy pushed out through gritted teeth and pinched eyes before pursing his lips and sighing.

"Really? The pain meds should have done kicked in by now. May have to up the dosage," Thedford said while eying and palming an IV bag.

"So, you think it was a bear?"

"For Pete's sake, it wasn't a bear Suzanne."

Thedford began a sentence but was cut short, "The wardens are sear—"

"It wasn't a bear! I'm telling you...I know what I saw."

Thedford rubbed his tie as if searching for a stain.

Suzanne adjusted in her chair.

"Look. People can think I'm crazy all they want. But I didn't see no dang bear. I told the wardens a hundred times and I told those fishermen that found me. You people have to listen to me. It wasn't a bear," Jimmy ended with a mumbled curse.

"Mr. Davis, no one is saying they don't believe you, it's just considering your circumstances—and you were attacked from behind—how can we be so sure your eyes didn't play tricks with you?" Thedford tilted his head with tight lips.

"Well what else stands over nine foot, as thick as two NFL linemen squished together and can run faster than a wide receiver? I'm telling you like I told those men in the woods, now I know what's been making the howls all these years. Don't think I'm the only one that's ever heard one of these things. And I ain't the first to have seen one either," Jimmy returned the gesture with a downward angle of his head and brows.

"So, you're saying you think it was Bigfoot?"

Jimmy grimaced and rolled his eyes, mumbling a curse beneath his breath. The tone in Thedford's voice, just wasn't sitting well.

"Call it what you want, but it was something I've never seen before and something I don't ever want to see again. It's only by the Grace of God I managed to survive this thing. All I know...is the wardens better take my word for it and not go out there looking for some Winnie the Pooh.

Cause these lashes across my back could just as easily wound up across someone's face. And I think they'd end up in a morgue instead of some stiff hospital bed with freezer burnt food."

Suzanne tightened her grip on his hand and raised her eye lids, "Jimmy."

"Mr. Davis, I can't begin to imagine the horror you must've felt out there, and I mean it truly is a miracle you survived. Regardless of what you saw, lets be thankful you're wearing a gown and not a toe tag. Get you some rest, you'll have plenty of time discuss your encounter later. You need your rest Mr. Davis."

Thedford patted Jimmy's shoulder once more, then nodded at Suzanne before heading for the door.

Jimmy was just short of growling as he watched him walk away.

"I'll have a nurse come shortly to bump your meds and I'll check back in a few hours. Get some rest Mr. Davis. You too Ma'am," he said as he stood in the doorway with a hand resting on the handle.

"Thank you, Doctor," said Suzanne with a nod and smile.

"Thanks," Jimmy said before rolling his eyes as the door shut and latched.

"Suzanne...of all people you have to believe me." Jimmy's eyes were strained, his lips quivering.

"Oh honey...I know the man I married. What you say you saw...you saw. I believe you."

"Thank you. Thank you," Jimmy managed to force past the growing knot in his throat.

"It's going to be okay...if no one else ever believes you...I will and I do," Suzanne said as she gently rubbed face.

He nodded his head and lowered his eye lids. A tear rolled off his cheek.

Omah

6

The headlamps to Les and Sam's 82 Ford Bronco struggled to cut through the darkness. It'd been a winding ride over and around the mountains from Myers Flat to a camping trail three miles southwest of Willow Creek. Les could only see about two car lengths in front of him on the one lane gravel road. Surrounded by trees and inky blackness, the secluded road carved through the forest like a two-year-old attempting to draw a snake.

The trail was tight with a steep decline to the right and a sharp accent up the woody mountain to the left. The light of the moon and stars were blocked by the thick canopy of trees. Darkness thrived here. So thick you could feel and breathe it.

After making a few more snaky cuts and turns, up ahead appeared a clearing. A lonely picnic table sat next to a rock fire pit. A wooden sign with a hand panted number eight was spiked to a tree with a rusty nail.

A strip of fog crawled over the table like a sloth and made its way to the wood line about the time Les and Sam had unloaded the Bronco and tossed their gear atop the table.

A light mist settled over the clearing, dropping the temperature by at least ten degrees.

"Dang...I'm going to have to find my beanie," said Sam as she gripped each elbow and instructed Les on how to make the tent.

Her long hair knotted in a bun would have to oblige. She let it down and crossed for the Bronco.

Having just fed the poles through the tent, Les just needed to tie it down. So, as Sam was busy rummaging through a backpack in search of the beanie, Les began driving down the first of four tent pegs with a hammer.

The hammer rang against the metal stake.

The loud thump and ding carrying through the air.

Thump! Thump! Thump!

What was that, was it an echo?

Sam pulled her head out from the passenger side of the Bronco and stood to listen.

Les wacked the stake, the metal rang out as it sunk into the soft earth.

Thump! Thump! Knock!

"Les stop!" she said in a raised whisper.

The metal rang out again.

"Les stop!" this time she yelled it, catching him before he struck the stake again.

"What?" he asked while wiping his nose with the back of the hand that clinched the hammer. Squatted on his calves, his pants had a damp spot around the knee.

"Did you hear that?"

"Hear what?"

"Sounded like someone knocking."

"What?" Les scoffed, "I didn't see any other cars around, I'm pretty sure we're—"

Thump! Thump! Whack!

Les snapped his head to the right and stood to his feet, hammer hanging by his leg.

A beat.

Omah

He turned and looked to Sam in the corner of the door and passenger seat, her hands rested on the Bronco's door frame.

Thump! Thump! Whack! Thump!

Les squatted and smacked the stake. Four times it rang into the night.

Sam hurried over and clung to Les.

"Honey I'm scared."

"Samantha...c'mon now. It's probably just another camper telling me to quieten down. You know...like how we used to knock on the ceiling with the broom in the old apartment when Heather would come in and be making all that racket. I'm sure it's nothing. They're probably just trying to sleep and me out here banging around done woke them up."

Les squirmed from her grip and squatted down to finish driving the other three stakes.

One by one he sunk them up, trying to be mindful of his whacks. All four were in. He and Sam fixed the tent to their liking. Sam being the lady that she is, made sure to comfy up the interior with about twenty oversized blankets. Which given the decline in temperature, might just come in handy.

Having secured everything for the night, the two crawled in and attempted to get some shut eye ahead of the big hike planned for the morning.

Maybe they'd come across the other camper and make amends for being such a noisy neighbor.

Les wrapped his arm around Sam, she yawned as she patted his wrist.

"Love you babe."

"Love you too. Get you some rest."

Couldn't have been more than an hour later, when she bolted from the sleeping bag, forming a L in the tent. Her breath in short gasps. Her eyes darting about the thick blackness, trying to adjust to the dark.

"What the heck wa—"

Waaaaaaaaahhhhhhhhhhhhooooooooooooooooooo

She went to smack Les, but her hand it the bumpy floor. He was sitting up too, eyes blinking, flashing, trying to adjust to the dark.

Limbs popped and cracked, leaves rustled, a tree snapped and thudded to the forest floor.

Waaaaaahhhhhoooooooooommmmmmaaaaahhhhhhh

Les jerked and foraged for his revolver.

His hands searched through the blackness and finally bumped into its cold metal. Sam was cutting the circulation from his left arm.

Les cocked the hammer and aimed to the tent opening.

Sam whimpered and buried her face into his side. Heavy feet slapped through the woods, snapping twigs and crunching leaves.

Les adjusted and regripped the handle with a greasy right, braced by his left.

Thump! Thump!

It was circling them. Les followed it with his aim.

His heart pulsing, his breath scarce, his thoughts all over the place.

"Hey! Who is it?!"

Silence.

They listened. Nothing. Just an eerie, smothering...silence.

A loud crash and shatter of glass emitted from their left. Les jerked the gun about four feet over and fired through the tent. Mostly out of reflexes. As the crash gave him such a jolt, his finger didn't have much of a choice. Not counting the thrust of Sam's face into his ribs.

OMAH

Heavy feet pounded through woods, knocking down any tree that dared stand in the way. Sounded like a herd of buffalo tearing through the forest.

The stampede eventually ebbed into the darkness. That eerie silence returned.

It was so still, even the crickets and cicadas knew to keep quiet.

Les forced himself into a crouch, having to pry loose from Sam.

"Sam...c'mon...let's go."

He tugged at her arm, as she wagged her head and sniffled.

"Sam...we got to go. We can't stay here."

She struggled to take a deep breath. She allowed her mind to ease and nodded.

Les scans the surroundings. Clear. The two crawl out of the tent.

His eyes fixed to the Bronco. The front windshield looked like the center of a humongous spider web.

His face wrinkles as he curses, then says, "C'mon...let's go."

They bolt for the Bronco, Les half dragging Sam as she was busy looking over her shoulder, being sure not to be flanked by such a monster.

Les released her hand, she whipped her head around and stumbled for the passenger door.

They hop in, Les fires up the engine and throws the gear shift in reverse.

Sam gasped.

Les focused his attention on Sam's gaze.

In the center of the bench seat, laying between them rested a boulder the size of a basketball.

Les swallowed hard, lifted his eyes to Sam, then turned and glared out the back windshield, foot hammering the gas.

Sticks and pebbles tinged off the metal underneath the Bronco as the tires licked up the earth.

Les yanked the wheel around, causing them to do a ninety degree turn. He slung the stick to drive, throwing sticks and pebbles, Sam clinched the seat with both hands, as they made it down the mountain a lot faster than they did up it.

Omah

7

Tuesday morning just after Legends and Tales had opened, Adam Lightfoot noticed an old Bronco skidding into the gravel parking lot. The front windshield shattered as if it'd taken a mortar. He gripped the counter and tucked his head beneath his shoulder with a twisted grimace, preparing for the Bronco to plow through the building.

Adam watched as a familiar couple hurried out of the Bronco and rushed inside. The bell above the door welcoming them. Their eyes wide and crazed, their hair a mess, looking like they'd just rode a time machine from the cavemen days.

"You're not going to believe this man," Les said as he rested his elbows on the counter and leaned over to catch his breath.

Adam wrinkled his brows, "Try me."

Brenda was in the back hanging up a new set of bigfoot shirts that had just came in from Redding when she heard the commotion.

Sam clung to Les' arm as he began.

He told them the whole account from beginning to end. Les was a fast talker to start with, but even more so when he was excited or spooked.

Adam and Brenda caught the gist of what he said, though at times it was hard to understand. They needed one of those signs with a number on it, so they could raise it and place a bid.

Les paused to catch his breath.

"I have never been that scared before in my life."

Adam took a breath and looked to Brenda. She caught his gaze and locked eyes with him. They nodded.

"Would you want to make a report about it? We could contact the local BFRO. It's a group of Bigfoot researchers, they'd be more than happy to come out and document your encounter."

Les and Sam thought for a moment.

"Nah...I don't want to do anything like that. But maybe at least we should tell a Ranger. Just tell them there's a bear in the area or something. That way they can warn other campers to be on the lookout."

"Okay...I tell you what, I'm buddies with a Game Warden here, Steve Phillips, you could give him a call and he could contact the guys up in Willow Creek."

"Yeah that'd be great."

Brenda smiled and said, "Steve's a great guy. We've known him for a while. He attends our Pau Wau each fall and spring."

Adam and Les were busy exchanging Warden Phillips number as they leaned on the counter, phones in hand.

"Well listen...I hate you had to experience that last night. I really don't think they would have hurt you. They're just super territorial creatures. They do that kind of stuff to drive you off their land. Like an old grumpy man yelling for you to get off his lawn."

Sam laughed as Adam and Les snickered while double checking the number and being sure the translation was correct.

"So, I guess we just happened to cross old Clint from Grand Torino, huh?" said Les with a grin as he held the phone to his ear.

After the fifth ring it went to his voice mail. Les left a message. Adam sent a text.

A 24' flat screen hung high in the corner with the volume low. A news reporter flapped his silent lips as a long box appeared to the right of him, with the words, "Bear Attack near Hoopa."

"Hey turn that up!" Les said pointing.

Adam hurried over and clicked the volume on the side.

The news reporter told a twisted story of Jimmy Davis' encounter as the scene cut to pictures of his shredded back.

They each winced at the gruesome sight.

Les rubbed his beard.

Adam sighed, "We've got to get a hold of Steve and find out what's going on. If a Squatch did that, then something's got them stirred up. That's not typical behavior for them."

Adam scrolled through his contact list and dialed out a number.

"He might be on duty," said Brenda.

"No, I'm calling Jack to see if him and grandpa have heard."

8.

Two days had past, since the Jacobs' were last in Texas. Thursday morning at seven thirty on the dot, Randy fired up the engine in a Walmart parking lot five miles south of San Francisco.

Having stuck with the plan, they were able to spend about three hours in Los Angeles and Hollywood, long enough to snap the pictures they wanted and get caught in a traffic jam from hell.

They made it to the Walmart parking lot around nine o'clock the previous night and now had plans to spend the morning sight seeing San Francisco before heading north on Highway 101 towards Myers Flat.

Bev fastened her seat belt across from Randy who stole a sip of his coffee and shifted the gear stick to drive.

The kids were asleep on the bunk above the driver's cab.

Passing through the morning commute, it took about thirty minutes for them to make it to the city and find a spot to park where they could walk around a bit.

"This should be good for a little while, shouldn't it?" Randy asked as he looked to Bev.

The look on her face, said the spot wasn't to her liking.

"Where do you want me to go?"

"Mmm...how about over there near that grassy area." She said as she pointed out the window to her right.

Omah

Randy leaned on the wheel and looked around her.
"All right."
The RV chugged about twenty yards over and settled in a cozier spot.
Bev and Randy unbuckled.
Randy planted his feet to the concrete and stretched.
Bev had to stand on an arm of the couch to reach the kids on the bunk.
"Hey…wake up. We're in San Francisco."
They moaned and squirmed.
Tyler lied on his back in the middle, mouth hung wide, arms straight out to his side and resting on Jennifer and Andrew's shoulders.
Bev jostled Jennifer's leg.
"Hey wake up."
She groaned and jerked her head away, burying it deeper in her pillow.
"C'mon…get up so you get some clothes on."
Tyler mumbled something about a Yeti.
Another thirty minutes passed before they stepped out of the RV and headed for a scroll downtown.
Red trolleys zoomed past, bells ringing as they climbed the hills and coasted down the other sides.
Crowd chatter was loud, the wind was brisk and the fog on the Bay hung low.
About a half mile into their walk, a large brick column with a pyramid top, a white clock with orange writing of *Home of the San Francisco Giants*" resting above it, came into view.
Randy's gut twisted, a lump formed in his throat, as tears stung his eyes.
He cleared his throat and cut to the right in front of an old barber shop.
"Hey, let's go this way."

The yank on Bev's hand caught her off guard.

"What are you doing?" she asked with a puff of air and crooked grin.

Randy wiped his face with his free hand before corralling the kids in front of them.

He leaned down and whispered in Bev's ear.

"The Giant's stadium is just over there. I didn't realize."

"Oh. I'm sorry honey."

Randy waved her off, tightened his lips and rested his arm around her to give her a good squeeze.

"It's just tough you know. I mean I had so many dreams of hitting my first homerun there and seeing my family cheer me on in the stands," he stopped and diverted his attention to a Ripley's sign.

"Hey, this should be fun. What do you think?" he asked Bev.

It caught the kids' eye about the time she answered.

"Can we please do this?" asked Andrew as he and his brother and sister came rushing to Randy and Bev as if begging for bread.

"I've heard this one's really good," said Jennifer.

Bev smiled, "Oh really? Yeah let's do it."

JUST AFTER nine o'clock that morning in the middle of Bridgeville and Myers Flat, two teenage friends, Rhonda and Robin were heading to a creek bed on Robin's grandpa's sawmill land.

It'd been two years since Rhonda had last been down here. Ever since what happened to her dad and brother, her dad had made it clear not to ever go back. But Robin's insistence gave way to Rhonda's objection. Robin wouldn't hush about all the arrow heads she'd been finding and even had a few to prove it.

As Rhonda continued to glance over her shoulder while following her friend, she asked, "You don't think our parent's will find out, do you?"

Robin wrinkled her brows and wagged her head, "No. Long as we're back by the time the bus stops by, we should be fine."

Rhonda nodded.

The girls passed a barn which wore rugged wooden planks that had curled outward from the weathering along with rusted tin atop the roof. It flapped and crinkled with the breeze.

Rhonda watched the rusted metal flap as they passed and asked, "Have your Uncles ever thought of reopening the mill?"

Robin tightened her lips and shook her head, "No. After Grandpa passed, they just decided to shut it down and do the cattle stuff instead."

Rhonda nodded as she looked on at the hundred-acre pasture down the rocky hill, filled with at least a dozen cows and calves, but only one Bull. Though his size made up for it. He was worth two any day.

A creek snaked around the pasture's perimeter. It was known for its catfish. Perfect eating size. Rhonda's dad and brother had fished it quite often but stopped after being chased off by that bear. Their fishing rods and tackle boxes might still be down here somewhere, they never did go back to get them.

If Rhonda's dad knew she was down here, he'd probably have a heart attack. She pulled out her phone and set a timer. They had to be sure they were back before the bus made it to the neighborhood.

"Girl. You don't know what you've been missing. That coffee can I showed yesterday..."

Rhonda nodded.

"...I've got another just like it. I'm telling you, I found the honey hole this time. They're everywhere down here. It's like arrowheads galore," Robin says with a grin.

Rhonda smiles back, then steals a glance or two over her shoulder.

They angle down the rocky dirt hill that fed into the pasture, being careful of their step.

The herd of cattle were gathered tightly, calves in the middle, the Bull by himself glaring across the creek. They paid no attention to the girls.

Rhonda and Robin were glad, the bull spooked them anyhow and they were always sure to never wear red around him.

They crossed toward the corner of the pasture, which was Robin's hot spot for the arrowheads. They'd have one hill to cross before reaching it. A small handmade cabin rested at the top. Smoke had ceased to billow from the chimney years ago. Matter of fact, Rhonda couldn't remember the last time she saw someone there.

Robin said her uncle's let it go after her grandpa died. It wasn't hard to believe her. The cabin looked to have been in a competition with the barn. Which one would rot away first?

They were halfway up the hill, when the snorting of the bull gave their heart a start. They spun on their heels and looked to the herd. Still packed tight around the half dozen or so calves. The bull stood out front, pawing at the ground, hot saliva dripping to his feet.

The cows mooed and groaned as they shuffled to keep the calves protected in the center.

"What are they doing?"

Robin's eyes wide, "I don't kno—"

The loud whoop across the creek, jerked the girl's attention to the right.

OMAH

"What the heck was that? Sounded like a monkey," said Rhonda.

"Yeah right. A monkey? This ain't Africa," Robin scoffed.

"No seriously. It did, didn't it?"

"C'mon, we're wasting daylight."

Rhonda sighed and followed Robin over the hill, stealing glances behind her to the cattle, then darting her eyes to the woods across form them.

They angled closer to the wood line, the creek rippling over rocks below them.

Rhonda moved forward, but her eyes were still looking over her shoulder when she crashed into the back of her friend.

She grunted.

"What? What'd you stop for?"

Robin didn't say a word but pointed to the soft sand in front of her, just above the creek bank.

Rhonda gasped when her eyes saw it.

A ginormous footprint was smashed into the earth, at least an inch or two deep. It was horizontal to them and looked like it'd came from the creek. It only had four distinct toes and was straight without any curvature to it.

The girls raised their vision to the right and two more were visible as they looked to have crossed into the grass of the pasture, heading towards the cabin.

"Robin...I don't know about this."

"Oh...its nothing, probably just Tommy four toes again."

A beat.

"Who's that?"

Robin glanced around, searching for the correct words, hoping Rhonda wouldn't catch on.

"You know...the old man that fishes down here?"

"No...I don't. And why would anyone be barefoot down here?"

Robin tightened her lips and shrugged her shoulders.
"I'm sure it's nothing. C'mon," Robin said turning away, but not without Rhonda catching her cut her eyes to the woods across the creek.

Rhonda's heart began to knock as her gut was quivering. The stark feeling of being watched didn't help. Keeping her head on a swivel, Rhonda's eyes jumped to every sound the woods could offer. Though it seemed to be just the wind passing through the trees, as the birds and critters were silent. Another thing that was unsettling. And judging by the change in Robin's demeanor, she was sensing it too. Something just wasn't right.

Robin stopped abruptly, spun around and said, "You want to head back? I don't feel right."

Rhonda was already nodding at the first sentence, "See, you feel it too. We need to get out of here."

They turned and headed back the way they came. Over the hill and back to where the cattle were.

The whole time feeling like they were being stalked. As if an invisible presence lurked behind, licking its lips, waiting for the moment to pounce.

Clinging tight to the wood line to avoid the cattle, the girls split their time between stealing glances into the woods and keeping an eye on the cows. Though mainly the bull.

The cows and bull looked to have felt it too.

What was it?

A bear?

No. A bear wouldn't be so sneaky would it?

Whatever it was, had no need to show itself, its mere presence was enough. The girls were a few feet from the bottom of the last hill, when the loud crack and fall of a tree, demanded their attention. They stopped and jerked towards the cattle about forty yards to their right.

The Bull snorted and huffed. The cows moaned and squirmed.

More thrashing across the creek.

Pop!

Another tree snapped, this one crashing into the creek. With that the bull charged down the embankment and the girls bolted up the hill. Their legs just wouldn't move fast enough for their liking.

They were halfway up the hill when they heard it. The bone chilling shriek sent a splash of ice water up their spine. The cows screamed and groaned, the bull huffing and snorting.

Heavy feet slapped the earth in a desperate pursuit. The thing was grunting and pounding after them. Rhonda could feel the vibration of the foot thuds, reverberate within her chest.

The thing was fast for its size. Its heavy breath grunted and growled.

It wasn't the bull; it was something much worse.

Visons of the most vile and wicked monster ever created by Hollywood filled Rhonda's mind. She could just picture something big and hairy with a mouth full of drooling sharp teeth. Surely, it'd shred them in seconds.

The girls bounded and clawed their way of the rocky hill, stumbling, groping, reaching, rushing to make it out. Their legs burning as gravity and fatigue pulled at their ankles in effort to bind them for the beast.

Their lungs gasping, hearts pounding—they have to get to the top of the hill. Keep going, can't stop, mustn't stop.

Rhonda broke past Robin and turned to give her a hand. Out of the corner of her she caught glimpse of a dark silhouette, a hundred foot down the hill. She struggled to pull Robin forward, her hand slipping, then grabbing for another hold. The dark image in her peripheral edging closer. The girls found their footing and bolted forward. Climbing and gasping, tears streaking down their faces. Faster, must go faster.

    They reached the top of the hill and bound into the road at the end of the neighborhood. Their feet pattering against the pavement as they raced home and never looked back. Rhonda heard the beast give one last shriek from the pasture, it peaked then ebbed away as they did their best to create distance.

🌳 Омаһ 🌳

9

The Jacobs had made it back to the RV after their morning of sightseeing. They reached the entrance of the Golden Gate Bridge just after noon.

Bev and Jennifer snapping pictures faster than anyone could blink.

Tyler was too busy aggravating his sister to see the view. Trying his best to give the world's greatest photobomb.

"Mom! Tell him to stop please!"

"Tyler quit pestering your sister."

"Okay."

The grand Pacific to the left with the glistening sun sending its rays across the sparkling white caps.

Honking horns added to the squawking gulls. On the outside of the road, people passed along the sidewalk like trails of ants.

People jogged, biked, walked, and gazed.

To the right, the Bay partially hid itself beneath a faint cover of rising fog. Under a wispy patch, Alcatraz peaked through at the bustling commuters and tourists.

Randy gripped the wheel with a greasy left and pointed out the passenger window across Bev.

"Look...there's Alcatraz!"

Tyler wrinkled his face and asked, "What's aca-trax dad?"

"It's a real old prison where a lot of America's most famous bad guys have gone. They say its haunted by the prisoners that died there."

"Oh...well I don't ever want to go there."

"If you don't stop aggravating me, that's where we'll take you," said Jennifer with wry smile.

"Hey...it'd be better than being around you when you're cranky," said Andrew.

That pulled a chuckled from the others.

Another four hours and they'd be in Myers Flat. Home of the giants.

ADAM AND BRENDA had ten minutes before they'd be closing the store for the day. Les was able to get in touch with Warden Phillips and after making a few calls, the verdict came back about a rogue bear being the suspect for Les and Sam's encounter and the attack on the hunter.

Adam spoke with his brother Jack and Grandpa, Kosumi Windburn from their Mother's side.

Jack and Grandpa both confirmed Adam and Brenda's suspicion. Someone must have injured or killed one of the creatures for them to be acting out in such a way.

Brenda was cleaning out the register and placing cash in a zip pouch as Adam walked the perimeter to be sure each door and window was locked. The sound of crunching gravel and the soft rumble of an engine caught their attention.

In the parking lot, a C class motorhome with a Jeep Wrangler atop a silver car hauler parked catty-cornered to take up less space. The engine eased. The side door popped open and one by one, three kids landed onto the gravel. The parents exited out the driver and passenger doors.

The husband stole a glance at his watch.

Adam looked to the wooden hand carved clock hanging to his right, 4:52

The husband wasn't a large man, but he wasn't a runt either. Average build for a white man. Black hair underneath a camo and mesh hat, flannel shirt and khaki pants.

The younger boy held the hand of his Mother, who favored a Native American. Slender frame, high cheek bones and black hair that almost shaded blue when the sun hit it just right. Reminded him of the lady from that TV show his wife likes to watch. The one where they buy old houses and flip them for people.

The family strode across the parking lot; the husband opened and held the door for his wife and kids.

"Howdy folks. How you doing this evening?" Adam asked as he rested his palms atop the glass counter.

Brenda tucked the money in a cabinet under the register.

"We're doing good, how about you?" asked the man.

"Doing well-doing well. Anything in particular you're looking for?"

"No, we just happened to be riding by and saw the sign out front, thought we'd swing in and check you out," said the lady, "Hey, we ain't holding you up or anything are we? What time do you close?"

"No-no, you're fine. We close at five, but we'll give you a bit to look around. No worries. I'm Adam Lightfoot by the way and this is my lovely wife Brenda," he said as he extends an open palm.

"Nice to meet you Adam. Randy Jacobs and this is my wife Bev, Andrew, Jennifer, and Tyler," Randy said as he placed an arm around his wife and tossed a thumb to the kids.

"Where you guys staying at?" asked Brenda.

"Myers Flat. Ehh...what is it? I want to say Giant...Redwood...RV park? That sound right?" said Randy.

"Yeah, okay. Great place. Nice view of the river too. Lot of good-sized Salmon in the South Fork," Adam stretched his hands apart to demonstrate.

Tyler and Andrew turned to Randy and started pleading, "Oh, can we fish? Can we fish?"

Tyler bounded next to Randy while squeezing his arm.

"Yeah, it'd be awesome dad," said Andrew.

"Of course. I packed our rods in the Jeep. Just got to get some rigs and bait."

"I think we can help you with that. We got a whole section against the wall over there," said Adam as he pointed over Randy's shoulder.

The family turned to follow his finger. About ten foot to the left, hung the large blown up photo of a hair covered beast striding across a creek bed, head twisted on a stubby neck, looking right to the photographer.

Randy chuckled.

"Bigfoot?"

Adam and Brenda nodded, not joining Randy's laughter.

Andrew and Tyler rushed to it, oohing and ahhing. Bev and Jennifer followed them. Randy rested one hand on the counter and another on his hip and with a crooked brow asked, "Y'all believe in that stuff?"

They nodded once more.

"I'm sure you being from the South, you've probably heard stories before haven't you?" asked Adam.

"How you know we're from the South?" Randy asked rhetorically with a grin.

"With an accent like that, I'd have to say...Georgia?" said Brenda.

"Close...North Carolina."

"But hey listen…there have been reports of some bear encounters recently in the area," Adam said just above a soft whisper as he leaned close, "Just be sure to keep an eye on everyone and don't go wandering in the woods too far. Cause take it for what its worth, there are some things out there you don't want to see."

Randy tightened his lips and sighed out a breath. "Bigfoot?"

Adam pulled back with a grin and raised hands in surrender, "Hey…you said it not me. All I'm saying is, pay attention to your surroundings and be smart."

A beat.

"But hey, enough with the debate, let's get you rigged for Salmon. Shall we?" Adam said with a slap to Randy's shoulder as he stepped out from behind the counter.

Brenda followed as the three angled to the bait and tackle section.

Bev and Jennifer busy themselves looking over the wood carved knickknacks and such, as Andrew and Tyler continue to be mesmerized over the Bigfoot stuff. Everything from action figures, to driver license, footprint cast, shirts, books, newspaper clippings, et cetra.

Adam showed Randy the rigs and bait he needed. The wall next to them was covered in pictures of trophy sized Salmon and Trout, all caught from the South Fork Eel River.

"Now when you catch a monster, be sure to get your picture taken, so we can put it on our Wall of Fame." Adam flicked one of the pictures with a knuckle.

"That'd be so cool!" said Tyler.

"Yeah, that'd be awesome," added Andrew.

Up high, watching over them, stood four hand carved Sasquatches, all made from a Redwood tree.

Omah

Bev looked them over, then located the price tag and quickly diverted her attention. Like the price tag, the beady black eyes of the creatures gave her chills.

Randy collected the bait and tackle Adam suggested, as Bev and the kids loaded up with souvenirs and gag gifts.

Jennifer being the book worm that she is, at least when she's not tapping Morse code on her phone, picked up a few books along with some cool t-shirts.

One of the books was titled, *Missing people of America's National Parks: What happened to them?*

10

After leaving Adam and Brenda's store, the sun still had another hour of daylight left to give, so Randy took the long way to the campground and followed the signs for *The Avenue of the Giants.*

A narrow two-lane road led them into a tunnel covered by the canopy of Redwoods tall enough to scrape the heavens. The light faded where the first patch of Redwoods began.

The road snaked its way like a river in the crevice of two mountains. Only these mountains wore bark, limbs, and leaves.

The scenery was breath taking. At the bottom of such giants, lush green fern filled the forest floor.

Squirrels and birds rummaged and scurried.

Randy quieted the radio and lowered the windows, allowing nature to sing.

Birds chirped, leaves mimicked a snare drum, and the tires against the asphalt resembled a roaring crowd.

Now fully engulfed beneath the giant's gaze, the temperature must've fallen by twenty degrees. The sun wasn't much welcomed in a place like this as it had to peak over and through the limbs to spread its warmth.

"My goodness, this is unbelievable isn't it," said Bev as she angled her head to the tops of the trees, where the sunlight looked like stars as it broke through the canopy of branches in little patches.

Randy winded around a long curve. To the left, the trees slimmed a bit, revealing a rushing river attempting to keep pace with traffic.

It wore a bluish green tint with a rocky shoreline.

Two men dressed in waiters, standing in about knee deep water, waved their poles before casting their flies into the river in hopes for Salmon.

"Oh, look they're down there fishing now," said Randy.

"What do you think they're trying to catch?" asked Andrew as he and Tyler had their knees pressed into the couch and faces peering out the side window.

Randy stealing quick glances down the ravine at the men, "Probably Salmon."

The curve straitened and the trees covered the view of the river once more.

An empty pull off spot about fifty yards ahead caught Randy's attention, "Hey, y'all want to stop and look around for a second? Get some pictures?"

The vote was unanimous.

Randy approached the empty parking lot and eased the motorhome to a stop.

Bev ensures the kids grab their jackets, including Randy. That's the last thing they'd need is a sick driver.

The side door opens, a brisk breeze and smell of nature welcomes them. Fresh pine and earth.

Randy brings up the rear as he plants his feet to the ground behind his family and turns to lock the door.

"Goodness look at all the pinecones," said Bev as they march towards a trail leading into a village of Sequoias.

Randy twist his key, locking the deadbolt.

By the time he'd turned around, he was by himself. Bev and the kids disappearing into the woods.

His heart pulsed a few aching beats as Adam's words resurfaced in his mind, "Hey! Wait up!"

He entered a trot and caught up with Bev as the kids were about ten yards ahead of her.

"Hey! Wait for us," said Randy with a raised tone.

The kids stopped at a Redwood which had a large opening in the front, as if it was missing its door.

Traffic hissed through the thicket, their glimmer through the trees like a shooting star.

Andrew leaning into the hollowed-out Redwood, "Wow. Check it out. This is so cool."

"Dad, do you have a light?" asked Jennifer turning with one hand braced along the tree's exterior, before glancing back inside the darkened dungeon.

"No. I sure don't, I left it in the RV."

Tyler rushed to Bev in a soft whimper.

She chuckled as he clung to her.

"What's the matter."

"It's scary in there."

They reach Jennifer and Andrew and take a glance inside. A large pile of brush and pine needles were neatly arranged like a comfy bed.

"Looks like someone's been living in there," said Jennifer with a glance to her dad.

Randy strode to her and peered in, "Hmm...probably a hermit or something."

"You mean there's a hermit crab that big?" asked Tyler, his eyes as big as golf balls.

Bev wags her head and giggles, "No baby, a hermit is somebody that lives in the woods and hardly ever comes out. Not a hermit crab."

"Oh...well shouldn't we be getting out of here? What if he comes back?" asked Tyler.

"Yeah, let's head back towards the RV," said Randy as he was busy leaning in and taking big sniffs, "Man, that dude hasn't had a bath since Edison invented the lightbulb. My goodness."

The bedding smelled like soured gym clothes mixed with a few hard-boiled eggs that'd been forgotten about.

"I know...that's what I told Andrew," said Jennifer between her giggles.

Randy pulled away and scanned the forest, "All right, well let's head back. We can look around some of the ones closer to the road."

The feeling of leering eyes hidden beneath the woodsy cloak, was enough to cause his palms to grease.

The vibe just didn't feel right. Like they were on uninvited territory, sneaking around something they shouldn't.

Randy ushered Bev and the kids in front of him, trying not to let them notice his nerves.

Once behind their eyes, he turned his head again to the dense patch of woods behind them. Scanning, searching for any movement. Listening for snapping twigs or branches.

The road grew brighter with each step as the RV eventually came into focus behind the bony fingers of limbs and lush fern.

Bev fiddling in her jacket, said, "Let's get a picture with one of the trees. Jennifer, you still got the selfie stick?"

"Yeah, it's in the RV. Can I go grab it?"

"Yeah, its locked though," Randy withdrew the keys and passed them to her.

She took them and bounded along the trail to the RV about a stone's throw from them.

"It's nice up here isn't it?" Randy asked as he placed his arm around Bev and brought her in close.

"It sure is honey," she said giving him a kiss.

"Oh, c'mon you guys," Andrew moaned as he and Tyler were busy playing baseball with a stick and pinecone.

Tyler noticed and covered his eyes.

"Sorry," Randy said with a grin and toss of his hands.

Jennifer came springing back, crunching any stick or leaf along the way.

She fastened her phone to the selfie stick and thumbed her way to the camera.

Bev beckoned for Tyler and Andrew.

They huddled close in front of a Redwood almost as wide as their RV was long.

They tightened their lips revealing toothy grins and leaned in to fit within the camera's reach.

Tyler wore bunny ears from Andrew.

Randy had one arm around Bev and the other draped across Tyler's shoulder.

What wasn't to love? A happy family. The great outdoors. Fresh mountain air. Beautiful scenery.

They needed this.

It'd do them some good to get away for a while and experience nature.

It'd be something the kids would never forget.

Snap! Snap! Snap!

THE SUN had settled for the night as a damp, chill breeze wafted down from the mountains. The headlamps of the RV cut into a patch of fog that crossed the gravel path to the check-in desk.

A small wooden cabin, no bigger than most people's bedroom sat to the right.

Randy parked in the designated spot for those checking in. Bev and Jennifer stayed behind, as the boys went with their dad.

Omah

Randy opened the door and a bell tinged above them. They make their way to a cedar hewn desk. The place was void of a human soul. Two cedar rocking chairs sat opposite ends of hand carved coffee table which presented various nature magazines. A TV hung along the wall to their left, the channel was set to a local program where an elderly man was busy teaching how to fly fish the South Fork Eel River. The volume was low, but the subtitles helped.

"Be right there," a flat, raspy and toneless voice came from the back. Sounded like a woman who must've smoked a pack a day since she learned to walk.

Randy scanned the room, admiring the handy work of whoever had put the place together. The place had a cozy feel, but an unwelcoming vibe. Quite ambiguous to say the least.

Feet pounded against the hardwood as it squeaked, begging for mercy.

A heavy-set lady, with graying cropped hair and a pair of glasses draping beneath her chin entered the room. An elderly man, in a flannel shirt and jeans held by suspenders followed.

He seemed to fit the bill for the one responsible for crafting the place. The hump in his back suggested he needed a cane, but he managed without one. He plumped down to a wooden stool and crossed his arms over a bony chest.

"What can I do for you?" the woman asked without an expression.

"We have a reservation."

"Name?"

Straight to the point.

"Jacobs."

She grabbed a mouse next to the computer and jimmied it to wake the screen.

The computer hummed as it breathed out a sigh of hot air.

The old man glared at them through his thick coke bottled glasses.

Randy smiled. The man didn't.

The woman clicked and clicked, then hammered out a password.

Click. Click. Followed by more taps on the keyboard.

"Randy Jacobs?"

"That's me."

"A seven-night stay...that comes up to four o'two with tax. Cash or card?"

"Card."

The man's glare became like a mosquito bite. Randy had to scratch it.

"You build all this yourself?" Randy asked as he handed the woman his card.

She grabbed it the second his hand left the wallet. Randy pulled his eyes from the man to look at the woman, who was busy typing in the card numbers.

"He can't talk."

The man continued to glare at him as if Randy had never asked the question.

"And yeah, he built this after he inherited the land from his Father. I'm his niece."

Randy nodded.

"He hasn't talked in over thirty years. My dad found him up on the mountain all tore up. Some say it was a bear, others say it was mountain lion. Dad always said he thought he stumbled on an Indian Burial ground and disturbed the spirits."

She handed Randy the card back.

"What's he say?"

The lady reached under the counter and fumbled through a stack of papers.

She held up the stack and found what she was looking for, then slid it across the counter.

The old man perked up and attempted to straighten his spine.

The paper was a rough black sketch of a large hair covered man with a mouth full of teeth. Brows angled above piercing black eyes.

The man grunted and mumbled, rising from the stool and reaching to snatch the paper.

The lady took it before he did.

His eyes locked on the woman's, his jaw set firm, his nose snarled, his fist in a ball.

Tyler and Andrew took notice as the commotion broke their gaze from the man on TV teaching to fly fish.

"Sorry. Sometimes he's picky about who sees it. Depends on the mood he's in."

Randy cleared his throat and rubbed the back of his neck.

"I'm sorry, I've just never been much of a believer in all this Bigfoot stuff."

"You stay around here long enough...you might just change your mind."

Randy bit the inside of his lip and cocked a brow.

The lady passed him a flyer with a map of the grounds along with the Wi-Fi information, "Just be careful. Enjoy your stay."

"Thank you. If I see one, I'll be sure I've left the camera in the car," Randy said with a smirk.

"Let us know if you need anything. Be careful," said the lady as she took the glasses from her eyes, allowing them to dangle under her face once again.

The old man furrowed his brows and eyed Randy and the boys on the way out.

The bell tinged and the door latched behind them.

"Man, they were some kooks huh?" Randy said as he folded and stuffed the brochure in his back pocket.

"That man was strange, daddy," said Andrew.

Randy scoffed, "Well...most people that claim to have seen a big hairy man wandering the woods, usually are."

The moon was crawling out from behind the mountain. Peaking at the campers below.

Crickets began their evening song as a lonely Owl joined in the distance.

AFTER FINDING their spot and getting settled in, Bev made some homemade spaghetti that they enjoyed while watching a new Goosebumps movie.

By 11pm, they were out cold.

It was a few hours later when Bev jolted awake to the sound of an awful wail high upon the mountain.

Sounded like someone was being murdered.

She rose and formed an L, twisted her head, waiting for it to wail again. She reached for her phone in the cubby next to the bed.

1:49

Randy laid on his side, eyes wide, breath stilled, ears alert.

The gentle shake of Bev's hand startled him.

"Honey...did you hear that?" she asked.

"Yeah...must be some lit campers. Probably some young people that ain't figured out how to handle their booze yet."

"I sure hope so. That sounded horrible. I've never heard anything like it."

"I'm sure it's nothing, get some sleep baby,"

Omah

Randy said as he reached behind him and patted Bev's leg.

She sighed, then lowered herself back to the comfort of the sheets.

She snuggled in close to Randy's back.

"All right, love you honey."

"Love you too babe."

Randy didn't sleep for another hour as his curiosity wouldn't allow it. Listening past the crickets, rustling wind, and soft rain lighting upon the roof, he waited for another wail. But his heavy eyes were sealed shut before the wailing woman ever cried again.

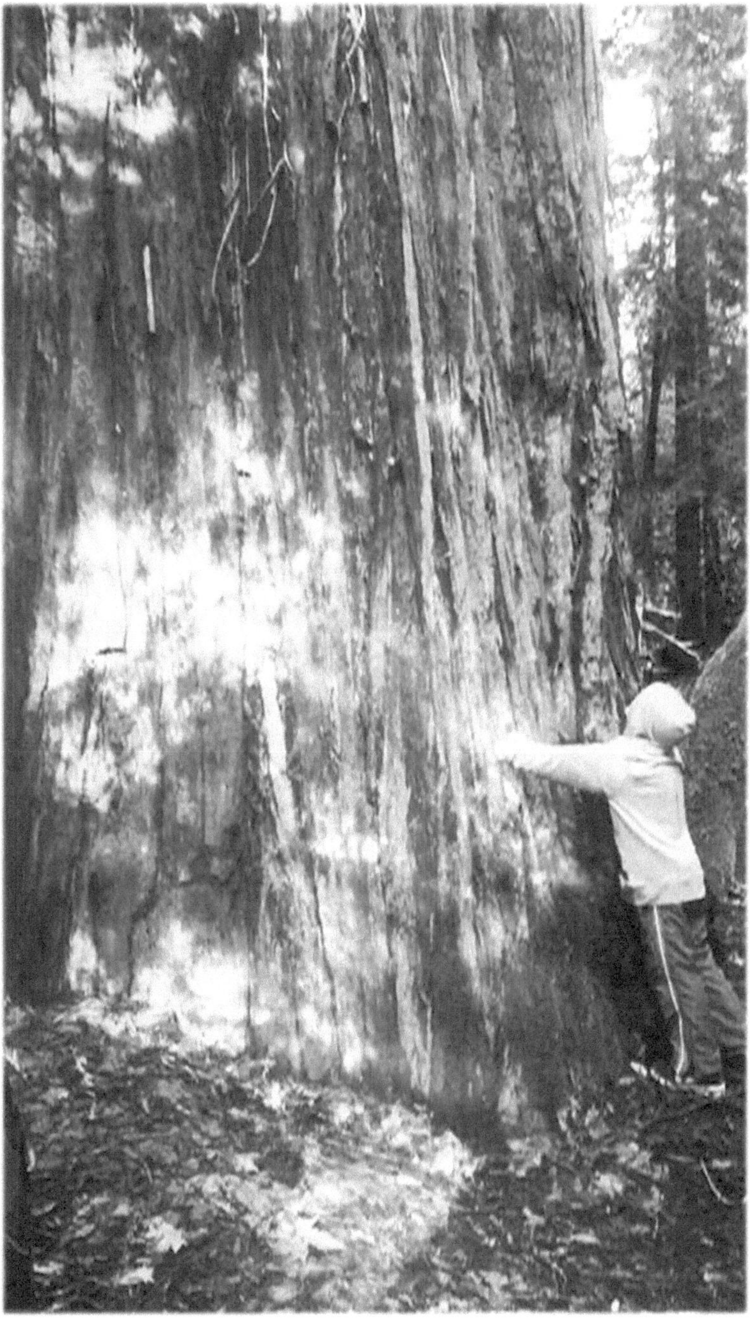

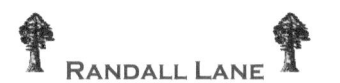

Omah

11

The alarm on Randy's phone began at 7:10 and after three snoozes, continued until 7:40. He hardly ever slept past three snoozes; Bev wouldn't allow it. Randy rose and twisted to the edge of the bed. His feet dangled for a moment before lighting upon the soft carpet. He took a deep breath, sighed it out long and hard, before giving his face a good rub down.

The sun had snuck through the blinds, casting a glowing ray upon Bev, still wrapped in the covers like a butterfly in a cocoon.

Randy patted her leg and grinned, before rising for the bathroom.

"What time is it?" she asked as if there was sand in her throat.

"Seven forty-two," said Randy as he relieved himself.

The toilet flushed with a hiss and the door creaked open. Bev cleared her throat, crawled out from the cocoon and spread her wings like a blooming butterfly, the sun caressing her back.

"You want to fix breakfast or lunch?" she asked in a half yawn.

"I'll fix the lunch and get everything packed up, if you'll take care of breakfast."

"All right."

Randy moved in and kissed her before heading into the kitchen.

It was *9:12* when they began the trek to the South Fork Eel River.

"Dad...did you get the bait?" asked Andrew.

Randy retrieved a white plastic bag and jiggled it, "I sure did. Got it right here."

The sound of rippling water filled the air as tall pines stood across the river, swaying with the breeze. Small pebbles crunched beneath their feet as they followed a trail to the river that descended an embankment.

Randy went first then turned to help Bev and the kids.

They continue to the river as it came into full view. A light fog settled above the trees like a top hat, just below the snow-capped mountains in the distance.

The gentle west to east flow of the river was easy on the eyes. The crunching of pebbles beneath their feet, ebbed as the ground was now a soft smush with the pebbles turning to sand the closer they got to the river's edge.

"This seems like a nice spot. What do you think?" said Randy as he scanned the river and mountain side.

The air was chill, but not enough for their breath to steam. The sun's rays cutting through the fog was a welcomed guest. Its warm hand stroked upon their cheeks.

A red tail Hawk flew overhead, chased away by two cawing Crows.

"The river's got a bluish tint to it doesn't it?" asked Bev.

Randy nodded, "Yeah...it's from the Cyanobacteria. A type of algae. That's what the sign said at the store."

"Oh really?" Bev questioned as she busied herself with unpacking an outdoor folding chair. Jennifer did the same. Randy was busy piecing the fishing rods together, while Andrew and Tyler studied the bait.

"What is this stuff?" asked Tyler.

"It's called Power bait. It's scented like Salmon eggs. The guy at the store said it was the best thing to use down here. Said it's what a lot of the guys in those pictures used."

Andrew spun the jar before his eyes, the mountains serving as a backdrop and asked, "Really?"

Bev crashed in her chair next to Jennifer and looked to Randy, "You do have your fishing license, right?"

"Yeah, I got them from the store. Here you go Tyler," Randy said as he passed him a rod, before preparing Andrew's.

Tyler practiced casting onto the sand and pebbles. Having grown up along the coast with a dad who'd done his fair share of fishing over the years, casting and using a spinning real, was second nature to the Jacobs boys. One of the many things Randy was sure to pass down, along with his skill and knowledge of baseball of course.

Randy chuckled at Tyler as he acted out hooking the fish of a lifetime. Only it wasn't a fish, it was a log that'd washed ashore.

Randy fixed Andrew's and passed it off, then prepared his own.

Andrew join Tyler in fishing for the biggest land fish known to man.

Randy popped the lid of the Power bait. A raw fishy scent introduced itself, causing Randy to slam his eyes, snarl his nose, and jerk his head away.

In a matter of seconds, Bev and Jennifer had gotten a whiff as the breeze carried it to them.

"Oh my gosh. What the heck is that?" asked Jennifer behind the cover of her elbow crease.

"Salmon bait," Randy said with a grin.

"I think I'm going to be sick."

Bev coughing said, "Whew. That stuff is raunchy."

Randy cleared the fumes from his throat, "Your telling me. It ought to do the trick though."

Andrew and Tyler had done placed their reels in the sand and was rushing over to the excitement. Randy stopped them before they reached him and pointed over their shoulders, "Hey. Don't leave the reels in the sand. We have to take care of our stuff now, remember?"

The boys spun on their heels and hurried to gather the rods before racing each other back.

"All right Tyler, let me see your hook."

Randy baited it, the stinky hooked ball swinging like a pendulum.

Randy watched as Tyler raced about twenty feet down from them, flipped the bell on the spinning reel, pinched the line with the crevice of a finger— just like his daddy had showed him—reared back and flung it out to the moving current.

Randy smiled, then turned and looked on as Andrew baited his own hook. He's at that age now, where he thinks he do everything on his own.

Andrew finished and wiped his hands on his hips, then hurried next to Tyler and cast a line.

Randy's turn. He baited up and angled next to the boys.

Bev retrieved her phone and began snapping pictures, while Jennifer was quick to check her Facebook.

"Hey...let's give it a break for bit huh? Look around you, isn't this gorgeous?" said Bev as she leaned on the arm of her chair and waved to the scenery before them.

Jennifer sighed and passed the phone to her Mama. Bev tucked it away in her bag.

"Once they finish trying to catch the Loch Ness Monster, we'll go into town and do some shopping and sightseeing."

Jennifer nodded.

"You know, this will be a trip you'll be telling your kids and grandkids about for years. I mean how many people can honestly say they travelled cross country in an RV?"

A beat as Jennifer shrugged.

"It'll be worth it. Trust me. I just want you to take it all in and enjoy the scenery while its here. Because in a flash, we'll be back in the Carolina's returning to the routine. Embrace the adventure and enjoy the scenery while you can," Bev smiled and rested her hand on Jennifer's arm.

Jennifer looked to her with her daddy's bright blue eyes and gave a smile back.

"Oh boy. It's a big one," said Randy as Tyler stumbled along the riverbank, the tip of his rod making big arcs like a small r.

His line jutted up stream, tight enough to pluck a tune.

"Woohoo," Tyler hollered, waving his hand as if riding a bucking bull.

Randy rushed over to lift the rod tip up before the fish had a chance to spit the hook, "Hey, pay attention now, don't give him any slack. Keep ya line tight."

Bev hurried to adjust her phone's camera and began filming. Her and Jennifer rose from their chairs and edged closer, eager to see the monster. Andrew sat his reel atop a log, being sure to keep it out of the sand this time and looked on at the action.

The fish made one last effort as it jutted back to the current before turning and racing to shore. Tyler adjusted and raced to wind the slack.

Now only arms reach from the bank, Randy squatted down at the waters edge, line in his right hand, he stretched with his left and grabbed the fish.

Black spots lined its back as a faint pinkish line streaked down its side.

"Haha. Ole man. Good job buddy!" Randy said high fiving a toothy grinned Tyler

"Is that a Speckled Trout?" asked Jennifer.

"No. I think it's a Cut-Throat Trout," answered Randy as he stepped away from the river's edge, gripping the greasy fish with both hands. He adjusted his grip and reached for the plyers on his hip.

Randy plucked the hook loose, Tyler handed the rod off to Andrew and stretched his arms for the fish.

Randy knelt beside Tyler, his arm around his back, with a straight thumb from his right. Andrew flanked the opposite end and wore a big smile with two stiff thumbs.

Tyler in the center, hanging on to the slippery, squirmy fish for dear life.

Bev took a step back to get them all in the frame.

"Say cheese."

Snap! Snap!

WITHIN TWO HOURS, Randy and the boys were one fish shy of their limit of Cut-Throat Trout. The cooler on the bank behind them, contained enough for a nice evening meal, just like Randy had hoped for.

Bev and Jennifer had already made the journey back to the RV to freshen up.

Tyler began to squirm and crossed his legs, "Dad, I got to pee."

Randy, with his focus on the nibble at the end of the line, said, "Okay, well just find a bush or something, where nobody will see."

"What about that bush around the corner?" Tyler questioned as he turned and pointed to a bend.

Omah

"Yeah, just hurry up."

Tyler wound his line in and propped the reel atop the tackled box next to Randy.

Tyler trotted to the bush, peaking over his shoulder, as Randy and Andrew grew smaller with each step.

"Oh, I got a big one!" Andrew shouted.

Tyler could now only see splotches of his brother and dad, as the brush done its job of concealment.

Tyler watered the pebbles and sticks, sighing as he did so.

"Tyler hurry up. Your brothers got a nice one!" Randy yelled, his voice faint for the distance.

Tyler zipped his fly, but the rustle in the brush gave his heart a jolt.

"Who's there?"

It rustled again.

A twig snapped, rocks tumbled into the river.

"Who's ther—"

12

"Tyler! Hurry up, you're going to miss it!" Randy yelled.

"Woohoo! Haha!" Andrew yipped while straining to reign the fish in.

"Keep it tight. Just like I taught you now."

Randy traced the line from the rod tip down to the water's surface. Eyes darting every which way, as the fish bounded left and right like a pinball.

"Tyler!" Andrew hollered.

Randy grunted as he squatted on his calves, "My goodness. What's he doing?"

"Must've had to do a number two."

The fish made a dash downstream near a fallen log. Oh no. Randy had a premonition of the fish wrapping around a branch and breaking free.

Randy bolted from the bank and reached for the rod.

"Nah ah. This is my fish," Andrew wagged his head and turned his shoulder to Randy.

"No. Look he's heading for the tree. Let me have it before he wraps you up in it. I'll give it right back."

Andrew gave it up with a reluctant tilt of his head. Randy took the rod and fought the fish away from danger. Then just like he promised passed the controls back to his son.

OMAH

Wearing down, the fish cruised to the bank, then gave one final tail slap.

"Ohhhh! My goodness! Will you look at that!" Randy exclaimed as he went in to grab it.

He cradled it against his gut. The head and tail extended about four inches past each side of his waist.

"Is that a Salmon-is that a Salmon?" Andrew asked, dropping the rod as he rested his hands atop his head and jumped in place.

"It sure is," Randy said with a grin bigger than the California and Nevada border.

"Grab the tape from my tackle box. Let's get a measurement on this bad boy."

Andrew drop to a knee and fumbled through Randy's bag full of lures and rigs in plastic compartments. It was easy to spot the tape measure. All the rigs and lures were organized by color and size, it all had its place, and everything was in its place.

He grabbed the tape and handed it to Randy. Like learning signs from the third base coach, Randy knew the size regulations by heart.

"He's got to be 21 inches to keep," Randy's tongue hung out the corner of his mouth as he laid the fish on the sandy pebbles and extended the tape measure.

He fixed the angled end at the fish's mouth and pulled the tape westward. Glancing back at the mouth, being sure the end of the tape hadn't moved.

A glance at the reading. A bead of sweat dripped off his forehead. A glance back to the fish's mouth.

"What is it? What is it?"

Randy looked up with a blank face and held it on Andrew.

"How big? How big?"

Randy sighed and dropped his head. Then snapped it up.
"23!"
He gave Andrew a stinging high five and ruffled his hair. Randy popped the hook loose and headed for the cooler.
"You ready to call it day? I think we got enough for supper."
"Yeah-yeah. Man, I can't believe I caught a Salmon."
"I know bud. It's a monster too."
Randy secured the cooler and zipped his tackle bag, sending his eyes to the bush Tyler had supposedly wandered off to.
"Tyler! C'mon bud, we're leaving."
No answer.
"Tyler!?"
Just the ripple of the current and flutter of the leaves bristled by the breeze.
"Tyler! Hey!"
Nothing.
"Man. What the heck is he doing?"
"I bet he's taking a dump," said Andrew with a snicker.
"He better not be," Randy chuckled.
Randy placed the strap to the cooler and tackle bag across his shoulder, Andrew grabbed the rods and bait.
"C'mon. Let's see what he's doing," Randy nudged with his head and marched off to the bend. Andrew followed behind.
"Tyler...bud, c'mon we got to go," Randy's heart picked up pace with each lack of a reply from his son.
"He's got to be playing. He's probably hiding in the brush going to try and scare us or something," Randy mumbled to himself, "Tyler...it's not funny, come on out. We got to get back to the RV so we can skin some fish. You ought to see what your brother caught."

Omah

The bush grew bigger as they were now about distance from the mound to home plate.

Randy swallowed and scratched an itch between his shoulder blades. The sand turned to small pebbles the further they got from the river bank. They crunched under his and Andrew's feet like someone chewing on ice.

They angled around the bend.

"Tyler?"

Nothing but pebbles and brown dying bushes.

Randy snapped his head side to side. His eyes darting, his pulse pounding, an electric charge sent a dose of ice water up his spine and across his flesh. His breath felt labored.

"Tyler!"

"Dad look at this," Andrew was crouched behind him, with his eyes focused into the murky water only feet from the bank.

Randy crossed to him and squatted to get a look.

Two footprints almost double the size of Randy's were pressed deep into the sand and pebbles about a foot beneath the water's surface.

Randy took a deep breath, covered his mouth and rubbed his beard. He stood over the prints with his eyes drifting to the steep hill across the river. Pines marched along the hillside, before giving way to Giant Sequoias and snowcapped mountains.

His eyes strained with moisture as his bottom lip began to tremble. His gut twisting in knots.

His gaze fixed to the mountain side for what seemed like hours.

"Dad? Where's Tyler?"

Randy cleared his throat, wiped an eye and said,

"Let's head back to the RV. Maybe he went back, because he knew that's where your mom and sister were."

Andrew dropped his head and climbed the embankment. Randy took a few steps backward up the hill, his eyes jumping from the prints to the dense forest of Redwoods.

His mind filled with yesterday's memories. Adam and Brenda from the store. Adam's warnings. The old man and lady at the check-in desk.

The wailing woman from last night echoed between his ears.

My God. What if they were telling the truth? What if there really is something out here? And what if it has Tyler?

No. Can't think like that. Don't go there. Not yet.

🌲 Оман 🌲

13

The Humboldt County Department of Natural Resources is a quiet, aged, brick building nested near the county line off US-101. Roughly a thirty-minute drive to Myers Flat, depending on the time of year and if you needed chains strapped to the tires or not.

It was a quarter after twelve, when Warden Steve Phillips was informed of the missing boy in Myers Flat. There were a handful of reasons Steve Phillips had plans to retire next year and having to deal with cases like this certainly made the decision a little easier. He'd seen enough to haunt him till he went to the grave.

In twenty-two years of serving as Humboldt County's Chief Warden, Phillips had directed seventeen missing children cases, and had failed to rescue five. Those odds have haunted him every night since Kyle Bouchard went missing back in 1997.

They found his body thirty foot up a pine, draped across its green needles. The smell of fresh pine has taunted him ever since. One whiff of it, and the face of little four-year-old Kyle Bouchard surges across his mind like a tsunami.

With little to no evidence, the coroner ruled it "death by nature." The speculation was and still is, a large cat. The other two—six-year-old Stacey Laeder and ten-year-old Dusty Holland—were found much in the same manner over the next fifteen years.

They vanish into thin air while hiking or camping with the family, only to have their body discovered some twenty or thirty feet in the air, resting in a pine.

No major wounds, other than a snapped neck and a few puncture wounds near the jugular.

For the other two—three-year-old Joshua Thomas and seven-year-old Wade McPhee—their bodies were never recovered.

Along with the kids, adults were mixed in as well.

Thirty-four to be exact.

Only thirteen were ever recovered. Ten of those were found scattered among wooden type structures in the woods. The other three in a hollowed-out Redwood.

The majority of the adults were male hunters. Twenty-eight of them with past criminal convictions surrounding unethical hunting practices, such as poaching and exceeding tag limits. The other six were fugitives with a history of violence.

Rumors among the locals have long since circulated about a possible serial killer, aliens, ghosts, Indian burial grounds...Bigfoot.

After hearing of the wounded hunter from Hoopa, the campers near Willow Creek, and now the missing kid in Myers Flat, Phillips forced himself to believe it was just a cat or bear. He found comfort in the thought.

Tracking and capturing a rogue cat or bear was included in his study and training. He and his guys were prepared for that. Which brought along the nagging, stinging question of...why these disappearances continue to happen even after taking a lurking cat or wandering bear? What if the rumors weren't rumors? Were the local's speculations really all that farfetched?

Enough with the non-sense. The kid needs help and Phillips and his men were his best chance.

The Warden slipped on a heavy, ribbed army green jacket, with the words, GAME WARDEN stitched in gold across the back. He grasped the gun belt from his Desk and looped it around him. Pistol on his right hip, he fastened the buckle.

He retrieved his phone as it felt like a bee in his pocket.

Phillips sighed and rolled his eyes toward the ceiling. The words, Sheriff Logan, appeared on his screen. He grimaced as he slid his thumb across the screen.

"Hello? Yeah…well I figure that much…when you heading out? No…not on my watch. I'll be there in half an hour. Ron, not today, okay? Not really in the mood. Get your best guys and we'll meet at the LKL…No. Not going to happen…. See you in thirty."

Phillips grabbed a back pack full of gear and hurried out his office. By the time he made it out to his dark green Chevy pickup with the warden signet on both doors, a dozen other men were marching behind him.

God, please keep this boy safe. There's no need to keep adding to the number. The gravel ruffled like popcorn as six State issued trucks roared from the parking lot.

Phillips leading the pack. His heart raced. His gut tight, but quaking, it was time to make a difference. Put an end to all this non-sense. Retire with pride.

OMAH

14

By 1:43, the Giant Redwood RV park resembled a hornet's nest. Flashing police cruisers had rushed in as a slew of Humboldt and Mendocino State trucks filled the campground to its limits. Multiple Sheriff deputy Tahoe's were scattered about, a handful of them were K-9 units.

German Shepherds cloaked with black jackets, panted at all the excitement as they tugged at their leashes, forcing the officers to pound their way to the river.

A Channel 14 news van whipped in behind a black Crown Victoria with tinted windows and state issued tag. The car crawled along the entrance to the park, crunching over gravel, eating away at the news van driver's patience as he trailed behind. The news driver adjusted in his seat and bit his lip. It took all he had not to bolt around the crawling Detective.

CSI were getting set up and busied themselves with snapping pictures of the prints, about a foot from the river's edge.

Rested upon a Sheriff Tahoe, a map of Humboldt County covered the hood as Sheriff Ron Logan marked it up with different colored pens. Biting off the caps and grinding his teeth upon the plastic as he scribbled wiggly lines here and drew circles there.

Warden Phillips did the same, bumping shoulders with the Sheriff more than once as he jotted down the miles from each attack and encounter.

Warden's, Deputy's, and Officer's formed a half circle around Logan and Phillips. By standers formed an outer layer as all the commotion pulled them from their campers like a magnet.

Channel 14 followed the Crown Victoria as they passed the information and check-in cabin where seated on the porch just big enough to hold a rocking chair, the old man bobbed back and forth like a buoy upon a calm sea. He chewed on a wooden pipe he'd carved from a Sequoia back when his hands could function without freezing up from the arthritis. He took a drag, the sweet smell of peach tobacco invading his nostrils and seeping into is his worn-out burgundy flannel.

He sighed out the smoke and watched as it lingered skyward, competing with the fog over the mountain. The old man tightened his lips and twisted his head to and fro, like a plank swing below an old oak.

His glasses fogged for the third time since the campground received its company. He rubbed out the smudges using his thumb and forefinger with the softness of his flannel. Pipe clinched with an aching jaw, the tobacco smoldered.

If only people would listen. Why it took something like this to open their ears, he'd never know. The man wagged his head once more and eased back into his rhythm with the squeaky chair.

He hoped they'd find the boy. And he hoped he'd still have a pulse when they did.

Omah

15

Sweat and tears drenched the tan carpet in the bedroom of the Jacobs' RV. Randy and Bev sat the end of the bed gripping each other as if they were tandem skydiving.

Their hearts heavy and sitting low in their gut, all they could do, was hold each other. Words were just too hard to form at the moment as their minds were racing faster than a spinning top. Salty liquid stung their eyes and taste buds.

Andrew and Jennifer sat motionless on the couch. Jennifer had her arms crossed and reddened eyes fixed to Tyler's stuffed monkey on the kitchen fold away table. Andrew nested his hands under his thighs and rocked with his watery eyes glued to the floor.

They both sniffled, but the moans of their Mother drowned it out. Randy sucked in a gasp of air through clogged nostrils. His lips quaked, his breath coming in spurts.

Bev sobbed and groaned, clinching Randy's shirt with balmy palms. When she wasn't crying and clinging to Randy for dear life, she was slapping his chest and casting blame.

Afterall, it was his fault Tyler had vanished. It was his responsibility to look after him.

"I should've known better than to leave him with you. Especially while you were fishing. Poor baby. Now he's out there all alone," her voice trailed off into another wail.

Randy forced himself to draw a deep breath, ease his mind and gain control of the situation. One thing at a time. Focus on the details. Don't look at the big picture just yet.

Details. Details. Details.

"Ssshhh...Bev. Bev...listen to me."

"It's your fault," she cried out like a wounded child, her voice dragging the inflection.

"WHY? WHY?" she gasped for breath and dug into his damp back.

"Bev. Bev. Listen. We're going to find him. There are two different County's worth of police and game wardens out there. This is what they do. They're trained for this," Randy braced both of Bev's shoulders and held her in front of him.

"We're going to find him. Trust me. Stay positive," Randy tilted his head and brows. Lines shot across his forehead. His eyes and cheeks were moist and puffy.

Bev was a mess. Her eyes wandered about the room, as if searching for the parachute's release cord to brace her from smacking the ground of her crashing world.

Her eyes landed on Randy's.

Randy brought her in close. His right hand resting behind her head, she cradled in the crevice of his neck. He kissed the crown of her head through the black shiny hair and said, "Trust me. We'll find him."

Still sitting on the couch beside her brother, Jennifer now held a hard cover book in her lap. She gazed at its cover as if it contained the secret to eternal life.

The cover art was that of a dense forest.

The title?

"**Missing people of America's National Parks: What happened to them?**"

Омах

16

Sheriff Logan and Warden Phillips were satisfied with the plan. They shared it with the chief K9-Unit officer, the senior Pilot of the search chopper, and with Detective Joe Stines whose pocket housed the key to the slow rolling Crown Victoria.

The five turned from the hood of the Tahoe and faced the crowd of search and rescue workers made up of officers, wardens, deputy's, detectives and volunteers.

"All right. Ears up. As you all know by now, this is serious. We have a six-year-old lost out here. He disappeared approximately two hours ago. Now, if we stick to the plan and stay within our organized search grids...we keep the odds in our favor," Logan scanned the crowd. His thin sliced eyes peaking beneath thick brows and a tan westernized wide-brimmed hat. His gold star pinned to his left pectoral.

Channel 14 waited behind the outer layer of spectators. Reporter Bobby Thatcher scanned the script and gripped a mic. Logan had promised a brief interview when he'd finish with his men.

Logan's thick gravelly voice continued on for another five minutes, laying out the search grids and assigning names to each. Warden Phillips flanked him with a firm jaw and hands stationed behind his back.

A chopper fluttered overhead, just high enough not to weaken the travel of Logan's voice.

Four of about a dozen or so volunteers tucked themselves away in the back. They were mostly in their mid-fifties, the youngest was forty-six. They each wore guts that had seen their share of adult beverages and could possibly be hiding kegs under all that hairy skin. Their tees and flannels were at least a size too small, maybe two. Beneath the kegs, army camo pants and to top it off, ruffled camo hats that'd seen their better days. Three of the four had high powered rifles stuck to their back, their fingers tucked beneath the shoulder straps.

The biggest of the four, had a cheek that resembled a squirrel preparing for winter. He spit a shot glass worth of black juice to the gravel. He wiped the Red Man blend from his lips and gave the wad another chew.

"Al. I think this might be our chance," said the young one to the biggest.

Al nodded in rhythm with his chewing jaw. The tobacco marinated and filled his cheek with another burst. He spit, then turned to the other two and said almost in a whisper,

"What'd you say boys? Think we can find the million-dollar man?"

Bud Nelson and Red Cromwell grinned and nodded. Neither seemed to know what a razor was. Though it did seem they at least tried to trim their scalp, but it was most likely done with a rock. They often betted one another about who'd lose it all first. At the moment, it seemed Red was in the lead.

"John, didn't you say you had that FLIR coming in?" asked Al.

Omah

"Yeah, I should have it in a few days. Got it off Ebay. It's coming from Montana, so shouldn't take too long, I don't reckon," said the forty-six-year-old, John Wallace.

The other three nodded with glowing eyes.

"Well...you fellas heard enough?" asked Al.

In agreement, they marched from the crowd and headed for the Dodge pick up truck, equipped with light bars, spotlights, a CB radio, you name it.

They'd definitely given Steve Phillips his fair share of work through the years. From hunting without a license, illegally taken a dear too close to a roadway, too close to a house, everything that drives a warden crazy, but keeps his job in tack.

Phillips eyed the men as they climbed into the Dodge. He sighed at the sight, then refocused on Logan.

"Cramer...Jarrickson...Higgensworth...Feltner...grid six-B. Grid six B...Matthews...Dayton..."

In spite of the history of cases like this, hope wafted through the valley, riding the breeze. Just has he'd done thirty-four times in his career, Phillips promised the kid he'd bring him back to his family.

And with God as his witness, he'd do whatever it takes to make sure that happens.

17

Jarred up and down with his little fists clinching to wads of thick, grungy, coarse reddish hair, Tyler felt like he was riding in his dad's center console boat as they bounded atop the ocean in search of King Mackerel.

Only this time, he was on land. Trees whizzed by like mailboxes on a straight away. His head bobbed toward the brown forest floor. His eyes jiggled and attempted to reign in the tops of the passing trees. Heavy foot falls drummed in his ears, as the creature's pads slapped flush against the ground. The beast grunted and snorted, seeking desperately to fill its lungs with precious air.

Each time he'd tried to yell, the creature covered his face with its leathery, slimy, and sticky hand. Tree sap almost glued his eyes shut once.

As he rode along, tucked against ribcage of a hairy monkey, he kept telling himself it was just a dream. Had to be didn't it? No chance this was real life. He should've listened to his Mama and not watched all those YouTube videos with his brother.

All the jarring had giving him a headache as nausea came in spurts, like the one now. He felt it build and crawl its way from his gut to his face. He tried to cover it with his flailing arms but was too late. It splattered

Omah

against the chest and belly of the beast for a second time.

The creature stopped and panted. Its head twitched about the forest, with eyes darting and nostrils flaring. Its lips curled as it gasped for breath. It dropped its gaze to Tyler and stared. Cradling him with its right arm, it took its left hand, full of pudgy fingers and toyed with his lips, nose, and eyes.

With the back of its hand, it wiped the vomit from his mouth, then sniffed. It grunted and snarled. Let out a low guttural gargle like growl, then shifted its eyes back to the cluster of trees and brush.

It readjusted Tyler and bolted once again. Tree limbs slapped across its burly chest. Its thudding, powerful, giant like steps vibrated Tyler's heart, like his brother's bass amp.

It has to be a dream. This can't be real.

Any second, Mama would wake him. No way, this is real. Everything seemed like a blur, just like in a dream. The jarring of his head and dimming of the light said this was the closing scene where he'd trade this dream for another or awake back in the real world.

The snapping twigs and branches and huffing of the beast, grew faint. His vision turned dark. His body felt numb.

All was quiet. His body floated out into the violent sea. His mind wandered in search of land.

18

As promised channel 14 got their interview with Sheriff Logan, however brief it was, at least it was something.

"Sheriff can you tell us the age and appearance of the boy?" asked Bobby Thatcher, mic angled to Logan.

"Six-years-old, short blond hair, brown eyes, three-foot-ten, fifty-five pounds, last seen wearing khaki pants and a black hoodie with the words Sunset Beach written across the front," the Sheriff drew a breath.

"Thank you, Sheriff. As I'm sure you are aware, do you believe this could be related to the hunter and campers who were attacked near Willow Creek and Hoopa?"

Logan eyed Thatcher without giving any expression.

A beat.

Thatcher tightened his lips and raised his brows. Logan slowly broke his gaze and looked to the camera.

"We're not going to think the worst here. We are well aware as to what has taken place over the last few days and are equipped to handle anything thrown our way. But at the moment..." his eyes shifted back to Thatcher, "...we are keeping things simple and going with what we have. Saying that, we have no indication that there has been any type of attack or struggle. Our best indication is that Tyler wandered off. Likely crossing the river at a large fallen tree down below where his dad and brother were fishing. If he was desperate enough, it wouldn't have been too difficult for him to do. That's what we have and that's what we're sticking to until evidence suggest otherwise."

Logan's eyes drilled Thatcher like a hornet.

Thatcher asked another question, but Logan refused to answer

Adam pointed the remote to the corner TV and turned down the volume just a bar or two.

Brenda had one hand tucked under an elbow with the other covering her mouth. She shut her eyes and wagged her head at the floor. She let a small breath escape through her nose. Its warmth rolled off her fingers.

Adam turned and looked at his wife, hands on his hips. He sighed and shook his head.

"I told that man to be careful. He thought I was jerking his leg. I should've been more blunt with him and told him what I know."

"Honey...don't think like that," she angled to him and wrapped her arms around him.

They held each other in that warm embrace as Thatcher turned his report back to the studio. A professionally dressed man and woman sat behind a rectangle table. Stacks of papers rested next to the few held in their hands. The follow up story?

Permit granted for new apartment complex just outside Eureka. Logging crews got the go ahead. The once lush patch of forest would soon become residential and teaming with life and modernization.

It'd be the largest housing effort the town had seen. The students at Humboldt State would sure be happy.

Brenda bit her lip and swayed her head as she pulled from Adam. He turned and looked at the tv screen behind him.

"That's not going to help the matters. There's no wonder they've gotten more aggressive over the years. We keep taking away their homes, they'll be forced to move in with the students."

He rubbed his eyes and pointed fingers at the lady reporter on the screen.

He finished his rant. His eyes fell to the floor.

"Brenda...we need to go up there and talk with the family. I need to be in the woods helping search for the boy. I couldn't live with myself if I didn't."

Brenda nodded and gave a faint smile. They embraced once more before gathering their necessities and locking up. They'd just have to take a loss for the day, but if it meant helping to bring that boy home, it'd be worth it.

Omah

19

The side door to the Jacobs' RV creaked open, a pair of brown Rocky boots landed on the metal steps. Randy took a deep breath and planted his feet to the cool moist soil.

He rubbed a nostril with the back of an index finger, adjusted his pants and marched to a trio of Warden's on the far end of the campsite. One stretched out a map with wide arms. The other two flanked him and took turns pointing at the paper scroll.

Randy crunched over the soft pebble and edged closer. The one holding the map peaked over, his eyes between the paper and his curled bill hat.

The three whispered amongst themselves. Likely wishing a superior officer would call and rescue them from facing the mess of a man.

The middle guy, short and fit, lowered the map, then rolled and squished it into a backpack.

"How we doing sir?" he asked.

Randy nodded and snorted a short gasp through his nose.

"Doing okay. Who can I join?" he eyed each of the three as his words were like a close bolt of lightning. Neither said a word, their gaze just lingered.

"Who I can join? Who do I need to talk to?"

"Umm...uh...you'll have to talk to Warden Phillips and Sheriff Logan. I...uh..."

"Where they at?"

Two of the men turned and pointed to a man angling for a black Tahoe. In golden letters, the words, Humboldt County Sheriff, scrolled along the side, next to a large star.

The man wore black aviator glasses, a tannish gray wide brim hat and a graying mustache that must've won its fair share of competitions in its day.

"Sheriff! Sheriff Logan!" the short one yelled, his hand cupped to his mouth.

Logan twitched his head, scanning the campsite. The short one waved and said it again, "Sheriff Logan!"

Logan spotted them, stopped in his tracks, removed his glasses and gave a Clint Eastwood like glare. He dropped his head with a grumpy tilt and waved off two men climbing in the Tahoe.

Logan stomped over. The gravel crunching like being ran over by a bulldozer. A slight arch in his back, that'd surely grow in the coming years. His face softened the closer he got. Logan drew in a breath and was careful to sigh it out. He placed his hands on each end of his belt.

"Mr. Jacobs," Logan said with a dip of his head.

"Sheriff. I want to join a search crew. Just tell me who to go with."

Logan wagged his head with tight lips.

"Look. I'm going to be in those woods one way or another. If you don't assign me to someone...I'll go myself."

Logan marinated his words. Clicked his tongue against his teeth then chewed on a lip.

He huffed out some air with a slow twist of his head. His eyes gazed to the mountain side. A hawk passed in front of the pines, swallowed by the vastness of the wilderness, looking only like a speck.

Omah

"Sheriff. I've got to do this. You'd do the same if it was your boy and you know it."

Logan pushed his tongue against the interior bottom gum on his left side. Dropped his head and drifted into a slow bob.

He raised his squinty eyes to meet Randy's.

"Don't make me regret this. I'll put you with Warden Phillips and his men. He's in charge, you're just along for the ride. Got it?"

"Thank you, sir," Randy stretched out his hand, Logan met it. They traded shakes and as quickly as Logan came to them, he marched back to the Tahoe, wagging his head more than once.

THE GOUGE in the rear woke Tyler with a jolt. His head bounced off the pine needles. A jagged rock had dug into his bony hip and cheek. He whimpered and squirmed for comfort, but there was none.

The grunting and huffing of the animal along with the horrible stench, opened his eyes. He yelped and rummaged across the ground, scooting on his injured rump. His back met a wall of bark. His hands stretched to each side. Scruffy bark caressed his fingers.

The beast sat on its haunches less than twelve feet away and glared at him. Nose snarled and teeth bared with tight lips. Its big black eyes scanned him over from head to toe.

Tyler cried and let out a screechy yelp.

The beast roared and thundered over on all fours like a raged Gorilla. It pounded the ground with its fist, barely missing Tyler's feet.

Tyler turned his cheek and screamed into the dense forest of car wide red trees. It was the same kind they got their picture taken with yesterday.

The creature huffed and snorted, its breath rolling gently onto Tyler's face. An odor like onions and boiled cabbage crawled on his face as beads of moisture and mucus gathered like maggots.

Tyler gagged and heaved, his gut jolting, his cheeks puffing with air.

Two leathery black fingers stroked his forehead, then traced his features. Starting with the eyes, the nose, mouth and ending with the chin.

The creature then traced its own face, as if comparing their differences.

Black wrinkled skin was decorated with a triangle shaped forehead, deep set sunken eyes, wide nose with no arch or bridge, thick brow lines like cliffs but no eye brows, black almost purplish lips that looked like two grub worms, but much larger. A thick black beard, but no mustache and tiny ears for such a big head.

The biggest difference was the chest. It was obviously a female. The beast grunted and nudged Tyler on his shoulder with the back of its stubby fingers. He winced. It was like being slapped by two Italian Sausages, but made from concrete.

The thumps vibrated his chest.

The creature sniffed, opened its mouth wide the huffed and grunted as it toyed with Tyler's hair. Intertwining its fingers and almost chuckling as it snorted and gasped with each twirl.

It started to hurt as the beast was getting rougher.

"Hey."

The beast snorted and jolted away at least a foot. It stayed a safe distance, crouched on all fours. Its domed head went lower and lower to the earth, setting its eyes at sharp angles, studying its pet. Its lips turned pouty and plump. It sniffed and nodded its head.

Tyler thought more than once of what this thing might really be but was too afraid to admit it. Is it really a Bigfoot? It had to be. It looks exactly like what him and Andrew had seen on YouTube. Was it an escaped monkey? What would it do with him?

A loud knock crackled in the distance. The dark red...Bigfoot, snapped its head to the sound and glared into the forest. So thick, you could only see for about the length it takes to reach first base in Tee ball. Then a crowd of brush and trees grew larger.

A crow squawked over head and hopped along a branch above them. It tilted its head and side eyed the two before bolting into the air to tell the others.

The Bigfoot raised its mouth and let out a cat like hiss, then made three loud clicks with its tongue.

Silence.

Bigfoot scanned the forest, eyes squinted, lips pouty.

Knock! Knock!

This time more to the right. Bigfoot jerked to the sound and bolted to its feet. It stood twice the height of Tyler's dad.

Ooooooooaaaaahhhhhhh! Thump!

A shriek and loud crash gave Tyler a start, before he could look, two hairy arms the size of logs had hooked under his armpits and was toting him like a football. Once again, he found himself clinching two fistfuls of hair and being jarred against a hairy, sweaty, stinky beast as they bounded through the forest. Leaping over logs and swiping away at passing branches that acted like the bars you had to pass through to enter Disneyworld. A loud crashing sounded behind them. Tyler craned his head and through all the jarring could see trees ruffling and branches swaying.

They were being chased. But by what?

20

Bounding. Leaping. Stumbling. Plowing. Frantic to escape the impending danger, the beast never slowed, but continued onward through the dense canopy of pines, ferns, and Redwoods.

It huffed and wheezed for breath, its chest expanding and collapsing faster than Tyler could even think. A briar thistle raked against Tyler's arm and shoulder but was ripped away by the time he felt the stabbing of its thorns.

The odor of boiled cabbage and onions were strong. Mixing in was the smell of rotten eggs and soured socks. The beast was ringing with sweat and so was Tyler. Being flush against its hot and hairy body was like wearing a fur coat in a sauna.

Coarse red hair slapped and slid across his forehead and cheeks. He would've rubbed it away but was fearful of losing his grip and plummeting from the hair covered skyscraper.

His little body still ached from when the female dropped him on that edgy rock.

The sound of rushing water grew with each pounding leap the beast took. Its own breath and grunts were quickly growing dim as the rippling water roared, drowning out all other sound. Tyler now had to strain to hear himself think.

He craned and twisted his neck in efforts to view the world right side up. The beast slowed and almost skidded to a stop. So much weight was hard to stop on a dime.

Tyler could just imagine the feel and taste of the water lapping against his parched tongue. The female loosened her grip, holding Tyler only with her right arm. She edged to the riverbank and squatted next to a calm pool nested behind jagged rocks.

Tyler eyed the sparkling water, the reflection of him being nestled against the female's breast like a football eyed him back.

The female reached with her free left and scooped up a bucket worth of water with a leathery black hand. She slurped it like a vacuum cleaner. It was gone the second it reached her lips.

"Hey."

The beast grunted and cut her eyes to Tyler, then made another scoop. This time she tossed it against his face. Its brisk chill took his breath. He gasped and licked its remnants as it rolled off his skin.

The female curled her lips and made a few pig-like snorts. Apparently, her version of laughter.

Tyler wiped his face and pointed to the water and did his best to mimic his captor's grunts.

She was stunned, almost appalled. She stared at him with icy, curious eyes. Mouth opened, brow lines angled, the beast was speechless. She swallowed hard and snorted. Then reached and cupped another bucket worth of water, sipped a tad herself before holding it gently to Tyler's lips.

The hair on her fingers tickled Tyler's chin, but the thirst allowed him to ignore it and wash away the dry cotton balls trapped in his mouth and throat.

The beast was thirsty too, because she gulped down at least a dozen or more of those gallon buckets she hid in the palm of her hand. If she'd placed both hands together, she probably could have scooped enough to fill a swimming pool.

She gave another scoop to Tyler and tried once more, but he turned his head. Another gallon would have been too much and besides now that his thirst had subsided, those hairy, prickly fingers were annoying.

Knock!

Sounded like a wooden baseball bat had whacked against a tree. Something him and Andrew done more than once back in North Carolina.

The female snapped her head and peered into the forest. Still squatted by the river with Tyler tucked under an arm pit, she craned her neck down low and sniffed the passing breeze that wafted from the knock.

She grunted and within an eye flash she was standing tall. It felt like he was standing on a two-story platform about to dive into a lake. Another thing he'd done back home. Summer trips to the lake were always fun.

Whirlllllloooooooo

The whistle pierced his ear. He jabbed his head into the damp hairy chest of the beast and was quick to cover his exposed ear. He squinted his eyes and glanced upward at the female. Her lips were pursed together forming an O, her head aimed to the heavens.

She carried the tune for what seemed like the time it took for his birthday and Christmas to roll around.

Her chest caved and finally her whistle tapered off. Tyler uncovered his ear and looked to the forest across the raging river.

The female locked her gaze to the forest and never flinched. She awaited a response.

She readjusted Tyler and moved him to her hip like a toddler. He clung with one fistful of back hair and another fistful of chest hair. They both glared across the river and listened past its rushing for a response.

Knock! Knock!

There it was again.

Splash!

Cold water pelted him like frozen marbles. He looked down at the rushing water—the same color of the river back at the campground— as it attacked the hairy log like shins of the female. They were half way across when he raised his vision. Within four or five strides, they were on dry ground and conquering a steep embankment like it was steps to a back porch.

The female slapped her feet against the forest floor covered with small patches of fluffy green carpet and knee high bright green ferns. It reminded Tyler of the jungles in Jurassic Park. Which made him wonder if it was some sort of dinosaur that was chasing them earlier. What else could frighten a beast this size? What would Bigfoot be afraid of?

Tiny bugs floated and fluttered about like dust when his dad cleaned of the floormats of the Jeep. Some of the bugs resembled mosquitoes, while others could have passed for that fairy on Peter Pan.

The female reached and pulled herself through the dense forest as each tug of pine just about ripped it from its roots.

Twigs snapped ahead of them. Something was scurrying and clearing a way for the beast. With Tyler bound under her arm again, she reached and tugged her way through the woods. Leaves crunched, twigs snapped, and ferns and briars slapped across Tyler's back. He'd learned to bury his face into her sweaty belly to avoid any limb or briar smacking across his face.

She stopped.

An eerie stillness followed.

She sniffed the air and did another one of those pig grunts.

A loud whooping and oohing came from up high. It sounded like a clan of monkeys. Bark raked and splintered off, lighting to the soft pine needles below. Claws dug into the pine bark and sounded as if they were gliding down like a fireman.

Tyler was too afraid to look and allowed his ears to fill in for his vision.

Thump!

A beat.

Thump!

Tyler's chest buzzed with each landing. It seemed to shake the earth. His pulse soared, his little heart knocked against the wall of his chest. His breath was quick and labored. He tightened his grip against the female and attempted to hide beneath all that hair.

He felt her lift a leg, then the other.

Snap! Crunch!

They were getting closer. The female grunted and was met with two separate snorts.

Snap! Crunch!

They'd been caught. Whatever was chasing them was now standing only feet away, maybe inches.

Tok-tok-tok-tok

Omah

    His female clicked her tongue and continued her stride. Perhaps an act of surrender. Tyler clung tighter and awaited their death sentence.

21

The release of the female's touch, as strange as it seemed, was horrifying. Tyler dug his fingers and nails into her hairy flesh, but it was no use. He slid down her body as if it was a slick brick wall. He thought he could have said the alphabet as long as it took for him to smack the ground.

He landed solid on his gut with a thud. His world spinning, his breath escaping him, he forced himself up. He made it to all fours, shook away the dizziness and looked up. Two dark figures were erect and attentive; about the distance Randy stood when he acted as the pitcher in coach pitch.

Tyler blinked and rubbed his eyes.

Pig grunts and snorts welcomed him. The figures, slouched at the back with long arms dangling in front, swung as if shooing him away. The female clicked her tongue and snorted out a huff of air. The two figures dropped to all fours and laid low, barely hovering over the earth. Their domed heads craning and tilting in wonder.

Tyler pushed himself up and clung to the leg of the female. Her palm the size of an average wall clock, but with attached wooly worms on steroids, patted his head and shoulder. Perhaps to soften him up to make him like a tender steak. The female marched to the two ape like creatures, which Tyler now realized were about half the size of the female.

He clung and rode along on her leg as they passed the two creatures who parted like an iron gate to a creepy cemetery. They glared at him with icy eyes and bared teeth. A low rumble emitted from their gut. The female paid them no attention, except for ticking her tongue and offering a few pig grunts.

Tyler twisted his neck and watched as the two creatures followed reluctantly behind him and the female. No doubt plotting an attack.

The female entered a thicket, swatting and pushing away limbs, briars, ferns, and bushes with waxy green leaves and red berries.

A thousand thoughts later, the female came to an abrupt stop. The creatures flanked her, which allowed Tyler to follow the trio's gaze.

A large pile of rocks the size of basketball's and beach balls made a rounded hump, covered with sticks and brush. The front door was about the size of the ottoman back home. The female grunted and flung her arms forward, beckoning the small ones to go first.

Tyler watched as they crouched to all fours and crawled through the open. Once inside they grunted. Then one of them coughed a half sneeze.

The female edged to the opening as Tyler clung tight against her leg. She prodded him with her hand, almost knocking him to the ground as he stumbled closer to his tomb. Surely this was it. She was feeding him to her kids, like a Robin dangling a worm to her baby chicks.

He could hear snorts and grunts inside the dark, cool cave. The next nudge forced him to the ground. His hands planted onto damp leaves. The knees of his khakis soaked through with brown moisture from the damp soil. A centipede the size of a garden snake, wiggle out from under his hand. He yelped and jolted backward against the female's leg.

She nudged him again.

The baby chicks' chirps echoed from the dark nest. He could see them clacking their mouths in his mind. A warmness soiled his pants. It stung as he tried to restrain it, but his body was shaking on its own now.

Another nudge. His head passed through the darkened opening. Nudge. He could feel the female's breath on the nape of his neck. It chilled his spine. Gooseflesh covered his body, or was it fire ants?

Nudge.

Monkey sounds grew loud.

Nudge.

It was pitch black now. He was on all fours crawling across cool dirt. Then, like the sun peaking out behind a cloud, a glimmer of light trickled into the tomb. He followed its rays. His head and eyes rising higher and higher.

The two creatures stood with bent knees and dangling arms only a few feet away. Their mouth's formed flat oval shapes, more monkey sounds.

He turned and was met with a gentle scoop of the female. She cradled him like a newborn baby and scooted her back against the right wall. The creatures moved around to the left, still amazed.

The opening sat at an angle like the left field foul line from the batter's box. The sun's light stood in a straight rectangle as it trickled in like the kitchen light into the basement back home.

The female held him tight and rubbed her fingers over his face. Lips curled, nose snarled, a big black tongue the size of a cow's rolled out with hot steamy breath and slid up his cheek.

Eeewww.

Sticky, stinky slime like puppy breath dripped off his chin.

He squinted and contorted his face and mouth, like a baby about to cry for its mama.

He peaked through a crack in an eye lid. Here came the big tongue again. He jerked his head and touched his chin to his shoulder.

The female grunted and huffed out a puff of hot air. She must've taken offense to his gesture. She made a snarled look of disgust.

The other two lowered their heads, craned and twisted with a curious gaze. Now only making faint grunts and rumbles.

Tyler was torn. One second he felt like dinner and the next he felt like a new pet. Stubby fingers raked across his nose and lips.

His sniffles startled her. Hot tears rolled off his cheeks and seeped through the hair to dampen her skin.

Tyler began to sob and wail like he'd just suffered a broken leg, but the pain wasn't in his leg...it was in his heart.

The two others stirred and began to dangle their arms as they returned to the monkey sounds. The female sniffed and leaned close as if to smell the source of his pain.

The emptiness in his gut only grew with each passing second. A void that only the warm embrace of his family could fill. Oh, how he longed for his Mother's arms. For only a second in her warm arms would feel like an eternity compared to this.

More tears soaked the female. She brought him in close, the warmth of her body flushing against his cheek. Her thick fingers caressed his face. She entered a gentle rock.

If only he could be in his Mother's arms again. His eyes began to sting as soft shadows and lines filled his vision. His body tingled with numbness. His body feeling light as a feather prodded his mind to drift onto a calm sea as his body seemed to float upon a raft. His eyes lowered. His breathing calmed. The shadows, lines
and hairy face was traded with dark red from the back of his eye lids.

He floated upon the gentle sea of red fur. The warmth of a mother's embrace made for a sound sleep.

OMAH

22

Closing in on three hours since Tyler's disappearance, Randy found himself ducking pine needle limbs and swatting away their bony branches. In front of him was Warden Steve Phillips, and in front of Phillips was Roscoe the burly German Shepherd and his owner and K-9 Unit Officer Chris Breeden. Roscoe tugged at the leash, pulling Breeden along aimlessly through the forest.

Behind Randy was Warden Jose Ortiz, and Sheriff's Deputy Nate Lindbergh. They'd been marching through the woods for the past half hour and Roscoe had yet to pick up a scent. Breeden let him smell one of Tyler's shirts again, but for whatever reason Roscoe was having a bad day. Just didn't seem himself. Every few minutes he'd stop, sniff, tuck his tail, pace in circles and emit a soft whine.

"Does he do this often?" asked Phillips.

Breeden stared at his K-9, wagged his head with raised brows and shrugged his shoulder. He didn't have much to say, other than, "No. I...don't know what's gotten into him."

"Well...if he don't pick up a scent, he's not really going to be much use for us."

Breeden nodded as Roscoe sniffed over leaves and pine needles, whimpering as his eyes darted to every rustle or twitch the woods made. The hair along his neck and back was spikey. A loud noise would've likely stiffened him like a fainting goat. He was spooked and nervous about something.

Did Roscoe know what Adam and the old man from campground knew? Did he smell one? Oh c'mon, stop it. It's a bear. Got to be. Which what would be worse a bear or one of those...things?

Stop it! Keep a straight head. Don't go venturing down some rabbit trail. Stick to the facts. Stick to reality. Reality? Yeah, well what's that? Tyler's missing. He vanished by the river. He probably ventured into the woods out of curiosity and couldn't find his way back. Simple as that, right?

But wait....what about him crossing the river? Would he do that? He can be a daredevil, but would he be that brave?

Randy?

If he didn't cross the river, then how...

Randy?

"Huh?"

Randy flinched and blinked.

Phillips stared at him, not saying a word. The others were now turning their attention and looking him over, obviously wondering if he was up to the task. The questions emitted from their eyes without them even having to speak.

Phillips sighed, looked to the ground and rubbed his chin.

"Randy...you sure you're up to this?"

He swallowed hard. Of course, he was up to this. He gave a short, quick nod and said, "Yeah-yeah. I'm good. Let's go," Randy gestured a hand onward and took a few steps.

Omah

He was stopped by Phillips hand as it landed on his chest.

"Hold on a second. Listen...I applaud you for wanting to be out here. It's what any dad would do...heck it's what I would do. But...I just want to make sure you know the risk your taking," Phillips lowered his gaze like a setting sun and glared into Randy's eyes.

Randy stared back, stuck his tongue below his bottom row of teeth and stared into the Warden's eyes.

A beat.

"Yeah...I know."

"Just..." Phillips took a deep breath, "...like we talked about earlier, if we come across something, let us look it over first. Can you do that for me?"

"That's not going to happen."

"You're right. It's not, but at the same time...I want to make sure we're all on the same page. Understood?"

Randy tightened his jaw, took a breath, glanced to the green needles of the tall swaying pines. Blue sky peaking through with a glimmer of a dusty ray piercing through both clouds and limbs. The rustle of rummaging critters above and cawing and singing of the fowls filled the air. The wind hummed a tune as it passed.

Randy returned his eyes to Phillips and dipped his head.

"All right good. Let's roll fellas. Keep your eyes and ears open."

With that they returned to their trek through the woods, Roscoe still leading, but undecided. Eager, but timid.

A MILE NORTH of Randy and his crew, Sheriff Logan and four others, including Deputy Jeff Anderson, Officer Will Carter, and Officer Mack Duggar followed closely behind expert tracker John Hildebrand.

The whop of a chopper cut the air overhead. It's engine and blades were faint and distant, but the pilot's voice wasn't. He squawked through Logan's black Motorola radio.

"Sheriff...be advised, winds are picking up. I won't be able to ride it out much longer. A cold front is rolling in off the Coast. I'm starting to feel it up here."

"10-4. Use your judgement. We're good down here." The radio beeped and crackled out a staticky hiss.

"10-4."

Logan zipped his black jack closer to his body. Its signature bright yellow block letters across his shoulder blades, SHERIFF.

Hoping they'd been done before night fall, they had only three to four hours before the sun would give up its ghost, allowing the creatures of the night to rule the forest. They had to get this kid out before then. He likely wouldn't survive a full night out here alone. He'd be lucky to survive a day.

The crew marched onward, as they crunched over sticks and scraped across fuzzy boulders wearing forest growth. Squished mushrooms, and flattened fern atop the browning needles covering the forest floor. The scent of fresh soil and moisture filled the air. Pine limbs stung their faces and hands as they passed through its crowd of witnesses.

John Hildebrand, with a rifle strapped over a shoulder and clothed in camo and an orange vest, scanned the ground with darting eyes, being careful where he stepped.

"You still got a hunch Hildebrand?"

"I'm starting to lose it Sheriff."

The man said as he followed a trail of twisted branches, crushed logs and deep impressions in the pine needles.

Omah

But it was all growing faint and beginning to look more like a deer trail than anything.

"That's not something I like to hear, John," Logan said as he sighed and pawed at his cheek.

"Hey...just keeping it real. I say if I don't have anything in the next few minutes, we maybe spread out until I pick it up again."

"All right. Sounds good."

Hildebrand melted lower to the earth, spine hunched and neck craning for evidence.

TWO MILES EAST of Warden Phillips and Sheriff Logan's crew, Al Frankford and his men were cruising deeper and deeper into the mountains riding along on ATV's.

Al led, as John Wallace, Red Cromwell and Bud Nelson followed behind. Dressed in bulky camo with rifles draped across their backs, coolers of beer and snacks rode along the front of the ATV's as they jutted over rocks, stumps and streams.

Al slowed, his fist held in the air, head scanning the thick forest off the trail. He killed the engine. The other three eased behind him and did the same.

Al fumbled through a back pack and retrieved a wrinkled map.

"This where we leaving them?" asked John.

Al remained silent as he traced the wadded, aging map with a calloused stubby finger.

His eyes narrowed, his lips twitched forcing out mumbles mostly to himself.

He sucked in a pocket of air through his nose and spit a cluster of green gunk.

"Yeah. Half a mile through that there thicket is Cashman's creek. I say we camp there for the night and set up surveillance."

"You reckon we'd be safe leaving these here?" asked Red just before relieving himself of Tobacco juice.

"Yeah. Ain't nobody ever come out this way," Al said as he lifted a leg over the side of ATV and planted it to

the ground. Readjusting his sagging pants in the process. He lowered his gaze and connected the zipper to his jacket.

John chambered a round in his Bolt Action Remington .280. Red loaded and spun the cylinder on his .44 revolver and holstered it on his hip, then tossed his black wad of Redman Chewing Tobacco to the ground.

Bud loaded his Winchester .308, eying the bullets, marveling at each one as he wondered which would make him a millionaire. He kissed the last one for luck. A metallic taste crossed his tongue.

"All right boys...you ready to get famous?"

They nodded with sly smirks.

"Bud, you got the knocker?"

"Got it right here," he said as he patted his backpack.

They hurled the bags onto their backs. Packed tight to the brink of popping the zippers. Pocketed the keys to the ATV's and marched off into the thicket.

A crow scoffed as it eyed them from a tall pine. An ominous cloud blocked the sun's ray. A sudden chill wafted between the trees.

The cawing of the crow dimmed as the men trekked deeper and deeper into the cold, darkening forest.

An hour had passed since their last break and Randy's ankle was beginning to remind him of its encounter with that outfield wall.

Omah

The ache grew with each step, forcing him into a slight limp. He was now bringing up the rear of the pack, just in front of Warden Ortiz.

"You okay there boss?" Ortiz asked through a slight accent.

Randy nodded and waved him off.

"Yeah-yeah, I'm good. Don't worry about—"

Knock! Knock! Knock!

The men stopped dead in their tracks as if they'd just entered a mine field.

Phillips held up a hand twisted behind him. Roscoe sat on his haunches, ears perked like the men.

Their eyes searched the trees, their ears deciphering the forest's code.

Silence.

Even the birds and critters seemed to listen.

They stood like statues for what seemed like hours, but in reality, couldn't have been more than a few minutes.

"What was that?" asked Randy.

No answer.

A beat.

Phillips turned and looked over his shoulder,

"I don't know."

"Sounded like it came from the west," said Breeden as he pointed through a patch of Sequoias.

If Randy's mind wasn't in another place, this would have made for quite the hike. They'd left the pines behind and was now surrounded by giant's that'd been witness to the way of the forest since the birth of Christ.

A few were hollowed out like the kids had stumbled upon yesterday. Randy shut his eyes and took a deep, painful breath. His heart resting in his gut. That memory stung.

Phillips cupped the radio and called for Logan.

"No. It wasn't us. Sounded south of us a bit. Figured it was you guys," Logan's voice hissed and crackled. Phillips had the volume low and did his best to keep it that way.

"Roger that. We'll check it out. Stand by."

"10-4"

They headed for the knock. Minds wondering, skin stinging from the scrapes and cuts of the forest.

Sweat trickled down the crease of Randy's back like rain running down a window on a cold morning. He was doing his best to stay positive, but flashes and whispers of doubt were hard at work.

His mind was like a raft tossed about in a raging sea of anxiety and fear. He clung to hope, wishing it to take him to dry ground. Because the sea of the unknown was a terrible thing. It wore on him with each passing second.

Enough! Keep moving. Stay positive. Control your emotions and keep you're head.

He took a deep breath and caught it before it escaped his grasp.

They continued the journey, stopping every few minutes to listen. They yelled out more than once, but no answer.

The forest grew thicker and the sun grew dimmer with each step. The snap and crunch of twigs were beginning to be drowned out by the crickets and cicadas.

The forest became alive the further the men trekked. Randy glanced at his watch, 4:56

Only another hour of daylight, before things got dark as the time zone under the Redwoods was a bit faster than that out from under their cover. Yesterday, when they'd stopped on the side of the road and ventured no more than they did, darkness came much quicker near the giants, than it did at the road.

Omah

Poor kid. He couldn't spend the night out here alone. Randy wouldn't allow. If it meant searching all night, then that's what he'd do.

He'd failed a lot in his life, but failing to find his son, was not acceptable.

Randy snorted a shot of air and wiped an eye with the back of his hand. He marched on in front of Warden Ortiz, calling out for his son.

The forest grew louder, and the temperature became low enough to reveal your breath. The Sun faded into a blood orange glare, but Randy fought with all he had not to allow his hopes to fade with it.

LYING LOW, hairy chest pressed against pine needles, a large dome shaped head attached to a thick neck and wide shoulders, tilted and gazed at a group of men, less than a hundred feet away. Big yellow teeth exposed by tight black lips rested below a flat nose and bulging black eyes. Its large body was spread out upon the ground like a lizard. Its nose twitched just below a narrowed gaze.

A low rumbled began deep within its gut. A putrid odor arose. The forest grew still as every bird and insect went silent.

23

"Knock back...see what happens," said Al.

Bud with a wooden baseball bat gripped in his right hand and a wrist strap securing it, swung back and *whap! Whap! Whap!*

They listened.

The forest was eerily still. A cool fog had begun to settle among them, making it difficult to see more than thirty foot away. Darkness came quick under its cover. The Sun's last beaming rays grew weak.

The silence and stillness were unnerving. As if the critters knew something was lurking just beyond the fog. Even the cicadas and crickets took notice of the eerie presence.

The men trained their ears to the forest, waiting for a response. John Wallace snapped his head to each shoulder more than once in a span of the few minutes while waiting. Bud steadied the grip on his rifle, Red unholstered his silver .44 with a black grip. Al poked the safety out of his .270 rifle that he'd taken more deer with than he could count. Most of them illegally.

It felt like a million eyes were on you at once, some hovering your shoulder, others nose to nose without your awareness.

Something was here in these woods. It knew they were here. It surely watched them behind the fog like a Panther in the night. Calculating when to strike. This was its territory, this was its home and they'd just broken in.

It sounded a little to the North didn't it? Kind of Northwest I guess?" asked Officer Breeden as Roscoe ducked his head and gave a soft whine.

Phillips turned with wide eyes and said with a stoic face, "Yeah."

"Tyler!!!" Randy yelled with his hands cupped to his mouth.

"Sshhh," Phillips waved him down with gritted teeth and narrow eyes.

Randy met Phillips tension, "Don't you sshhh me, you—"

Crash! Thud!

The men snapped their heads to the dense patch of Redwoods, now hiding behind a stretch of fog. It sounded as if a tree had just been felled and soared to the earth. Branches snapped and trees popped in the distance.

Phillips called for Logan.

Pow...pow...pow!

Scattering throughout the maze of Redwoods and fog, John and Bud darted between columns of trees. Fern bushes and service berry plants swiped at them like a crowd of hungry fans. Briars pierced their flesh, their tiny thorns like needles.

They thundered through the brush, leaping over fallen logs and swatting the branches. The fog and darkness seemed to only grow. Screams and groans emitted behind them. Red fired off two blind rounds with his revolver. Fire bellowed from the barrel, a flash of orange just in front of Red's face as he stumbled backward.

A demonic roar returned the crack of the gun, followed by big pounding footfalls. More screams, more agonizing moans. They were slowly muffled out with gurgles and two coughs.

Red fired once more before turning and thrusting forward in effort to catch up to John and Bud, the lighter of the three.

Red's heart knocked against his bones, his pulse soared, his breath like a fleeing chicken, the harder he fought to grasp it the further it slipped away. Through the fog he could make out the two silhouettes of John and Bud.

"Wait up-wait up!"

Red pounded onward, his bum knee screaming in protest of such a rush. That demonic wail bellowed once more from behind. Thudding, pounding feet edged closer. John and Bud slowed just enough for Red to catch up. They waited with outstretched arms and snatched him by the shoulders when he reached them.

A low rumble and growl right on their tail. They trudged forward, the air becoming scarce, their lungs begging for breath, their hearts begging for rest. They couldn't stop now, must keep moving.

OMAH

24

Thrashing and rustling tore through the thicket like a stampede of buffalo fleeing a freight train. Warden Phillips and his crew stood firm with greasy hands gripping the rifles and aiming into the fog.

Roscoe barked twice before cowering and wrapping tight around Breeden's legs.

Randy stood behind the four gun wielding men. He rubbed his eyes in quick manners. The whole world was moving in slow motion. Like when you see a car run the red light and know you're about to take a hit, but all you can is brace. Randy anchored his feet and bent at the knee, bracing for impact.

The thrashing grew louder as the forest grew darker. The fog thickened and the sun winked out below the tree line. Still visible out from under the canopy of Redwoods but hidden under their glare.

"Steady. Steady. Wait till we have a visual," said Phillips out the side of his tight jaw.

Twigs snapped, limbs popped, and rotten logs crunched. Breathing and gasping followed.

Phillips squinted his eyes and pulled his head from the sight of his rifle, scanning the fog.

It's people.

"Hey—"

Three dark figures emerged from the fog and barreled into and past Phillips and his men. Phillips and John tumbled to the dirt like football players. Red plowed into Breeden sending him backwards with his feet nowhere to go from the confinements Roscoe had put him in. Randy stood back, arms stretched forward and feet peddling backwards. He caught Bud by his camo army jacket, sending them both into a tail spin.

Red had broke loose from John and Bud's grip and stumbled passed everyone but managed to somehow keep his balance.

Everyone scrambled, searching for their weapons to guard against the strangers and the beast plowing closer, snapping branches and small trees like toothpicks.

The things roar rattled their chest and shook their gut. It pounded to the right, remaining behind the cover of fog. It tore through the woods like a rabid elephant but roared like something deep in the Amazon jungle.

Pow...pow!

Ortiz and Lindbergh fired off numerous shots. The thing plowed on, wailing like a banshee and destroying every tree mother nature had to offer.

Within a matter of seconds...*it* had vanished.

THEY ENCROACHED on a dang Grizzly," said Deputy Anderson as Logan barked into the radio.

Waited. Then barked again.

"C'mon Steve...tell me what you got."

Nothing.

"Maybe we should head that way. Didn't sound too far," said the tracker, Hildebrand.

Omah

Logan nodded. His jaw rock solid with acne scars lining the upper cheeks. He tried again for Phillips. The radio hissed and beeped as he waited a reply.

It crackled, but took a minute to emit Phillip's voice, picking up about mid-sentence.

"...it's a big one. Tore past us and bolted East. It may be injured, god knows there were enough bullets flying. Its mad as all get out now, so keep your eyes open. We bumped into some men, they say the bear got their buddy. We're going to scan the area...I'll be sure to mark it."

The radio hissed, a red light winked, reflecting off Logan's face and uniform. Daylight was fading quickly, as a faint purplish orange glow streaked above the towering Redwoods. Serving as a canvas behind the green cedar limbs.

Being out here in the dark with a wild Grizzly would be a bad idea. It'd risk the safety of the men. As terrible as it is to lose a kid out here, it'd only make things worse to start losing men.

"10-4...Steve...I say we call it day. If the winds die down enough, we could have the choppers scan with the FLIR...but I don't want my guys being out here at night with a mad bear. I'm sure you don't either. What do you think?"

A rustle and crackle, like torn wrapping paper.

A moment passed.

Logan tapped the black antenna to his shoulder. Eyes scanning the dirt he kicked with his boot.

Phillip's voice rasped back, "Yeah...10-4...let's just plan to be back out at dawn. See you at the camp."

"Roger that."

Are you kidding me? You sorry—"

"Randy...listen. I can't imagine how hard this is for you. But you have to think about the safety of the men. It won't do anyone any good to be out here...in the dark...on its territory. We have to keep the advantages in our favor."

Randy grinded his teeth and wagged his head. His breath huffing into the cooling night. He planted his hands to his hips and scanned the ground.

Thoughts racing by faster than a 95-mph fastball. He can't leave Tyler out here in the dark. He's still alive and if he calls it a night...that might not be the case.

"I'm staying. I'm not going back to the campground without my boy," Randy said with a sternness that dared to be challenged.

Phillips sighed.

The others glanced about each other and stole glares to the darkening sky. The moon was full and trudging to relive the sun of its duty and give a glimmer of light.

Phillips looked to his watch, 6:03

"Randy...you know I can't let you do that. It'd be unethical for me to allow to stay out here by yourself. These woods are nothing to play with. They've swallowed more people than—" he stopped his persuading, reminding himself of the very reason they were out here to begin with.

Randy looked deep into Phillips eyes. Sensing that even the Warden had his doubts.

Phillips grimaced and attempted to redeem himself, "Listen...my point being. I don't want to have to be coordinating a search crew for you too. When we find Tyler, I want that to end it."

Randy bit his lip and looked away.

"Randy...c'mon man. Thank about your boy. I know you want to be out here but think if something were to happen to you. You don't want him or your other two kids and wife to have to live with that. We'll try to get some choppers in the air to tonight to do some scans. Then we'll be back out at daybreak."

Randy snorted in a shot of air through hot nostrils and rubbed his beard. He lifted his eyes to Phillips, pursed his lips and nodded.

Phillips and the men trekked to where the attacks took place to make a quick sweep of the land, in search of Al. They reached the spot, Phillips marked it on his GPS and called in the coordinates to the command post back at camp.

They searched for a solid half-hour, but the forest was empty of any evidence. With the night setting in, they headed to where Al and his boys parked the ATV's. About a hundred yards parallel to the worn-out trail, was service road 12 where Phillips and his men parked their side by sides.

Phillip's gut seemed heavier with each step as the dread of likely not just finding the body of another hunter, but that of a child as well...weighed on him. It was one thing to find the body of a man or woman, but a child. That's hard to overcome. That's what he was fearing most. He couldn't let another family down. He had to find the boy, and gosh darn if he allowed another victim to be added to the list of the missing.

25

Darkness had covered the earth. Accompanying it was a chill breeze that caused the limbs and leaves to shudder. A lonely hoot owl in the distance served as John Revere and warned all of creation that *it* was coming. A squirrel rushed to take cover in a hallow knot of a Hemlock tree nested next to a patch of Cedars.

A racoon scurried from a trash bin, heeding the owl's warning and seeking shelter from what was to come. Crickets and cicadas pleaded on behalf of the critters, but another owl comforting its lonely friend, quieted them down.

The two owls carried their conversation back and forth, sounding like two monkeys. They finished their chatter. An eerie hush lingered down from the mountain like a spirit searching a place to dwell. A horrid odor drifted alongside it, passing in between the remaining campers and RV's in the Giant Redwoods RV Park. By the looks of it, only a handful had decided to stay after all the excitement. There was space for eighty-two visitors, but now, counting the Jacobs, there were only two dozen spots that were filled. Everyone else had packed house and hit the asphalt.

Steam emitted from the furnace vents atop the Jacobs RV. Mixing with the thickening fog. Their 4-door Jeep Wrangler was parked along side the car hauler still attached to the hitch on the RV. Next to it was a black Ford Sport Trac. The bed of the truck was filled with scraps and pieces of Redwood logs and trimmings. Parked nose to nose with the back bumper of the Sport Trac, sat a white Toyota Rav4.

A peek inside the RV would reveal four Native Americans seated and circled around a mother with her daughter and son. A few of the adults caressed a cup of coffee as they cradled it between their hands.

The daughter clutched a hardcover book which presented a dense forest on the front and back. The boy held onto a stuffed gorilla. The Mother clung to a small gray beanie which had been discovered just on the other side of the South Fork Eel River. It belonged to Tyler Jacobs.

"I knew I should've never left him alone with Randy. I should've known better," Bev said with a hoarse voice and strained eyes. She smelled Tyler's beanie, shut her eyes and swayed her head in small to and fros.

"Mrs. Jacobs...you can't think like that," said Brenda as she rose from the small recliner across from Bev and sat next to her. She placed her hand on Bev's knee and attempted to soothe the grieving Mother.

Bev sniffled, turned to Brenda and gave a half smile. "Thank you. You can call me Bev."

The fear of the unknown was worse than knowing. The thought of her little boy wandering about the cold, dark forest...tore at her heart and mind like a rabid beast unleashed from hell. The pain was so deep and heavy, her heart felt like someone had it in a vice grip and with each passing second, they twisted the bolt, tightening its grip. Stay strong. Stay positive.

She took a deep breath through her nose with closed eyes, straightened her spine and carefully opened her eye lids, then sighed the breath away. The tightening stopped where it was. Her heart still ached, but her breath seemed to slow the ghostly tormentor from making another revolution with the vice. She rubbed her forehead. Brenda gripped and squeezed her left hand. The gesture was comforting and soothing. Bev turned and hugged her.

"Thank you," was all she could muster under the pressure of the vice. They rubbed one another's backs as a few warm tears dripped to their shoulders.

"It's going to be okay," said Brenda softly, before pulling away. Bev tightened her lips and nodded.

"Thank you."

The oldest of the four, cleared his throat and struggled to scoot to the edge of the recliner. His red complexion and sharp cheek bones were filled with wrinkles like the lines streaking up a giant Redwood. He'd about been around as long as one of them too. At least that's what he liked to tease everyone with. Kosumi Windburn was the brother of Adam and Jack Lightfoot's mother. Uncle Kosumi was all the blood family they had left, as both parents had passed a decade back.

"Ma'am...in all my years, I've yet to comprehend the mystery of the forest. Like a rip current, it sometimes chooses to take people out to its world. It pulls and tugs...until eventually the sight of land has disappeared. Now I'm not going to ignore the reality of nature's harsh environment, but I'm also not going to ignore the fact that the greater number of people that get sent out there, the better chances of bringing your boy home safe. The more lifesaving rings we toss to the sea, the better chances your boy has of surviving," Kosumi's sharp native accent was in full effect. He rested a calloused palm atop a hand carved cane, dressed in feathers that dangled from the wrist strap and burned engravings of a fearless Eagle.

His dark, narrow eyes zeroed in on her, "I don't know what your beliefs are about what all lives out here in these woods. But I know what mine are. And I'd be a fool not to share with you what I know."

Bev swallowed and angled her brows, curious where this was going. Andrew and Jennifer sat motionless to the side. Hanging on every word of the old man. Adam sat on the far end of the couch below Brenda and Bev, while his brother Jack leaned against the kitchen counter, one foot on the steps leading out.

"There are rules in these woods and there are those who are tasked with protecting such rules. They oversee everything that takes place, often times without our ever knowing. They guard and protect the forest and all of its inhabitants. They are the guardians among us, though few ever see them, like a spirit their presence is often felt more than seen. They keep things in order and anytime someone comes to violate the sacredness of the forest, they protect what they've been given authority over. And God-forbid should one ever be taken before its time in the hands of a human."

Kosumi paused to catch his breath.

"What are you saying? *Bigfoot*? You're kidding me right?" Bev's countenance shifted as her gut heated. "Look...I'm sure you mean well, but if all of this is to get me to believe in your crazy stories about giant apes roaming the woods..." she let out a disgusted huff, "...well I think there are more important things to be thinking about than some...folklore."

Kosumi breathed deep. A gentle smile stretched his lips. His eyes were harmless and seemed honest. But you never can tell.

"Listen...I know this all sounds foolish...because I thought it did too while I was growing up. I figured it was just the elder's way of keeping the young'uns from roaming off in the woods. But that all changed when I saw one with my own two eyes."

Bev scoffed and wagged her head; her eyes scanned the red oak kitchen cabinets as far away from Kosumi's gaze as possible.

"Mom...we need to listen to him. You've always said to respect our elders...right?" said Jennifer as she still clutched the book in her now balmy hands.

Ouch. Nothing like getting a correction from your offspring. Bev sighed, lowered her head and caressed the bridge of her nose between her eyes. "She's right. Mr. Windburn...I apologize. I hope you can understand my grievance with all of this. It's just the last thing I want is to fall for something I'll regret later when I'm less vulnerable."

"I understand. And on my word, with all that's within me...I can assure that what I'm saying is the truth as to the best of my knowledge and experience."

"Mom...I've read some in this book. I think there's really something out there. Whether that's what happened to Tyler or not, I don't know. But I really do think there might be something out there," said Jennifer as she turned the book over and showed it to the adults.

"Yeah...there's some good stories in that one. I remember reading it when it came in last year," said Adam.

"These creatures have been given the authority by the Great Creator to guard the forest and protect the earth from evil. They do however seem to have a hard time getting past wrongdoings. That's one thing they really struggle with...forgiveness. Often times, if one is provoked or god forbid injured or killed, their spirit will haunt and terrorize the woods...sometimes resulting in the death of the prideful and wicked. They do not kill, just to kill. There is always a reason for it. They don't like hidden agendas, they know when someone is out to get them," Kosumi flicked a long braid of hair from his shoulder.

"Although there have been quite a few cases of missing children and hikers reported over the years, there have also been cases of those people showing back up and claiming to have seen or sometimes having been taken captive by the hairy men. Their stories rarely get told. But there's plenty of them if you know where to look. These creatures can be gentle and caring if left to themselves. Some of the kids that have reappeared after a few days of their disappearance, say that they spent the days with a family of bears..." Kosumi raised his brows and craned his head, "...I've heard some say a family of giant monkeys. Then there are older kids and even a handful of adults who have claimed that the hairy men took them and protected them from the dangers of night."

"Great. So now you're telling me my son is held captive by a bunch of sasquatches? Look I really don't mean no disrespect, but..." Bev breathed deep "...I'm just having a hard time believing there's a hoard of giant apes roaming the woods."

"Bev...I wouldn't be telling you this, if it wasn't true," Kosumi's eyes were just too honest looking to tell a bold face lie.

"And you all believe this too?" Bev asked as she scanned her finger to Brenda, Adam, and Jack. They each gave her a reassuring nod.

"We've all seen them before. We *know* they're real. Trust us," said Adam.

"Well, you said you saw one with your own two eyes earlier. What did you see?" asked Bev as she trained her gaze to Kosumi.

"Mama, they really are real. Remember all the YouTube videos me and Tyler showed you?" said Andrew who sat Indian style at the feet of his sister in the swivel passenger seat.

Bev nodded, "Yeah...I remember."

Kosumi cleared his throat and set his eyes to the top of his cane where next to the Eagle, was burned a large Redwood. His eyes and brows narrowed. His sharp jawline tightened. Taking a deep and steady breath, he allowed himself to enter a dense forest worth of memories.

Omah

26

Smoke billowed from a hand hewed log cabin but angled to the snow-covered earth under such cold and dense air. It crept along before disappearing among the sea of giant Sequoias. Filling the forest with a thick gray cloud. Tall pines circled the cabin, giving it insulation from the elements. There wasn't much of a yard as most of it was angled down the mountain. But there was a small flat patch off to the side with enough space to split wood and till a garden. Other than that, it was pretty much up or down hill.

Sitting next to a warm fireplace nestled in the little log cabin smaller than most people's living rooms nowadays, Kosumi and his two older brothers were thawing from a hard day's labor of chopping wood. As they sat rubbing and massaging the feeling back into their toes, an array of sudden bangs sounded from the front door. It shook and rattled the hinges with each thud. Their Mother halted her knitting and eyed her three boys with a trepidatious glare. She swallowed hard and gently sat her needle and thread aside, then rose a slow finger to her lips and looked to her boys with angled brows.

She reached for the single shot rifle loaded with a musket ball, which leaned in the corner behind the door's swinging entrance. Now gripped tightly between balmy hands, the door thudded thrice more.

Heavy breathing, gasping, banging. It was loud. And it was hours before her husband would be home from his hunt. Something just didn't seem right and with all that'd taken place in the past month, she was more than hesitant to open the door, she was terrified. Her hands quaked and struggled to keep her grip on the rifle.

Bam! Bam! Bam!

"Who is it!?" Mother asked with a stern voice like that of a general.

More heavy breathing. Panting.

"The creature's back...he's down in the valley tearing things up. The village is gathering a hunting party now..." more breaths and painful gasps, "...four of the strongest men were fatally wounded and two children are missing...please we need Mr. Windburn's help."

His words stung her heart like a hornet. Her gut churned and buzzed. She gave it some thought. Took a deep breath, rolled it out through hot nostrils, flipped her long black braids over her shoulders and opened the door one inch at a time.

A thin, harmless old man, likely older than he looked stood at the door. One hand against the log cabin to brace himself. Worn overhauls over a rugged flannel and thick fur jacket. Gray hair underneath a thick wool hat, gray beard, bulky glasses that rested on the edge of his nose which made him look to the heavens when spoke with you. His eyes and smile reflected his gentle heart which wouldn't allow him to even harm a fly.

One hand upon the cabin, the other on his knee, the old man bent at the waist and was paying his dues for having just made the journey from the valley village below. His eyes were glassy, and his face was flush with rushing blood when he craned his neck to look to Mother.

"Mrs. Windburn...we need your husband. Please...he's the only one that knows anything about these things."

Mother sighed and hooked her hands under Mr. Stone's armpits, helping and half dragging his limp body into the home for warming.

She shooed her three boys away from the door as they stood tightly beside her. She had the oldest move her chair next to the fire. She eased Mr. Stone over to it. He plopped down like a bag of flour.

The boys gathered around, sitting native style, and glared at him as if were a man from the moon. The fire crackled and hissed, its warmth a pleasant friend. A whiff of smoke wafted by. Trailing it was the strong aroma of an herbal tea.

Mother turned from the wooden counter and passed off a fresh cup to Mr. Stone. He welcomed it with glee. The mere sight of the steaming liquid floating in the wooden cup seemed to give him warmth. He adjusted his glasses and sipped it with a few gentle slurps.

Satisfied and warmed, he held it between his knees with his left and used his right to remove his glasses before rubbing his forehead. He shook his head and shut his eyes as the stark reality of what had taken place in the valley below began to set in.

"Mrs. Windburn...what do we do? How do you and your family survive up here? This thing is a monster from hell."

Mother looked to her boys for a moment, then looked to Mr. Stone, "We mind our own business. We leave them to their selves and respect them for what they are."

"And what is that?"

A beat.

"Guardians of the forest. They were put here by the Great Creator to guard our precious wildlife and environment. It's only when they feel threatened or are encroached upon, do they act out in such manner like in recent months.

"They live among the Giant Cedars of old which are the protectors of our Spirits, they guard us from all evil in the spiritual realm, but the hairy men among the forest guard us from evil in the physical realm. When they witness someone take more than need from the forest or waste what they've hunted...they take vengeance into their own hands. Much like us humans, they can be quite stubborn when it comes to forgiveness. It takes a long time for these creatures to forget such wrong doings. Until man performs the sacred rite, it will continue like this...getting worse with each attack."

Mr. Stone dropped his eyes to the wooden floor, placed his glasses back to their spot at the tip of his nose and stole a sip from the tea.

He swallowed and gave a refreshing smack. His breath seemed to have slowed, but the fear in his eye and tongue remained. Cradling the tea in his lap, he raised his vision to Mrs. Windburn.

"What do we do?"

A long pause.

"Hair. You find hair or any other article belonging to the creature and you bring it here. It's the only way to put an end to all of this. As for the children, they tend to care for them as one of their own, in most cases...now there have been times...that children were harmed too, but that's the rarity, not the norm. It's man that has wronged them or the forest and that's who they have a grudge against. Not the children."

Omah

    The room fell silent among the crackle of the flame. Its tinder warmth like that of a mother's embrace. Although just beyond the cabins hand crafted wall, lurked a mysterious creature that was a force to be reckoned with. Its presence and mood could shift quicker than a gust of wind blowing in the vilest tempest.
    A long, deep guttural, anguished howl bellowed from the forest. Penetrating heart and spirit with dividing sunder. Seeping beneath the flesh and wiggling its way deep into the soul. It was out there. Make no mistake...it was out there.

27

"You sure you'll be okay till the morning?" asked Warden Phillips as he and the men spread about the Giant Redwoods RV Park, heading for their vehicles.

"Yeah," Randy said as his eyes never left the ground in front of him.

"Okay. Well get you some rest," Phillips patted Randy's shoulder, "The search crew will be out just before dawn. We'll launch at sunrise."

Randy nodded.

"I'm going to try and get a chopper in the air tonight with a FLIR. I'll give you a call if there is anything you should know. Otherwise, I'll see you in the morning," Phillips extended his aging and calloused hand.

Randy shook it. His mind anywhere but the present.

"Thanks," Randy nodded a half smile and headed for the RV.

The air had chilled about ten degrees since their trek through the woods. A gray hazy smoke hovered the park like a spirit. Two owls in a domestic dispute in the distance. Crickets singing along to their favorite tune. The rustle and ripple of the river roaring in the background. Which caused the memory from earlier that day to scrape across Randy's mind as if it were nails to a chalk board. His heart stung and began to throb with a gut-wrenching ache.

His vision blurred as hot salty tears streaked down his cheeks. Randy stopped between an empty fifth wheel and small camper—that looked to of had been there since spring when the leaves were bright and green— and bent at the waist, placing his hands on bony kneecaps. The nausea was too strong to hold back. He huffed and sniffled, then wiped his mouth with the cuff of his jacket. He wasn't sure he could make it to the RV, this seemed like a nice place to crash, curl into a fetal position and sob till morning.

His shoulders quaked and jolted as more tears gushed out. If only he hadn't of gotten so caught up in that fish, none of this would have happened. His youngest son was now paying the price for such a stupid mistake. He's supposed to be the protector…the guardian of the family…how could he ever live with himself? He'd failed Tyler, he'd failed the family.

A light flicked on in the kitchen of the fifth wheel, the side door jimmied. The sound of a dead bolt sliding open, sent movement into Randy's feet. He shuffled onward with an arched back and craned head angling toward the earth.

"Hey, are you all right?" a scruffy, aged voice asked as the door opened and slammed against the side of the camper, being caught by a quick breeze.

Randy continued his slow gait, never turning, but raised a thumb in the air over his head. The man mumbled and chattered with a woman as her curiosity got the best of her. They uttered something about, "Must be a drunk."

The door latched, the dead bolt slid home. The cool breeze ripped against Randy's back. It's going to make for a cold night. Tyler would be lucky to survive it.

Somebody was cooking hamburgers as its aroma meandered throughout the park. The thought of it attracting the bear or whatever that thing was that came barreling through the woods back there, crossed his mind more than once. Which would be worse? It being a bear? Or the "Bigfoot" that the Indian at the store and the lady at the desk talked about?

Either one sent a shudder down his spine. To think his boy was out there all alone, not only in the elements, but with the creatures and animals of the night...it was too much. He breathed out a deep sigh and raised his head for the first time in twenty paces. If it wasn't for the Sport Trac and Rav4 in the driveway of Randy and Bev's RV spot, he would have likely turned around and trekked through the woods in search of his son. But the two mysterious vehicles demanded otherwise.

Who could that be?

IF IT WASN'T for my Mother and Father, the rampage in the valley below us, would have likely continued for years. My Father being the expert tracker and hunter that he was and having learned about these creatures since his youth, was able to gather a group of men willing to listen and within two days they had what they needed. They brought the hair to Mother, and they conducted the—"

Foot steps thudded on the small metal steps below the door, a hand gripped the knob, giving it a twist. Bev slid to the edge of her seat, ready to force herself up, curious of who was on the other side of the door. Kosumi stopped his words and struggled to twist himself to face the door. Jack took a step up and angled to the kitchen table. Andrew whimpered and gripped his sister's arm.

The door opened, revealing a shadowy silhouette. Two street lights in the background shone on his back, leaving his face in the dark, until the man conquered two steps and stood at the bottom of the doorway. Quick to shut out the cold air rushing in, Randy
slammed the door shut behind him. A little harder than he intended.

With a dozen eyes glued to him awaiting an answer, shame and guilt washed over him when he couldn't provide the one they wanted. He wagged his head and tightened his lips. They each allowed their breath to escape. Randy locked eyes with Adam, now standing next to his brother Jack.

"Randy…" Adam said with a soft tone and gentle nod, "…we heard on the news. We can help," Adam said with steady eyes before glancing to his brother, wife and grandpa.

Randy took a deep breath, rubbed his forehead and angled to the couch where he sat next to his wife. Brenda scooted down to make room.

He and Bev hugged and wept gently in each other's arms. The others remained quiet, respecting their sorrow. Randy and Bev both snorted air through moist nostrils and rubbed their red streaked eyes. Their faces flush.

Randy breathed out through his mouth as his nostrils were clogged from the mucous and asked, "Will you help me look for him tonight?"

28

The soil was damp and cool, soaking through his khaki pants. The raw odor of earthy leaves, soiled and soured hair, and rotten eggs filled the air like three puffs from a can of Febreze. The temperature was dropping rapidly as each breath emitted thicker and thicker puffs of white clouds that huffed into the darkness like enlarged periods on a black chalk board. Grunts and groans and clicks of enlarged tongues emitted from the blackness. At times the creatures even engaged in what sounded like a foreign language. Fast moving chatter and lots of tongue clicking. The two younger ones would go back and forth, before the big female would chime in to end the gossip. They'd bark their displeasure, but they'd soon be hushed by what could only be their mother.

The big female lay on her side, Tyler was nestled close, her body heat and thick but stinky hair gave him warmth. It was like clinging to the dog's blanket. It stunk, but hey, it kept him warm.

The moonlight lit the entry way with a slim glimmer of light that only entered about three foot into the cave or den, whatever it was. Outside, nature was alive and well. Twigs popped, bushes thrashed and rustled about. Coyotes yipped and cackled faintly like a distant crowd. A few deep snorts from what must have been rowdy deer getting spunky from the cold front, blasted into the air as they rummaged about. Owls hooted, crickets sang, and the wind howled.

How could one sleep like this? Between the stench, the cold, the noise, the ache of missing family, loneliness...sleep would be impossible.

Tyler rose to his haunches and placed his hands to the damp dirt next to him and the female. His palms now cold and wet. He huffed and sighed, before crossing his arms. Lips trembling, heart hurting, eyes stinging with hot tears.

"Mama? Mama?" he began to weep.

The big female rose in a huff. The other two must've done the same, though he couldn't see them, he felt their glare and heard their movement.

The female nudged him in the side with a stubby finger. He flinched and winced.

Ow!

She grunted. Nudged him again, this time with more thrust.

Arrgghh

It felt like she was jarring his guts, her fingers dug in his side and prodded as if they were hairy tree branches jabbing him out of the dark. He grabbed at the place she poked just in time to catch her finger before it dug into him again.

"No!"

She growled and snatched her finger back as if insulted by his disproval. The other two hissed and clicked their tongues, still hidden somewhere in the shadows.

Pop!

The sound of the popping branch got their attention. Loud and heavy feet thudded over leaves, pines, logs, and branches. Crunching. Cracking. Popping. Its breath in a huff. The critters of the night went silent.

Tyler scurried close to the big female, burring his face deep into her thick, curly and stinky coat of fur. She moved and forced herself to her feet. Tyler allowed his fingers to slide across her thick, hair covered body. He clinched to her leg that was like the size of the Redwood he tried to hug yesterday with his family. His mother had even snapped a picture of him. Surely it won't be the last.

The other two creatures emerged from the darkness, miles away from where Tyler thought they were. They edged close, crouched on all fours, keeping an eye on Tyler with craning necks, but also shifting to keep an eye on the entryway. They galloped to their mother like two baby gorillas, knuckles digging in the dirt. They disappeared on the other side of the large female.

More pops and thuds echoed outside, before coming to an eerie halt. Silence. For what felt like the time it took to travel from North Carolina to California, the woods were quiet. No creature talked. It must be forbidden.

The quick, short growl caused his heart to skip. It wasn't the thing outside that'd made it, it was the big female inside. Evidenced by the patch of white smoke venting from her Grand Canyon of a mouth.

Silence.

A few moments pass, before the female's gesture was returned with a much deeper and lasting growl that seemed to rumble Tyler's gut. He clung tighter to the female's leg, gripping it as he were trying to bear climb a tree. Which he might just have to do in order to survive.

Twigs popped and crunched. Heavy breathing. A black shadow filled the moonlights glare in the

Omah

entryway. Standing on two feet like a man, the huge shadow stood there as whatever it was sniffed the air in a ferocious manner. It let out a deep rumble again and kept it going, even while it eased into the den. The shadow moving and extending into the darkness. A pair of humongous hairy legs and feet stepped in and stood, sniffing the air and growling from what sounded like a slimy throat and hungry gut.

    The feet edged closer, revealing hairy knees that were as wide as a telephone pole and maybe even as tall. Tyler couldn't watch. He buried his face deeper in the hairy and matted fur of his captor and protector. Mama. If only his real mama were here. But wait, maybe she is. Kind of. He squeezed fistfuls of fur and dug further into the female's thick leg. Just like all the times he'd ran into mama and daddy's room during a thunderstorm. This one too would pass. The beast thundered out a bark and growl, heavy feet thudding lower and lower into the cave. Mama would protect him, she had to.

29

"I think I got something," said the pilot known for his heroic days in Vietnam. He was the only one talented and experienced enough to handle the winds.

The quick white blip on the FLIR had grabbed his attention, but now he struggled to find it. His co-pilot scanned the area over but could never pick up what Hank Bayloff—the Pilot— said he saw.

The blip disappeared as if it were never there. Which caused Bayloff to wonder if perhaps it was one of the two victims they were searching for, either the lost hunter, or boy. Maybe they'd hid under a shelter. Only problem is...why would they still be hiding?

With the chopper overhead, you'd think they'd be out waving and garnering attention. Something didn't seem right. Maybe it was just an animal. But it sure looked like it was standing upright before it vanished. Weird.

THE BREEZE had grew going by the sound of the rustling leaves. Heavy whop-whop-whop sounds coming from up high. A soft but loud rumble. At first Tyler thought it was the creature lowering into the cave, but even its beastly voice and growl were overshadowed by the thunder above. The creature now stood flat footed in the entryway. The moonlight shining around its broad back. It was only visible from the chest down. As the rest of it was covered in the shadow where the moonlight stopped. It was crouched over, as it likely didn't have enough room to stand straight. Long, lanky, hair covered arms draped along its thick knees. Thicker than Mother's. This one was bigger. Much bigger. The way it stood and acted reminded Tyler of a defensive dog ready to attack.

    The thunder above eased into the distance. The whop-whop-whop now like an echo. The deep grotesque growl, resembling a cat's pure in texture and pace, but a diesel truck in depth. It huffed and kicked loose dirt with a wide foot, slinging the soil on Tyler and the Female. It dusted Tyler's face and chest before he had time to take cover. The beast grunted and snorted, then slumped over onto all fours and began slapping the ground with tight balled fists. Its face now visible. Much like Mother's, but darker and leathery looking. Maybe it was just the shadows playing across its face, but it seemed older and rougher. A long scar stretched from its left eye over the bridge of the nose and down the cheek. Its shoulders were as wide as two or three of the biggest men Tyler had ever seen combined. You could stand three men side by side, and this beast would still be wider. It was a living and breathing King Kong.

    And the stench? Whew.

    He thought Mother and the kids stunk, this one was ten times worse. Like soiled sweaty clothes mixed with rotten eggs and decaying flesh. His gut turned and protested once it registered from his nostrils to his brain. He covered his nose with the neck of his hoody.

The beast didn't flinch but kept a death stare on Tyler, nostrils flaring, hair bristled, and eyes angled downward. Tyler had seen enough and turned into Mother's fur for safety. Surprisingly she'd been quiet so far. And the young ones two.

Woah!

Roarrrrrr!

The female's sudden jolt shook Tyler from her fur like a coconut dropping from its tree. He tumbled and rolled a time or two across the damp dirt. Wet leaves and earthy soil sticking to his face and body. A wet, salty iron taste filled his mouth. He spit and coughed to rid it of the dirt. A small clump of it had packed in his jaw like tobacco, forcing him to reach in with his thumb and forefinger to remove it.

Thrashing about in the dark, the two beast growled, snorted, huffed, barked and fumbled for a grip. It was as if wrestle mania had plopped down right before his eyes. Emerging from the shadows, the hairy back of one of the creatures appeared.

Was it Mother?

No.

The other one. It struggled on wobbly hairy tree trunks, its huge feet slapping the soil for a good footing. Two large hands gripped its shoulders as it seemed to do the same to Mother. The two fought and scuffled, twisting and struggling. For the other one to be twice Mother's size, she was doing more than holding her own.

They vanished into the inky shadow again. More grunts and groans and snorts. Slapping feet and pounding fist cutting through the dark void.

Tyler scooted across the ground, kicking with his feet and pulling backward with his hands. A loud wail pierced the air and seemed to have jabbed his ear drums. He cupped his ears about midway through the wail before it tapered off with a hiss.

Tyler squinted and shook his head, ears ringing. He continued to scoot backwards. Something tickled his hand. What is that? It was hard but seemed fluffy. He felt blindly in the dark, hand shuffling across the dirt.

He hit it. It was hairy. It was a bony, hairy leg. It flinched when he first grabbed it. Its owner roared, hissed and spit like a kitten when threatened.

Tyler yanked his hand back in fear of it being bitten off. He shifted his angle and scooted some more before finally finding the root and dirt covered wall. A hard rope like root dug into his back, but he made do. At least he knew where some of these things were. Mother and the big one still fought and grappled in between the shadows and glimmer of moon light streaking in. One of the young ones sat to his left, as long as it was still there. But he didn't know where the other one was.

A grunt.

Sounded like one of them got the wind knocked out of it. A thud. It must've been pressed against the wall opposite from him and the young one. The young one whimpered and whined to his left. On the tail of that one's cry, came another whimper to Tyler's right. Great. Now he was sandwiched between the two young ones.

A god awful, hair-raising shriek that had to have come from the big one, filled the cave. Its deepness and thrust was enough to rattle Tyler's heart and gut like a subwoofer. A sudden streak of black bolted for the door and conquered the opening in two steps. It happened too fast to tell who it was. Surely Mother wouldn't leave them here all alone.

It sounded like a freight train plowing into the woods as whoever it was thrashed and tore through the forest as if running from a soon to be explosion. Did Mother flee knowing she wouldn't get the upper hand in such a battle? Had she left them alone with the evil beast?

A grunt. A huff. A tongue click.

Whoever was left here in the dark dungeon was moving closer. Its hot breath puffing white clouds out of the darkness. A faint silhouette appeared. Whoever it was, was on all fours again. Another white cloud of hot, steamy breath. A low rumble, edging closer.

30

Huffing. Grunting. Gasping for breath. Little white puffs continued to rise from the shadows. The silhouette grew with each passing second. It emerged from the darkness, hunched back, big knuckles scraping across the dirt as it edged closer. Its face was down, but by the size of the creature it had to be Mother. It wasn't near as big as the one that'd entered. It raised its head and with an open and gasping mouth looked to Tyler, then scanned the blackness for the other two. It was Mother.

She crawled over and rolled to her rump next to Tyler. Flopping next to him, still catching her breath. Her arms and legs were limp. Her kids emerged out of the dark and scooted close to her. The one to Tyler's right, grunted and nudged him away. The two nestled up against her hairy and sweaty fur. They whimpered and whined. The one on the right even started licking at Mother's knee. Her breath was raspy and labored, wincing here and there.

Must be her battle scars from defeating Goliath. Man, Mother was a tough cookie to survive all that. Which when giving it thought, offered both comfort and fear. Comfort as for the fact that she could defend and keep them safe from about near anything after seeing her take on a creature so big. But also fear, because if she could do that to him, what could she do to a person? Let alone a kid? Best not make Mother mad.

You got what now?" asked Warden Phillips. He and Sheriff Logan among a crew of others were seated around a cherry oak conference table between white boards with taped maps and photos of Tyler Jacobs and Al Frankford, the missing hunter.

"I said...I had a visual," the pilot's voice crackled over the hand-held radio.

Phillips looked to Logan who sat with his fingers interlocked at his belt buckle with extended legs and crossed feet. He wore brown rugged cowboy boots that could hold up in both a rodeo or trek over the mountains. His head was tilted and so was his brow. He was only here, because it'd look bad if he wasn't.

Him and Phillips had never gotten along much, especially since their dispute over what happened to that missing boy a decade ago. Phillips swore on his grave it wasn't a bear, but Logan swore on his, it was. Ever since then, they only spoke to one another when it was beneficial to the job.

"Well what do you mean? What did you see?" asked Phillips.

"I marked it on the GPS..." a static hiss. "...I got a blip on the FLIR..." more static and crackle. "...but it disappeared before I got a good look at it...it was definitely upright."

"10-4. Is it enough to send some guys out or no?"
A beat.

"Listen...I don't want to be held accountable for anything if some..." static. "...thing happens out here. I'm just tel..." crackle and hiss. "...ling you what I saw."

Phillips took a deep breath, then scanned the eyes of the men in the room. He started with Logan who sat looking like Sam Elliot with his graying mustache, white hair, and stone face. K-9 Officer Breeden sat at the edge of his chair, elbows on the table forming a teepee. Deputy Jeff Anderson wrinkled his brows and glanced to Logan next to him. Detective Joe Stines sat across from the two, still wearing his black suit, tie and slacks. Taking a break from scribbling notes, he leaned to one side of the chair, elbow propped, hand holding a pencil to his teeth.

"10-4. I understand. It'll be on me and Logan, not you. Send over the coordinates as soon as you can."

A beat.

Crackle and hiss.

"Wadyasay about Logan?"

"I said it'll be on me and Logan, not you. Send me the coordinates ASAP."

"10-4. We'll do."

Phillips turned the volume down to ease the hiss from the radio signal. He sat it down on the table in front of him, black rectangle with an assortment of red and white buttons and dials. A bony black antenna extending to the ceiling. The men stared at it as if it held all of life's secrets. A moment passed and not a word was spoken.

"You can't send guys out at this time of night. Too risky," Logan's firm and deep gravel filled voice pierced the silence.

Phillips took a breath before answering. Attempting to cool the steam building in his gut. He adjusted his curved bill black baseball cap which wore a golden cut out of the state of California on the front. He scratched his five o'clock shadow. The flame within was growing hotter...hotter...hotter.

Phillips slapped the table and bolted to his feet. Causing all but Logan to flinch. Phillips hunched his back, hands pressed tight against the wooden table and unleashed his tongue.

"What choice do we have? I mean...there's a kid out there alone who very well may not survive the night. Not too mention Frankford who could be fighting for his life this very moment. Now I don't know about you...but I couldn't live with myself if something happens to this kid because we were to afraid to risk our safety in fear of what's happened in the past! How are we going to keep this from becoming another statistic? We have to take the risk."

The floor was his. All eyes were locked on his lips.

"I'll admit...at first, I thought it'd be best to wait till morning, but the more I keep thinking about it, that's the same mistake we've made time and again for the past ten years since the Landry boy. I'm not going to wait around for it to happen again. I say we launch with our best men and resources tonight and find the boy now. Not tomorrow. *Now!*"

Stines and Breeden were nodding, but Anderson kept a stoic face much like Logan.

"Steve...I know you want to bring this boy home to his mama, hell we all do. But the fact is...he's most likely dead by now. Face it, this isn't a rescue...it's a recov—"

Phillips cursed and swiped a stack of papers from the table, pointing a bony finger across it to Logan.

Years of guilt, anger, blaming, ego and protecting territory had all led to a clashing of heads such as this. Logan pushed from his chair, sending it spinning backward. His outstretched hand grasping for Phillips neck, but Deputy Anderson reached him before he took hold. Phillips was restrained by Detective Stines. To be such a clean cut, quiet man, he had quite the muscle.

Omah

Phillips and Logan barked out spit filled curses and insults to one another as it took all Stines and Anderson had to keep them from locking horns.

Breeden cursed and smacked the table, rattling the half empty glasses of water.

"Hey! This is nuts! We've got a—" he cursed, "—boy and hunter out there who need us. We don't have time to be tearing at one another's throat. Now I don't mean no disrespect as you both know I look up to each of you, but guys...we've got a job to do. Whether we agree or not, our job is to bring this boy and that hunter home. Differences and grievances aside, that needs to be our focus."

Logan and Phillips huffed and eyed one another with a searing hostility. Their pulses were slow to ebb to a normal beat as Stines and Anderson loosened their grip.

Logan jerked free and made three quick swipes at the wrinkles in his uniform. Phillips sighed and lowered himself back into the chair with a thump.

"You're crazy Steve. I won't have any part in night searches, and neither will my men. At least not until I know we're rescuing and not recovering."

Phillips nodded.

"You do your thing. I'll do mine."

"And as for Randy...he's your responsibility, if something happens...and god forbid he's with you when you find the kid...well, that's on you."

Phillips nodded again. Eyes narrowed, lips tight and jaw trembling, steam rising from his gut into his throat. He swallowed to cool it. It sizzled as it sank down his windpipe and settled back into his bowels. His mind was racing, his heart was pounding, but he was doing his best to keep a strong bridle on his tongue. It wasn't worth it. Logan was a tough man like himself, likely why they didn't get alone, though they had their differences, they certainly had their similarities as well.

Like himself, the guilt and shame of losing another to the ever-hungry forest, had taken its toll. The difference though, was Phillips was determined to end it. He was tired of wasting time with excuses and fears of what might happen. There's a kid out there roaming the dark, with a family that loves him, grieving for his return. He couldn't—and by god he wouldn't—bring bad news to another family. This is where it ends. This is where the tides turn. He'd do everything in his power to make sure that happens. Starting tonight.

Omah

31

A long, drawn out wail that could've came from the deepest pit in hell, sounded off from the thick forest and enveloping darkness, seeping and slithering its way into the dungeon, right to Tyler's ears.

Mother perked to attention, her ears bending at sharp angles, her nostrils flaring, she squinted and eyed the opening. There it was again. Another long, deep wail. Like a mix between a Lion and a dying woman. Sounding as if it were in mortal agony, Mother must've done some damage. More than the thing had done to her.

She stood and eased to the moonlight streaking in. There she stood, head tilted upward, eyes scanning the trees and stars. Nose filtering every scent. Ears filtering every sound. The forest was silent, except for the wail and now distant whop-whop-whop sound.

KnockKnockKnock

Three quick thuds sounded off near the wail. Mother jerked her head so fast, it would have given most humans a cramp. She grunted and snorted, then took a few steps closer to the slant leading out of the dungeon. Tilted her head back, snarled her nose and upper lip, made a tongue click just before entering a long flowing whistle, that sounded sort of like a tea kettle, but much deeper.

The whistle trailed off into the forest, lingering as the echo carried it. She finished with a huff once her lungs were exhausted of air. She stood motionless, looking like the carved statues Tyler had seen at some of the stores they'd passed on the way up from San Francisco.

Breaking the silence was a deep grunt like whoop which seemed closer than before. With that Mother snapped around and pounded to Tyler and the other two. In the blink of an eye, Tyler found himself scooped up by Mother as if he were a dog that'd escaped the yard. She toted him like a football and bounded out of the dungeon and into the moon lit forest. Her gait was out of balance a tad as she favored the bummed knee. The other two trailed right behind her. They were off again, running, leaping, panting, sweating, and darting through limbs and branches. Following trails where there were and plowing new ones where there weren't.

The creature wailed again, sending Mother to dart to her right as if the track this barreling train was on had just been shifted. The whop-whop-whop in the distance could have been coming closer or could have been going away. Hard to tell between all the jarring, clinging on for dear life, and the wailing from a demon.

Scared. Confused. Tired. Cold.

When will it ever end?

OMAH

32

Four miles to the north of Myer's Flat in a small town called McCann, Jessie McDaniel, his ten-year-old son Tony, Jessie's friend Bobby Morgan and his nine-year-old son Michael were fishing in McCann Creek off Dyerville Loop Road just upstream from Devil's Elbow.

They'd been fishing for Salmon and Trout since sundown and was planning to stay until midnight, which would be in another hour and a half.

Wearing his lucky orange hat with the word STIHL written on the front in big white letters with a white mesh back, Bobby Morgan had caught his fair share during the evening. Though none of the fish were of the legal-size limits, that didn't stop Bobby from packing his cooler.

Jessie warned him more than once, but Bobby wouldn't have it. There weren't any wardens out here at this time of night, what'd it hurt to take whatever he wanted?

Would he ever eat that many fish? Probably not, but what the heck, it was always more fun to keep a fish than to toss it back for the next guy to catch. Like a personal trophy, a reward for his efforts. Afterall, what's the point in fishing if you don't come home with something? Even if it is illegal.

Besides, he always enjoyed skinning and gutting the rascals anyhow, that was just as much fun as catching them.

Always full of stories and tales, most which were nothing more than bold face lies, Bobby hadn't stop yapping since he'd cast the first line. He rambled on with stories of how he'd once killed a bear with just a pocket knife after chasing it through the woods in the middle of the night. Another time he caught a fifteen-pound bass and a ten-pound bass all on the same lure with the same cast.

"Dad...we know you didn't really do none of this stuff. You know that right?" asked his son Michael.

Jessie and Tony couldn't withhold their laughter. They'd been dying to say the same thing all night.

"Now boy, what you trying to say?"

Michael chuckled and said, "So you're saying you really chased a bear one time and killed it with your pocket knife?"

"Yeah...and I—"

His words were cut short by the loud pop of a crashing tree across the creek from them. It snapped like a toothpick and came thudding to earth with a loud thump. Tearing away any branches or trees that may have stood in its way.

Every cricket, cicada and frog went silent. Even the rustle in the trees were quiet. No breeze, no chirping of the creatures, no nothing. Just quiet...eerie...silence.

The boys dropped their rods and clung to their Dads. Bobby looked to Jessie with wide eyes illuminated by the flame of their lanterns hanging in the tree just behind them. Jessie shrugged his shoulders and wagged his head.

They each stared into the darkness beyond the flames light, listening...watching...waiting.

Nothing.

"Aww, it's probably just a—" Jessie started to say with a wave of his hand, but the loud splash downstream interjected.

It sounded like it could have been a bowling ball. Droplets of water crashed to the surface as they fell from their ascent of the splash.

"What in the devil's hell?" Bobby mumbled.

Bowussshhh

Another splash. This one closer than the last.

Twigs snapped. Leaves crunched.

It was coming closer whatever it was, and it was coming quick. Like a bulldozer tearing through the woods, trees crashed, and heavy feet pounded the dirt.

"Go-go-go!!" Jessie screamed.

Everyone dropped whatever they held, whether it was a fishing rod or a soda, it all crumbled to the ground. They bolted up the embankment towards Jessie's truck.

Clawing and grasping for roots and rock crevices, Tony was first, as Jessie pushed him onward. Michael was behind him, prodded along by Bobby bringing up the rear.

A horrible wail that could have only came from the mouth of a demon filled the air. The scream was so deep, yet so high pitched, it pierced every square inch of their bodies at once. It vibrated within their chest causing their hearts to knock against the ribcages. Bones shuddered and rattled without restraint. Hair stood on edge, skin crawled with gooseflesh.

This must be what hell is like.

The four of them stumbled and pushed their way up the hill. They reached flat ground and just to their left was the trail the truck was on. Another wail emitted from their right. No way that thing could have crossed the creek that fast.

Either it was a spirit or there was more than one of them. Neither was a comforting thought.

Is this what Jessie's grandpa meant by the

Creek Devil all those years?

Can't think about that now. Must keep moving. With a hand on his son's back, pushing him onward, the dark silhouette of the truck came into view. Jessie fumbled the keys from his pocket, felt for the black remote. Hit every button in effort to unlock his Toyota.

The sound of heavy feet thundered behind them, gaining more and more ground with each passing second.

The headlights to the truck blinked followed by rapid blast of the horn. The creature behind them belted out an even deeper and more heart piercing wail.

Jessie and Tony reach the truck. Jessie slings the driver door open, Tony clambers in.

"C'mon...get—" Jessie was screaming his words as he turned around to face Michael and Bobby, but Michael was all alone.

"Where's your dad!?"

Michael with wide eyes and a dumb found look, spun to look behind him, stumbling to the door.

The creature wailed again, deep and long.

Michael climbs in next to Tony, both of them gasping for breath, tears wetting their cheeks.

Jessie takes two steps from the truck, cups his mouth and yells for his friend. The beast screeched again, feet pounding closer. No answer from Bobby. Jessie climbs in the truck and turns the ignition over. He pounds the horn, but it only seemed to send the beast into an even deeper rage.

What does he do? Does he leave his friend to ensure the safety of the boys? He couldn't just leave him out there could he?

The sound of shattering glass followed by a

pelting of the remnants of his back window, seized his thoughts. A large rock landed on his dash and smacked the bottom of his front window where it rested.

Jessie slung the gear stick to drive and gave one last glance out the driver window. A dark silhouette raced toward them, tucked behind a cover of shadows. The thing screamed that blood curdling, hair raising wail once more, before Jessie slammed the gas pedal, slinging rock and dirt behind the tires as they bolted out of the ravine.

The only thought on his mind now was protecting the boys, surely Bobby would understand.

33

Travelling along service road 12 just off Highway 101, Adam, Jack, and Randy were packed in Jack's Rav4 with enough gear to survive in the wilderness for a week. And that's exactly what they'd do if that's what it took to bring Tyler home.

Bounced around with a few pot holes disguised in the dark, Randy leaned up from the back seat and asked, "So you guys really believe in this stuff?"

By stuff, of course he meant "Bigfoot", but he had yet to feel comfortable enough throwing the word around. Especially when his boy could have possibly been kidnapped by one.

Listen at him. It's nuts.

Adam twisted from the passenger seat, looked to Randy and nodded. Jack with hands at 10 and 2, looked up at the rear-view mirror, peering at the dark silhouette sitting in the back seat, "Listen man...I know it can be hard to believe in something you've never seen before, but I'm telling you now...I've seen it...we all have," he said aiming a thumb to his brother.

"These things are real, whether you believe it or not, makes no difference. They're out here."

Omah

Randy leaned back, resting his elbow against the door, hand to his chin, eyes glaring out at the passing darkness. He'd taken two Ibuprofen before they left, hoping it'd relieve the pain in his ankle. Whether it did or not, he'd just have to tough it out.

Once he got out in the woods and got some adrenaline pumping, it'd ease off.

Hopefully.

The tires crunched over rocks and splashed in puddles, jolting the cab each time. A backpack full of food and supplies tumbled off the seat, Randy bent over and readjusted it.

The whole car smelled of fresh pine and some sort of seasoning Adam had used on the rice and bean mixture. The pine came from the air freshener dangling from the rearview mirror. A snapshot carving of the famous picture of one of the creatures crossing a creek bed. It swung with the rhythm of bumps on the road. Its eyes seemed to glare at Randy.

A long drawn out shriek as if from a dying woman entered his mind. Is that really what that was he and Bev heard last night?

Is that what took the old man's voice at the check-in desk? Is that why he won't talk? As terrifying as it sounded in the safety of the RV, imagine being in the woods when one of them did that. Is that really what plowed by them in the woods earlier? Is that what terrified those hunters? Those were some big mountain boys, one would assume it'd take a lot to spook them that bad.

The carved creature slowed its dangling. The squealing brakes and touch of Adam's hand on Randy's forearm pulled him back. Randy flinched and batted his eyes.

"Randy? Randy? Hey?"

"Yeah-yeah."

"This is it. This is where we'll launch."

Jack cut the lights off and killed the engine. Randy opened the door and stepped out. His feet landed on the shifting gravel, soft from the recent rain.

His eyes raised to the wood line. This is it. This is the point of no return. He wasn't coming out of here until he had his boy. One way or another, Tyler was coming home.

34

They'd ran full force for what seemed like an eternity but was likely less than half an hour. But none the least they'd probably gained as much ground as the average man could in two hours. With long thunderous strides, they must've conquered twenty feet with every two steps. Even with her bleeding knee, Mother kept a solid pace. The two young ones pounded right on her heels. The wailing had ceased.

The sudden sliding halt almost shook Tyler loose. The two young ones plowed in her rump and grunted. She turned, gasping for breath, her thick chest widening and shrinking rapidly. She clicked her tongue twice before angling through a thicket to the right.

Her nose high in the air, pointing to the night sky. The stars were in abundance, shining through thin clouds. One wispy cloud attempted to cover the full moon, but its light was too bright.

A stale, metal like taste filled Tyler's mouth. He swallowed hard. His stomach ached and growled. Almost sounding like one of the creatures. Goodness was he already becoming one of them?

He tightened his grip as Mother still carried him like he were an inflated ball wrapped in pigskin and white laces. Maybe she thought he was a pig. Maybe she was planning to feast on him at the proper time.

He whimpered with trembling lips. Mother waded through slappy, sticky branches, swatting them away like bees. She looked down at Tyler, her gaze a tower length above him. She clicked, then let out a thin hiss like whisper, trying to form a sentence, but it came out like another language spoken in a hushed tone.

She raised her gaze and continued deeper into the thicket. A horrible odor arose, reminding him of the one that'd entered the dungeon earlier. It also reminded him of the trash soon after Easter with all the leftover boiled eggs. Soured, rotten and loud.

He buried his face in Mother's fur. Which didn't offer much relief, but it was at least bearable. The other smell was sure to make him puke. She stopped and stood motionless for at least a solid minute. The odor grew worse as now even Mother's sweaty, soured fur couldn't fend it off.

Tyler twisted his head to see why they were so quiet. It was another opening, like the one before. A doorway hidden behind pine branches and leaves. Another dungeon? Had they stumbled upon the other one's home? Mother's step forward and clicking tongue startled him. He turned and hid his face against her hip.

Darkness covered him so thick, he could feel it. The air was damp and cool, just like the other place. Heavy, raspy breathing grew the more they entered the darkness.

The sudden shriek stabbed his heart as a wave of trembling terror washed over him. It was the wail of the demon. They'd just entered its lair. What was she doing?

Omah

It thrashed about. Too petrified to look, he tried his best to hide within Mother's thick fur, but there just wasn't enough. Grunts. Snorts. Huffs. Hissing. This thing was mad, and Mother had yet to say a word. Is this it? Is this where they shred him to pieces?

35

The things roar was like that of a Lion. It bounced and crawled through the dungeon. Judging by how loud the noises were, this dungeon must be smaller than the last one. As if there wasn't enough air to go around. And after this thing's roar, it may have used it all up. Its rumbling growl grew as the sound of heavy feet slapping the earth floor edged closer. Mother spun, taking a blow across her back, just in time before Tyler had his head knocked off. She grunted and stumbled, still gripping Tyler under her right armpit. She swatted with her left, smacking against hard, hairy flesh.

The thing huffed and lost its footing. Mother let out a series of deep raspy barks like a horsed dog.

Silence.

It was just the beast's breath as it huffed and snorted powerful thrust of air. Mother took Tyler in her arms and forced him to the ground next to her.

Hanging on for dear life not wanting to leave the safety of her stinky fur coat, "No!" She grunted and forced him to his feet. He clinched to her leg.

Heavy footsteps moved left to right. Sounding as if they stopped in the moonlit entryway. Tyler gently raised an eye lid and leaned out from around her tree trunk of a leg.

Omah

There it was. The wailing demon. But with a scrunch, and focused glare, Tyler noticed something.

This one was different. Much different.

It had a beard. A long one at that. Long and gray. And there was no scar across its face. It seemed about the same size as the one Mother had fought earlier in the other dungeon, but its features were different. It was much grayer. Its face wore more wrinkles, especially around its black deep-set eyes. The face was still super leathery, kind of like an old worn out baseball glove with all the cracks in the hide. A wide, flat nose. And that long gray beard. It looked as if it were mimicking a Bible character.

Kind of like Moses.

It stood there at an angle in the light breaking through, leering at Tyler from the corners of its ginormous eyes. It seethed at his presence, its breath a raspy hiss. Sounded like a person with a bad cough, like something was fluttering in its lungs.

Was it sick maybe?

Its sudden jerk toward the opening caused Tyler to flinch. It climbed its way out, thrashed around on heavy flat feet.

Was it leaving? No. Sounded like it was hanging close by.

What was it doing?

The sound of branches scraping across the ground told of its whereabouts. It was coming back. Its shadow stood in the moonlight for just a moment before it lowered its hair covered feet into the dungeon.

It came in backside first. Arms and hands full of leaves, it covered the opening as it backtracked lower and further inside. The light slowly fading. The moonlight tried to enter but was blocked by all the branches.

The creature continued to block out the light, the cold earth room grew darker with each passing second. By the time it was finished, Tyler could barely
make out the creature's silhouette. Once it moved from the opening, it blended into the dark.

Becoming an ever-fading shadow, before completely disappearing as it moved closer. By the sound of it, the thing plopped to the earth next to Mother.

Following suit, she did the same. At least by the feel and sound of it, she did. If it wasn't for sound and touch, she could be standing right in front of him and he'd never know it.

With heavy eyes, cold flesh and a pounding heart, Tyler eased down and cradled in closer to Mother's side. It didn't make much difference if he shut his eyes. He almost couldn't tell the difference between them being open or shut. He might just sleep with them open.

Omah

36

Miraculous stories of kids missing in the woods and being found days later, rare though they are, do happen. One such story wasn't that long ago. In the mountains of North Carolina, a three-year-old boy vanished while out hiking with his parents and older sister. No trace, no sound, just...gone.

After a dozen or so counties had entered the search efforts, it was four days later when the boy was discovered. Not a mark on him, though slightly dehydrated and famished. The boy claimed to have spent the past few days with a bear. But remember, he wasn't but three and kids that young can have quite the imagination.

At least Jennifer, Andrew, and Tyler did when they were that age. Andrew and Tyler still do. Another story that came to Bev's mind was that of two sisters lost in the woods of Maine about a year ago. Five and eight-years-old if she could remember correctly. They were missing for three days and claimed an old hairy man took care of them, which prompted police and DNR officials to continue to search the area, believing this "old hairy man," may be the one that had taken the girls captive. But they insisted they weren't taken, and simply just wandered too far in the woods before losing sense of direction.

Then there were the stories from Jennifer's book. Those are people and children who never made it back.
Something had happened to them. But what? What if these kids were right? What if the stories Kosumi told were true? Could that be what these kids were talking about? A bear? An old hairy man? What if the creatures were real? What if they had her son? Oh God no! Please no!

"Ssshhh...Bev...it's okay. Everything is going to be okay. Adam and Jack know everything there is to know about the creatures and they will do what needs to be done," said Brenda as she gently stroked Bev's arm, sitting next to her on the couch in the RV.

Kosumi sat in the recliner while Jennifer and Andrew were laying down in the bunk over the driver cab.

"Right, Kosumi?" asked Brenda.

Bev sniffled and wiped her eye with a Kleenex. Kosumi nodded. His long braids now draped across each shoulder in the front, sharp cheek bones and stern face that were not at all like his warm spirit and personality.

"Yes. Once I have some strands of hair, we can perform a peace offering."

Whether it'd work or not, who knows, but it would at least be worth a try, wouldn't it?

OMAH

37

The constant beep and hiss of numerous machines did all they could to override the volume on the TV. Jimmy Davis and his wife Suzanne read the subtitles with squinted eyes when their ears failed them. A young brunette news reporter stood with mic in hand out in the cold, dark, half empty campground of the Giant Redwood RV Park.

The headline below her, read, "Officials search for Missing Boy"

The small white clock with black numbers and outer trim and reddish orange hands, towered proudly above the tube.

It read, *11:32*

The young brunette recounted the recent events, then turned and looked to the scattered campers and RV's. The camera panning and zooming before cutting to footage of Logan and his men addressing the vast crowd of searchers and volunteers from earlier in the day.

The video faded as a picture of Tyler holding a Trout appeared on the screen, then faded to a picture of the family standing in front of a Giant Redwood. After that, the scene cut to a map of the surrounding area. A red X appeared in Bluff Creek showing Dave and Travis Hodges encounter, before two more red X's appeared where Jimmy's attack occurred just north of Hoopa and the place of Les and Sam's attack, just south of Willow Creek.

Then lastly, a red X appeared in Myers Flat representing the missing boy…Tyler Jacobs.

A gravelly voice crackled on the heels of the reporter, the camera faded to an older gentleman, gray mustache, firm jaw, tan cowboy hat with a Sheriff star in the center above a black and firmly pressed shirt. A black hand-held radio was attached to his shoulder. He wore black sunglasses to hide his icy eyes.

A blocked line appeared below the man as he spoke, it read, *Humboldt CO Sheriff: Ron Logan*

He kept it short and sweet, answering only what needed to be answered, nothing more. He ended with, "We're going to hit it hard and quick before this cold front settles in. With predicted lows being in the teens, we don't have much time to waste."

The scene cut back to the lady reporter who stood with a blank face for a second as she waited for her cue. She got it a tad late, then broke the awkwardness with, "Live Coverage from Myers Flat. Channel 6 WSOC, I'm Samantha Wheeler, back to you Doug."

Volume bars appeared at the bottom of the screen and shifted one at a time to the left.

"Honey…there's something out there. That poor boy doesn't stand a chance. You see what it did to me."

Jimmy said before having to readjust the irritating oxygen tubes running to his nostrils. He sat at an angle, still in his hospital gown. Doc said he was doing good and would be able to leave in the next few days. Hopefully, tomorrow.

Omah

Suzanne nodded and took a deep breath, "Jimmy...you're lucky."

Her eyes strained and misted over. She squeezed his hand and caught a tear with her free hand.

"I'm worried about that kid, honey. If they don't get to him soon...he won't make it. Either that thing will get him or the cold will," Jimmy said wagging his head.

A beat.

"Honey...I need to talk with the Sheriff and Warden. They need to understand what this thing is capable of."

38

Being out in the woods in total darkness, other than moon light, was nothing less than daunting to say the least. Randy listening and darting his vision about. A thousand eyes watching them from the shadows, at least it felt that way. There were plenty dark spots and trees to hide behind. The forest was teaming with chatter when they first entered. As if they'd just stepped into a busy high school hallway. Crickets, cicadas, owls, rustling leaves and branches, and what must have been a sleeping deer they startled. Whatever it was, leaped to its feet and dashed through the thicket.

But now after a few hours of trekking through the woods, the air becoming more frigid by the minute, their breath creating thicker clouds with each huff, the woods were eerily...quiet.

"Guys hold up a sec," said Randy.

He stopped and leaned against a Redwood, rubbing his ankle, wincing out his breaths. He'd be all right, he just needed to massage it and get the kinks out. Though of course the cold air never seemed to help.

Adam adjusted his black wool hat, eying the dark forest. They had lights but would only use them if

necessary. Much like the .270 Remington Rifle strapped on the back of Jack's shoulder and the .357
revolver on Adam's hip.

Jack shifted his rifle and gripped it between his gloved hands. Eyes scanning their surroundings. Adam continued to do the same with his hand just over the holstered gun, like a nervous deputy.

Randy swallowed and said, "I'm good gu—"

"Ssshhh..." Jack said with a finger to his lips.

Adam turned and looked over his shoulder to Jack and Randy. His face only a mere silhouette, even so, Randy knew something was off.

Pop!

They flinched and jerked to the right. Jack brought his rifle to aim at eye level. The rustle and flapping of leather, told Randy, Adam had unholstered his revolver.

Feeling at a disadvantage, Randy needed something too. Though it wasn't much, it was better than a bare hand, he retrieved his pocket knife and fixed the blade.

No one said a word. Neither the men nor the forest. It was as if an eerie black cloud had washed over him, so dark he could feel it creep along his flesh. Tiny cold bumps festered across his body. A drop of cold sweat trickled from his neck to his navel.

A horrible stench arose. A cross between a dead deer and rotten eggs. It meandered through the air seeming to take the place of oxygen. The men were forced to cover their faces beneath the neck of their shirts.

Pop!

Something was snapping trees like twigs for a fire, but these pops were loud and more dense sounding than just a twig.

The men stood frozen, attempting to blend in with the trees. Maybe these things had sight like humans and couldn't see that good in the dark. Or maybe they had sight like a ca—no don't think like that. If they are real, they're likely just another species of Gorilla, so they're sight shouldn't be nothing too special. Right?

Whoooaarhhh!

The men jerked around to their left this time. How'd it get over ther—

Pop! Back to their right.

There was more than one. They were surrounded.

"Stay calm. They have to know we mean no threat," said Adam as he holstered his gun. Jack lowered his rifle and slung it back over his shoulder.

Are they nuts?

Randy stood there, still squeezing his pocketknife with a cold hand and numb fingers encased around the handle. Randy wagged his head.

Whooooarhhhh! Another grunt to the left again.

"Randy..."

He swallowed and conceded to fold it away. He stuffed it in his right hip pocket.

Silence.

A moment passed of complete...eerie...silence.

It was pierced with a series of quick, sharp chatter that emitted on each side of them. It sounded like they'd been dropped in the middle of a Japanese interrogation. The tone and angle of the dialect sent a chill down Randy's spine. His breath felt labored in the presence of such unknowns.

Their voices were raspy, deep, and tended to end each syllable with a god-awful hiss. It began to sound otherworldly, it just didn't seem natural. Then as quickly as began...it ended. The odor lifted and oxygen returned.

Omah

"Tyler?" Randy beckoned. Jack and Adam hushed him as soon as he reached the L.

Quiet. Nothing.

Twigs snapped, leaves crunching on both sides of them. The sounds ebbed away with the stench. The insects returned to their chirps and screams. Even the leaves returned to their rustling as a soft breeze wafted passed them.

Adam took a deep breath and scratched his chin, "That was them. They're out here. I say we camp here tonight."

39

Stealing glances over their shoulders into the dark woods every few seconds, the men had their base camp established within half an hour. It was too early to call it a night, it was only a quarter past midnight. There was really no point in entering a tent, because there was no way Randy could ever get any sleep. How could he until he found his boy? A handful of times, he could have sworn he heard Tyler scream for help, but he was the only one to hear it. And after listening for a few minutes, he'd come to realize it was either a lonely hoot owl or a distant coyote that had wandered from the pack.

The chatter of the night bugs clawed at his mind, raking across his sanity. Half of him wished they'd hush, but he also knew what it meant if they did. The forest didn't grow silent for no reason. He'd learned that its silence served as a warning. Something was coming and you best pay attention. Kind of like an alarm really. As long as the crickets and their cousins continued their chatter and singing, all was okay, but the second their voices faded...well...you better have your head on a swivel.

So far, the forest had yet to send another alarm. Since their interrogation of the two beasts, the woods had ceased to shut up. As if it were making up for the moment of silence earlier when the creatures were around. Now, the critters seemed to not just chatter, but at times...scream. Some of the bugs sounded hoarse.

The sound of crunching leaves and twigs added to the night's song. Adam led the pack, Randy in the middle and Jack bringing up the rear. They stepped over logs and fern bushes, some they saw, others they only felt with their feet. They still didn't use any light.

Branches swatted against their chest, sticky needles from a Pine bristling upon their cheeks more than once. Their breath looking like steam from an old train. They trudged onward, eyes darting, ears ciphering the many squawks, screams, and chitter-chatter the forest had to offer. Randy kept waiting to hear those Japanese beasts again.

"How bad is this cold front supposed to be?" asked Randy after taking a branch to the teeth. His words spitting in a mumble at the end as the needles stung his lips.

A beat.

Adam drew a breath and glanced over his shoulder, "I think they might be calling for snow tomorrow night."

Snow? Oh, for Heaven's sake, could it get any worse? Randy stopped, Jack bumped into him as his eyes were scanning the woods behind them. Randy and Jack stumbled forward causing a stir in the brush.

Adam swiveled, his heart picking up pace, his hand edging to the revolver on his hip, like metal to a magnet.

"What are you doing?" asked Adam

"He stopped."

"Snow? Are you serious?"

Through the darkness, the silhouette of Adam's head moved up and down in a slow fashion before angling to the

ground, hands on his hips. He took a deep breath and sighed it out. A long white trail of
steam billowed skyward, "Randy...you know as good as I do...we need to get your boy before then. We got tonight and tomorrow before it sets it. We don't get snow that often, but when we do, it's usually more than a dusting."

"Silence.

Nobody said anything for a good minute. The reality of the predicament was slowly setting in. A quick gust rustled through the trees causing the leaves to shudder. Randy pulled his wool hat down a little further on his head. He clasped his gloved hands and breathed into them before rubbing them together.

"All right...well let's get to it."

They continued deeper into the forest, listening, smelling, and watching. They'd stop every few minutes to catch their breath and listen to the woods whisper and screams. What was it telling them? Adam and Jack seemed to understand such language, but it took some concentrating for Randy to pick it up. A gentle breeze meandered above them, whispering like a Spirit as it passed. What did it say? Had these trees seen Tyler pass below? Had these critters and bugs seen his boy? If only they could talk. And if only he'd understand such language.

"How far are we going to wander from camp?" asked Jack.

They stopped again. Their breath in cold huffs. "Not too far. We're about a mile now. I say we try and do a mile radius of it. What do you say?" said Adam as he looked to Randy.

Randy nodded and not sure if the two could see him in the dark, he added, "Yeah. Let's do that."

Omah

Sudden movement sent Tyler tumbling from the thick warm fur to the thin cold dirt. Cold damp leaves stuck to his body and face. A raw earthy smell and low grumble like growl filled his senses. A sharp acrid odor trailed not far behind. Causing him to cover his nose. It was still too dark to see as it was hard to even tell if he had his eye lids open. It felt like he did, but it sure didn't look like it.

He squirmed and twisted, trying to gain his sense of direction, scanning for the opening where those faint trickles of light had seeped in.

Where is it? Where is it?

C'mon. Ahh hah. Found it.

His heart jolted at the sight of a large shadow standing just next to the glimmer of light piercing in. The thing seemed to be hunched at the shoulders, its head tilting and peering out the branch and limb covered opening, as if watching for an intruder.

Tyler darted his head about, searching for Mother and the other two. Mother was crouched on all fours in the dark a few paces behind the bigger one. Head craning and stretching to the opening, as if something demanded her attention. He didn't know where the other two were. Maybe sleeping or hiding in the shadows?

Tyler flinched.

What was that?

Sounded like a twig snapped. There it was again. Something's out there. It sounded like more than one. Had the one Mother fought off earlier went and got its brothers?

Could Mother and this older one fend them off? What is that?

Sounds like someone talking. It doesn't sound like the language Mother used earlier. Its different. A little too far to make out the words, but it did sound familiar. It was growing louder and so was the crunching of leaves and twigs. It was coming.

Omah

40

The sound of heavy feet drew closer. Twigs snapping and popping as leaves continued their crunch.

Mother and the other one tensed and shifted their footing as if preparing for battle. Something was coming and Mother and the one that looked like Moses were ready for a fight.

A low grumble like hiss emitting from her mouth. Foam and slime probably followed it. Tyler pictured it drooling like a monster from some horror movie. That hissy growl continued from a deep slimy throat that could likely swallow a human in a matter of seconds. But if they were worked up this much, what was out there? What had chased him and Mother earlier? Was it the one with the scar? Another creature he'd never seen before? What else is out there?

Crunch. Snap. Pop.

Whatever it was...was gaining ground and Mother was ready. She stopped her hiss.

All was silent. The two were nothing but big hair covered shadows with a mouth full of teeth, ready to strike.

RANDY STOPPED. The feeling in his gut made him uncomfortable. His heart pumped harder, something just wasn't right. Call it parental intuition or whatever you like, something told him Tyler was near. He could feel his presence.

His eyes scanned the darkness. His ears listened for his voice. Jack saw him stop in time to avoid bumping into him again, "What is it?" he asked stopping a few feet from Randy, who stared to the black sky with a million tiny beads of light staring back through the branches.

Adam stopped and turned.

"I feel him. He's close. I know he is. Tyler!"

"Ssshhh!" said Jack.

"Don't shoosh me! My boy's out here. He's close, I know he is. Tyler!"

TYLER SNAPPED his head and tried to force himself to his feet, but his cold tight muscles said otherwise.

"Daddy," his voice a faint whisper, emitting over cold cracked lips. He swallowed to wet his windpipes and tried again. "Da—"

The wind was knocked out of him as a hairy wrecking ball plowed into him, crashing him into the cold, damp dirt. He landed with a thud, gasped, but his breath wouldn't come. Cold leathery hands covered his mouth and eyes. Its heavy body resting on top of him. It was one of the younger ones. Tyler fought and scrambled, trying his best to gather his breath through aching lungs, but no matter how hard he tried, it just wouldn't come.

RANDY..." said Adam as he made his way back to him and Jack.

"Randy hang on a second man—"

"Tyler!"

"Randy...dag gummit. Listen to me," Adam finally grabbed hold of his shoulder. Randy jerked away and gave Adam the look.

"Randy...listen..." Jack tried this time, "If he's with them...we have to do it their way...*not ours*," Jack said with a comforting touch to Randy's elbow. He didn't jerk away, but took a deep breath and lowered his head, white fog swirling to the stars.

A beat.

Finally, "What should we do then?" Randy asked. "Cause I'm telling you...I think he's here."

SCRAPPING AND WRESTLING for breath, Tyler squirmed and grasped for the creature's face, hands, whatever he could get a grip on. But it was useless, like trying to catch the wind. His lungs burned, begging for air. He tried to bite and scream but couldn't. His eyes stung and became heavy all of a sudden. His body felt numb, like he was floating. As if drifting on a rocking sea. Blackness covered him like a blanket. The sound of the creature's breath, the smell and taste of its dirty, nasty hands...ebbed away like a slow setting sun.

TYLER IS likely not here, or he would have heard us. We need to leave something as a gift, to let the creatures know we're not here to harm them. They need to know our intentions," said Adam as he dug in his jacket pocket.

"What's that?" asked Randy as the darkness between them wanted to keep it a secret. For the first time since leaving the car, Adam flicked on his flashlight. Their eyes took a second to adjust. That irritating sting lasted just a few moments, long enough for Adam to show Randy what he held in his palm. He was quick to wink the light out.

A long, black and white feather, looking to belong to that of an Eagle or Hawk was rested in Adam's palm, but now burned in Randy's mind as his eyes readjusted to the darkness.

"It's an Eagle feather", said Adam as he waved it up and down, side to side over Randy, Jack, himself, and ...the woods, "It represents Peace, Prosperity, and Happiness."

Adam and Jack got quiet. They uttered hushed tones, sounding like they were in prayer. After a brief moment of sacredness, Adam angled to a Redwood to the right of them. His steps were light and barely audible, causing Randy to realize just how loud he walked himself. Adam fidgeted with the feather against the tree for a moment, before crossing back to Randy and Jack.

"Let's leave that there for now. I'll put out some more at the camp."

"You think that will get the point across?"

"It should. These creatures are smarter than you think. They know the significance of such a feather...they see that...and hopefully they'll be willing to trade.

Omah

41

Still dark and gloomy when Tyler awoke. How long he'd been asleep, who knows. The last thing he remembered was something big and hairy on top of him, its leathery, stinky hands covering his mouth. All was quite except for the sound of heavy, raspy breath entering in and out of a snore. His own breath had to be labored for as the cold, damp air stole it from his lungs. It was if one breath came for the work of two. His throat felt scratchy, his lungs burned and had a soft rattle with each gasp. His teeth chattered without his approval and so did his legs. He couldn't feel his toes or fingers. His nose and ears were like ice cubes, numb and stiff. Tyler craned his head about, eyes attempting to pierce the dark. If he could find the trickle of light beaming in from the opening, he could find his bearings.

Where is it? C'mon where is it? Hah! Now, if he was looking at the opening that meant Mother was likely to his right. Wait...no...that's his left...left...yeah because it's the hand he wears his baseball glove on. He's a righty...not a lefty...so yeah...Mother should be on his left.

Tyler stretched out a trembling left hand and patted the cool, moist earth. Nothing. He kept feeling through the darkness, eyes scanning. Something tickled his knuckles. Fur. Must be Mother. Oh...the fur was so warm. Like a heated blanket. It rose, then fell, a raspy snort shot out when Tyler curled up next to her. His cold, frail body must've startled her and given her a jolt.

Tyler snuggled in close, burring his fingers and face deep into the pleasant maze of hair. Mother shifted and rolled from her back to her side.

"Hey," Tyler said as he had to readjust before being toted along for a ride. A rush of chill air greeted him, he was quick to find the warmth at Mother's side. She grunted and scratched the lower part of her leg without even having to bend. Her arm could have reached across the room if it wanted to.

Eyes heavy, burning, and thick with sandy boogers, he did a quick wipe of them, then hurried to burry his hand back into Mother's hairy side. He took a deep breath and within minutes, he was back on that boat drifting lazily out to sea.

FOUR HOURS HAD passed since Adam left the Eagle feather on the Redwood. They had just finished the one-mile radius of camp and were heading for the tents. The temperature had fallen and was now likely below freezing.

The plan was to get back to the tents and attempt to get a few hours of sleep before sunrise, then hit it hard when the sun came up. But Randy already had plans of staying up, keeping watch, and listening for any sign of Tyler or the creatures.

A branch swatted across his chest. He pushed it away and continued on through the thick, dark, loud, frigid forest. Twigs snapped and popped under his feet, silhouettes of trees—some big like a Redwood, others small like a Pine—passed by as they maneuvered around them like rocks in the way of a canoe. Short, broad shadows of fern bushes and service berry here and there, mingled in with vines that tried to tie around Randy's neck and chest more than once.

Omah

"We should start gathering wood for the fire, so we don't have to do it when we get there," said Jack.

The sudden crackle of his raw voice caused a stir in Adam and Randy. They both stopped and spun atop the leaves and twigs.

"Dang it, man," said Randy.

"Yeah...good idea," Adam said as he retrieved his phone and looked to the map. The place where they'd set camp, was marked with a yellow star, the place where they were now was marked with a blue dot about a sixth of a mile to the Northeast. Another 900 feet to the Southwest and they'd reach camp. Adam bent and grabbed a handful of small twigs, stuffing them into his jacket.

Randy found two broken branches the size of a tee-ball bat, that felt dry enough to catch flame, then filled his jacket with leaves and sticks.

Jack followed suit. He managed to find a small log that'd likely keep a flame until Sunrise. And like Adam and Randy, stuffed his jacket with remnants from the forest floor.

It was just after four in the morning and with enough hope, they may just find Tyler before noon. At least that was what Randy was thinking, but he'd do his best to find him before then.

It took them another twenty minutes or so to reach camp and less than five minutes to get a fire going. They each agreed that with the falling temperatures, their best chance at staying warm would be to vacate the tents and sleep as close to the fire as they could. They each had thick sleeping bags, so between that and the fire, they should be able to make do.

RANDALL LANE

THE FIRE CRACKLED and hissed, its embers rising to the heavens as Randy sat on a log next to it, stoking it with a sturdy branch. Adam and Jack tucked away in their bags, looking like warm cocoons. Randy just couldn't allow himself to slip into such warmth, not while his son was lost in a sea of cold wilderness likely learning to speak Japanese like the creatures.

Eyes glued to the orange flame at the tip of his prodding stick, Randy's chest felt like it was carrying a bowling ball. His heart ached and longed for his boy. If only he'd paid attention and not allowed him to wander off, none of this would have happened.

Randy dropped the stick to his feet, the other end lifting and kicking embers. He rubbed his forehead and heavy eyes. His shoulders began to quake as his heart attempted to release its pain. Not now. Stay strong. No matter how large of dam he tried to make to hold back the river of emotions welling up within...he couldn't build one fast enough or large enough to withstand such pressure. The dam broke.

Hot, salty tears fell to the earth, his shoulders moving more rapidly, he sucked in air through blocked nostrils, his heart ached and moaned in utter agony. He bent over, crossing his arms at the waist and began to rock to and fro. Gosh, why was he so stupid? How could he just let Tyler venture off like that?

How did he not hear anything? Looks like he would have heard something thrashing in the brush or splashing through the river. Better yet, how did he not hear Tyler scream for help? Surely, he did. Wait...wait a second.

What if that wasn't where Tyler was taken? What? What if Tyler wasn't taken by the river? What if he was lured back into the campground by someone? But who? Who would have—

Omah

Randy raised his vision in a slow, mechanical motion. His eyes locked on Adam and Jack asleep in their bags. No...no way. But wait...it makes sense doesn't it? What if all of this Bigfoot crap is all a cover up? What if they are the ones snatching all these people? What if the authorities are involved in it? It makes sense doesn't it? Run a small shop that is sure to attract tourists, fill them with garbage about some hairy biped roaming the woods, terrorizing and snatching people and kids. Then wait for the perfect opportunity, take what you want and sell them into slave trafficking.

What if this was all a setup? What if they'd led him out here in the middle of nowhere, to murder him and blame it on the creatures? No...c'mon.

Randy needed sleep; he couldn't trust his mind when it was lacking it. Better yet, who could he trust?

Adam rolled, his back now facing Randy. The fire dancing between them. Jack, just to Randy's right, was curled on his side, face aimed to him.

Randy wiped his wet and tired eyes. The sleeve of his jacket smelled of smoke. The fire crackled and breathed out a hiss of embers as the log Jack had collected, fell and rolled to the edge of the fire. Randy stood and kicked it back to the center with his boot.

Pop!

At first, he thought it was the fire, but when there were more thrashing and popping, he knew by the look of the fire, it wasn't. It sounded like footsteps. It sounded like they were more than one.

Crack! Pop!

Twigs snapped and crunched. A team of feet edged closer.

42

"Hey—" Randy's voice was met with another that said the same. The voice was quicker than Randy, and asked, "Who is it? State Game Warden, let me see your hands!"

Adam and Jack wrestled themselves out of the sleeping bags, almost busting out the zippers. Randy raised his hands and tilted his head, "Phillip's...is that you?"

No answer.

Leaves crunched and sticks popped. Whoever it was, was coming closer. The flame next to Randy, made it difficult to see into the darkened forest.

By now, Adam and Jack were on their feet next to Randy, hands in the air.

It sounded like they were coming from their two o'clock, but it also sounded as if they were at their ten. They'd surrounded them. Was this where it all goes down? Caught in a crossfire of someone posing as a Warden? Or what if it really was Phillips? And what if he was in on it too?

The loud crack of a stick came from his two o'clock. Two dark silhouettes emerged from the dark. They eased into the light of the flame. Rifles drawn and pressed firm against their shoulders.

Two other pair of feet came from the left. Their dark out cropping piercing through. Weapons drawn, they crept forward.

"Phillips? It's me Rand—"

One of the men to the right, cursed, then said, "Randy...what in the devil's hell are you doing out here like this?"

"I could ask you the same, Warden. Thought you were giving it up for the night?"

All four men were now visible and so were Randy, Adam, and Jack. The four men lowered their weapons, which releasing the tension in the air.

Phillips took a deep breath, letting it out as a thick white fog. He wagged his head and said, "Randy...our chopper said he got something on the FLIR...I wouldn't be able to sleep unless I launched a crew."

"What did they get?" Randy's voice quick and strained.

"They thought they had a person about half a mile to the south, but it disappeared. So, we really don't know what it was. Could have been the bear for all we know."

Randy lowered his head and scanned the dirt between him and Phillips, his mind racing and more than alert.

"Adam...Jack...be careful out here with him, will ya," Phillips said as he slung the rifle over his shoulder, "And for the record...I don't know you're out here. Right fellas?" Phillips said glancing to each of his men. They nodded and likely wore tight lips behind the wool face mask.

"Are you staying here for a bit?" asked Phillips.

"Yeah...until Sunrise, then we might move and set up somewhere else," said Adam.

"All right...well...I reckon I need to tell ya."

Randy scrunched his brows and asked with a stern voice, "Tell me what?"

Phillips took a breath, "We got word about two young girls being chased off by a bear while messing around up near Bridgeville. It's just a few miles north of us. Then...we got a call from a man who says he and his son were fishing with some buddies in McCann and got ran off by something...the other man disappeared. We've got a unit out there now."

Randy sighed with a balled fist to his lips.

Adam and Jack cut their eyes to each other. Adam gave a slight wag with a tight mouth. They had so much to say, but it wasn't like the men would believe them anyhow. They chose to let the men believe what they want. Besides if they stayed out here long enough, Adam and Jack wouldn't have any need in telling them what really lurks in these woods.

"We're going to be to the north of you, maybe a mile at best. Keep your eyes and ears open. You fellas know what's out here, so keep that in mind. If we need you, I'll fire three shots about two seconds apart. I expect you to do the same," Phillips said with a tilt of his brows.

Randy nodded as did Adam and Jack.

"All right...you boys be safe. Randy...you're in good hands with these guys. We're going to find your boy," Phillips said with such assurance, it seemed to lighten the bowling ball that'd found itself in Randy's chest. What is that? Is that hope? It might very well be, and it'd be best to hang on to it, because he will sure need it.

Phillips motioned with the tilt of his head to his men and like whistling for hunting dogs, they followed tight behind them. Within seconds, the four of them faded into the darkness. Their steps ebbed away like a falling tide as they were enveloped by the sounds of the creatures of night. Within minutes their steps had dissipated into the night.

43

If he was lucky, Randy may have dozed for a few minutes. Not by choice but by demand of his heavy eye lids and tired brain. He just couldn't allow himself to sleep, knowing Tyler was out there in the woods all alone. What if he hollered for help while Randy was sleeping? As hard as it was, he forced himself to stay awake, other than the few dozes he recovered from with a start. His back ached and so did his hip and pelvis from sitting and slumping over on the hard log all night. And of course, his ankle wasn't too happy either.

A purple streaked wave of light hung just beyond the thick canopy of forest. The Sun had begun its accent and every creature known to man, knew it. Birds thrashed about in the brush, chirping and singing to welcome such beauty. The savior had arrived to light up the darkness. The relief radiated through the entire forest; no more shadows for the beasts and creatures of night to hide behind. Light was spreading and licking them up and all of nature took notice.

The fresh scent of pine wafted through the air, followed by an earthy smell, perhaps damp tree bark. A squirrel rummaged about above him, knocking a pinecone loose as it free fell from at least three stories.

To think that such danger could abide in a little piece of heaven such as this, is hard to believe. The sights and sounds before him, could easily be adapted into a kid's fantasy story. This place knew heaven during the day and hell by night. The polarity that existed here was hard to comprehend.

A stir behind him pulled his attention to Adam who was rising in his bag, rubbing his eye lids. Jack was squirming, on the verge of waking.

Adam yawned and arched his back, then said, "Guess it's time to get to work."

Randy nodded.

"Hey...wake up. The sun's peeking through. We need to get started," Adam said as he stuck a heel into Jack's leg, giving him a brotherly nudge. He tossed and turned, moaned and mumbled something. Adam nudged him again.

"Hey...get it up. We got to go."

"Awwyarrryeeaahh..." Jack jolted, eyes flinging open. He flashed up, forming an L. His eyes darted about, feeling through the faint light trickling in through the trees. He unzipped his bag as it gave a quick swipe sound. He stood to his feet, a tad wobbly, like a drunken sailor. The barely two-hour sleep still had him feeling tipsy.

Adam forced himself up and bent down to gather his sleeping bag. Randy sat on the log, arms crossed, head craned to the squirrel above. He'd already gathered his things and secured them on his back. Even with his thick jacket and wool cap, he was still a bit chilled. It looked like there could be a few snow clouds rolling around in the distance. The air felt like snow weather. It wouldn't surprise him to see some in the coming hours.

Within a few minutes, Adam and Jack were packed and ready to go. They kicked dirt upon the fire, Jack relieved himself on it to cool the coals. They hissed and sizzled, emitting steam into the cold, dense air.

Adam marched to the front of the line as Randy and Jack filed in behind, just like last night. Randy stole a glance at his watch, *6:19*

Good. Randy had decided before Adam and Jack awoke, that he'd call Bev around eight, that is if he could get a signal. So far, it'd came and went more times than he could count. Hopefully, there'd be good news to share.

They journeyed deeper into the forest as the Sun continued to rise and throw more light past the branches and limbs. The birds sung louder, and the wind howled greater. The limbs above shuddered with each passing gust. A storm was coming and by the look and feel of it, it'd be here soon.

Must've been a half hour later when Adam stopped. Not saying a word, he lifted a spread hand and held it at eye level behind him. Randy almost stepped into it. Jack pulled the rifle from his shoulder and steadied his grip.

With his left hand and arm twisted behind him, Adam's eyes were trained up ahead. He slowly moved his right hand over the revolver holstered on his hip.

Randy breathed deep and scanned the woods ahead. A thick patch of serviceberry and fern rested in between three Redwoods. One was hollowed out but placed in front of it were numerous teepee like structures crafted out of small pines and branches. Four of them to be exact. Each pine had been snapped like a piece of celery and laid against one another to form a teepee.

A gentle breeze wafted from the south. Toting with it the pungent odor of death and decay. The men covered their faces and crept forward. Adam now clasping his revolver with both hands and aiming just in front of each step. Jack chambered a round in his .270, as Randy felt for that pocketknife.

The reason for such odors, were now visible. Dozens of carcasses were strewn about inside the structures. Looked to have been a feeding sight, now turned into a cemetery of not so lucky victims. Some of the bones still had hair and rotten flesh attached to them. Likely deer or elk, judging by the color of the hair. Other bones were stripped of such accessory. Those could have been anything. Bear? Dog? Human? Who's to say?

The vibe this place emitted was nothing less than eerie. Much like the feeling of passing by a graveyard at night. An unwelcome feeling, as if you really shouldn't be here, hovered the place like a fog. The feeling of being watched by a hundred invisible eyes was overwhelming.

Randy cleared his throat and for the first time since stumbling upon the sight, words were spoken, "Uhh...you think you should leave a feather? You know, let them know we don't me any harm?" his voice in just a faint whisper.

Adam turned and faced him for the first time in the last few minutes. His face was drained of blood, his eyes wide and wandering. He nodded and said, "Yeah...I think that would be a good idea."

Adam reached inside his jacket and retrieved another Eagle feather. This one wore a small leather strap around the white shaft. Adam crossed over to one of the structures and tied the feather to a branch. Stepping back, it dangled in the wind.

"Hey guys...come check this out," said Jack standing outside the hollow Redwood, about thirty feet behind Adam and Randy.

They angled to him, eyes scanning their surroundings. They reached Jack who still held his rifle firm toward the earth, his eyes locked on something within the tree.

Omah

Randy followed his gaze.
It was a nest. A bed. Pine needles atop branches filled the space. On top to the right was a piece of torn clothing.
A slashed camo shirt and remnants of an orange vest.
Next to it? A piece of torn black cotton with a white S. Much like the black hoodie Tyler was wearing with Sunset Beach written across it.

44

"Randy?" Adam said in a soothing tone while placing his hand upon Randy's quaking shoulder who heaved and gasped, moaning like the bereaved parent he was.

Jack stood a few feet back from the two, his head low and gently wagging with one hand rubbing his forehead.

Adam patted and rubbed Randy's back, but how could that ever soothe such loss and grief? They'd just stumbled upon the beast graveyard and a piece of his son's hoodie lay in the creature's den. It was evident now...Tyler had joined the others. He was now a number to add to the statistics. His bones and the hunter's were likely scattered about before them. They may have even stepped on them, tucked away under the leaves, swept away like dirt under a rug when no one's looking.

Now what? It'd probably be best to call the officials. This was now a crime scene. Though the police and wardens would never consider the possibility of it belonging to the hairy men of the forest, it would likely go down as another bear attack. Or Mountain Lion, they'd used that one before too. No matter what they chose to label the attacker as, it wouldn't be true.

But if the creatures did do this...why? They would never commit such atrocious murder without reason.

Omah

Something had them worked up, they were repaying an eye for an eye, tooth for a tooth. And until they resolve it, this will continue to take place. Tyler won't be the last victim. This is only the beginning.

"Hey—" Jack's voice came with a quake and touch of apprehension from behind. Adam and Randy turned to see him squatted upon his calves, Rifle laid across his thighs, one hand covering his nose and the other poking inside one of the teepee structures with a stick.

"It's a body."

45

Jack called to Warden Phillips with three shots from his rifle, spread apart by two seconds each. Adam called Humboldt County Police Department and Randy called Bev.

Within half an hour, a chopper flew overhead before slowing to a hover. Another half hour passed before Warden Phillips and his men came trekking through the forest.

Randy sat on his haunches, back against a Redwood, knees close to his chest and face buried into his palms. Adam and Jack stood close, eyes scanning the forest floor, searching for the right words.

Phillips and Officer Breeden walked over the entire graveyard searching for evidence, while Roscoe sniffed and pulled on the leash. Officers Nate Lindbergh and Jose Ortiz marked the area as a crime scene as they rolled yellow tape around the entire site.

Voices squawked over Phillip's radio asking for coordinates, it could have been Sheriff Logan. This place would be buzzing with people shortly. Phillips satisfied with his combing of the area, crossed back to the body tucked away under the wooden structure, faintly buried by a few pine needles and rocks.

Omah

The last he'd checked, bears don't burry their victims, only humans do that. So...do they now have a killer out here? Boy, talk about causing a stir. A killer out here in these woods. He could hide for days, even months maybe, before anyone would find him. If he's smart that is. Hank did say he thought he saw someone last night while he was scanning with the FLIR in his chopper, maybe it was the guy responsible for this?

Phillips slowed his racing mind and returned to the man hiding under the leaves and stones.

A bloody and twisted arm stuck out from under the covering of a failed attempt of a proper burial. The arm was tan and full of thick black hair, streaks of flaky dried blood ran down it. Attached to the end was a right hand which wore a gold wrist watch. The glass on the front was shattered and it no longer ticked. It stopped at 6:02

Close to the time Al Frankford was last seen. Is this him? Could that be his time of death?

It took all he had to restrain himself from digging past the leaves and stone to uncover the man's face, but Phillips knew it'd be best to leave that to the detective and coroner. This had to be Al Frankford. If it wasn't, who else could it be?

46

It must have been just after midnight when Kosumi and Brenda left the night before. Jennifer and Andrew slept with Bev as they were all too emotionally distraught to sleep alone. The ringtone of Bev's phone could have been mistaken for an alarm, but she knew otherwise, because she didn't remember setting an alarm. She reached for her phone. It was Randy. Why is he calling so early? She swallowed hard.

"Randy...what is it? Where is he?"

All was silent but Randy's raspy breath.

"Talk to me...Randy." her voice breaking, tears stinging her eyes.

"We haven't found him yet."

Bev swallowed hard and rubbed her tired and strained eyes.

Jennifer squirmed next to her, awaking to her voice. Andrew being the hard sleeper that he is, would take an earthquake to wake.

"Honey...we found the hunter."

A beat.

"He's dead."

Bev breathed out a muffled cry. Hot tears ran down her cheeks. One rolled to her mouth filling it with its salty taste. She wagged her head as it rested in her palm. She sniffled and breathed deep.

"What are we going to do?" her voice tapering off at the end, her words failing her.

"Our baby is out there all alo—" she couldn't finish. She broke.

Randy on the other end, sighed and tried to remain strong for his wife.

Jennifer rose and hugged her mom as they embraced one another in a tight hug. Neither wanting to let go. The sheets damp with their tears.

"Bev...Bev...listen to me."

She sucked in a gasp of air, wiping tears from her eyes.

"I going to find our boy. As long as it takes, I will not give up searching until I've found him. I'm going to bring him home. Let's stay positive...we have to keep believing."

Bev nodded and said, "I know."

"Stay strong Bev. We're going to get through this, and we will get through it together. Tell the kids hey and I love them."

"I will."

"I think we are going to come back for a little bit. The county officials and a bunch of the other surrounding counties are ramping up the search efforts, the woods will be buzzing with them in the next few hours...Warden Phillips said I needed to take a break for a bit. As much as I tried to fight it, I know he's right."

The line was silent for a moment except for Bev's staticky breath.

"I trust your judgement. I think we all could use a regrouping."

"I agree. So, the detectives and coroner will be here any minute. I think we're going to follow them out, Adam and Jack want to be there when they conduct the autopsy. Jack knows the coroner pretty good and says we shouldn't have a problem. I'll call you when we get on the road."

"Okay...be careful. I love you."

"I love you too. Call you in a bit."

"Okay...love you, bye."

"Love you too, bye."

Omah

47

Having been jolted awake and slung upon the female's back, Tyler dug his fists deeper into her fur, clinging with all his strength. He almost lost his grip a time or two, which caused her to reach back and readjust him. She and the other three bounded and bolted through the forest as if they were prison escapees. Something had them worked up. They could be chased again. It sure felt like it. Despite the frigid air, the female rung with sweat. Tyler's hands were like icicles, his nose, cheeks and ears burned with a stingy numbness. Clouds of white fog emitted with each quivering breath.

Tyler and the female were in the lead, with the two young ones sandwiched between her and the old one that looked like Moses.

They dodged and swatted away limbs and bony finger like branches scraping across their body and face. Dark clouds broke through the forest's canopy, the sun hidden by the abundance of tree branches.

Then for the first time since being awoken by Mother, they stopped. She hobbled over to a Redwood, her breath in quick huffs, her lungs expanding and collapsing with rapid pace. She pulled at Tyler and managed to retrieve him from her back. Plopping him down with a thump.

His eyes were still heavy and not fully equipped enough to keep them open without allowing a few soft closures here and there. His legs still numb and weak, they quivered as he walked. His head spun as if he'd just hopped off a merry-go-round. He couldn't stand long. He had to sit. His back resting against A tree.

He crossed his arms and squeezed tight, lest he allow any heat to escape his frail body. If only he had a fur coat as thick as Mother's. She stood less than a few steps away, eying him with caution, erasing any thought he had of fleeing.

The two younger ones—who were both about the size of his real Mother, Bev—strode up next to the female before clinging tightly to her side. The older one who reminded him of Moses stood further back rotating shifts of glaring at him like he could eat him and stealing glances about the forest as if to be sure something else doesn't eat him first.

Moses seemed like a good name for this one. He looked like a Moses, but what about the others? Well, the kids...he could name them Andy and Jenny, like his real brother and sister, but different. As for Mother...what should he name her? Hmm?
Well...sticking with Biblical names such as Moses, he could call her Mary? Afterall she was quite the Mother. Jesus' mom as a matter of fact. But Mother just felt right, it meant more to him. It was comforting to call her Mother. Mother will have to stick. So, now there was Mother, Moses, Andy and Jenny.

With the naming process out of the way, his mind returned to wondering just what it was they were running from? Was it the one with the scar again? But Mother didn't seem all that afraid of him. She acted different from then to now. Like the first time they were running from something when it was just her and him. What on earth could have such a creature as this afraid it had to flee?

That's the thing, he keeps calling these things creatures and beasts as if trying to dodge the question.
What are they? Well…they sure look like the bigfoots from all the videos him and his brother had watched. But…his mom and dad always said it was just a hoax…a myth. How can that be true? What else are these things? Escaped Gorillas? No. Too big. Too tall. Cavemen? No.

They're bigfoots. What else could they be? Just like the bigfoot in the film on YouTube, they kept calling Patty and like the bigfoot in the beef jerky commercial. Whatever those are, is what these are, because they look exactly alike.

They're bigfoots. They have to be.

A sudden thrash to the left, made them all flinch. Moses jerked his head around and eyed the forest in the direction of the rustling leaves. He tilted his head back, his nose high in the air, upper lip curled tight against his nostrils. Teeth bare, he sniffed four times, then lowered his head and let out a low grumble, gurgle type sound, much like Mother had done before, but deeper and longer.

Mother's hair bristled and fought against the cool breeze that brushed past her. A raw, soured odor arose, like dirty feet mixed with boiled eggs. Her pupils grew and a corner of her lip curled. Then came that guttural growl once more.

Andy and Jenny clung tighter to her side. She lowered into a crouch position, arms wrapped around her kids. She twisted her big dome shaped head over her shoulder like an owl, looking to Tyler with a threatening Mother like glare and grunted.

She didn't have to tell him twice. Tyler slid his back up the tree and bolted to her, digging into all that fur, wishing he could hide beneath it.

Andy and Jenny snarled and growled, but Mother quieted them down with a look.

Moses took a step forward, knees bent at weird angles. Long, muscular arms dangling past his waist, similar to a chimp.

The loud crash gave Tyler's heart a start as his breath escaped him.

Moses thrust back his head and let out a chest pounding roar. Tyler's heart knocked against his ribcage, his bones rattling beneath his skin as it crawled like a hundred caterpillars were beneath it.

Moses charged.

That was the last time he saw him, as Mother snatched him up and bounded through the forest once more. His body upside down and fighting to revert to an upright position. Terrible screams and thrashing emitted from behind. But above was only passing limbs with dots of gray clouds piercing through. Similar to a starry night, only the black were tree branches.

Trees popped and crashed to the forest floor, wailing and deep guttural howls echoed through the air. Whatever was taking place behind and whatever Moses was fighting, there surely could only be one survivor of such an ordeal.

48

After having bounded through the woods long and far enough for the howls of Moses to fade, Mother stopped at the crest of a hill. It sounded like a river rippled below them. Other than that, the woods were quiet. Eerily quiet. Too quiet.

Mother sat Tyler down once more, though he tried to suggest otherwise, she wouldn't have it. He, Andy, and Jenny clung to her big powerful legs as she strode to the hill. Head jolting side to side, eyes darting, nostrils flaring and twitching.

They reached the top. Mother crouched low and proceeded to lay on her belly. She poked her head up just enough for her eyes to see. Tyler, Andy, and Jenny did the same.

Below them was a river that had a greenish tint to it, much like the one he'd fished in with his family yesterday.

His eyes grew wide as a flicker of hope ignited within. Though it wasn't the same place where they'd fished, at least he didn't think it was...it was at least the same river. He saw this river yesterday when he and Mother stopped to get a drink before coming to Andy and Jenny. If they kept staying close to the river, maybe they'd end up back at the campground. Tyler hoped so at least.

Mother grunted, her eyes scanning for any threat. Her tongue protruded out, dangling past her chin. Though her face was dark, her tongue was a pinkish white. It looked dry. Her steamy breath rode out, pushing along a horrid stench. Ten times worse than puppy breath.

"Eeewww," Tyler grimaced and turned his face.

Mother grunted once more, then poked a stubby finger into his side. It dug in like a pointy rock, those fingers could tear muscle and likely pierce bone without her even trying. Can you imagine what would happen if she did?

"Okay-okay...I'm sor—"

Rarrhhhh. She barked with a short breath then entered that low grumble once more.

Tyler quickly lowered his eyes from hers, realizing he'd crossed a line.

Man...Mother was ornery, that was for sure.

She slipped backwards down the slight hill, grasping roots and rock for balance. Her kids did the same, so did Tyler.

He kept waiting for her to throw him on her back, but she didn't, she just marched down the hill with Andy and Jenny following close behind.

Had she forgotten? Was this a test? Did she feel comfortable enough with him now that she didn't need to have him on her back every second? Should he make a break for it?

He stood frozen to the dirt, eyes following Mother, Andy, and Jenny as they continued down the hill, gaining distance and growing smaller with each passing second.

He looked to his right. A cold empty forest stared back. He looked to the sky. Dark clouds pierced through as a fog hung around the branches in the tops of the Redwoods.

Omah

It looks like it could snow any minute. Should he stay with Mother and hope they're somehow found? Though that seemed highly unlikely, after all, how many Sasquatches had been found so far?

He didn't like his chances with that. What if he fled and took his chances of surviving out there? Moses and the thing that had them all scared, and fleeing might still be out there. And the one with the scar might be out there too. His spine shuddered at the thought of encountering one by himself. There's no way he could ever survive such an encounter without the protection of Mother. He'd also have to face the cold without the warmth of Mother's fur.

But if he stayed with her, he'd likely never be found. If he wanted to see his family again, he knew what he had do.

He looked again to where he'd last saw Mother and her kids. They were gone. Only their footfalls told their whereabouts. He looked to the forest, then looked to the sky.

What choice did he have?

He looked one last time to where Mother's footfalls sounded, a tear snaked down his rosy cheek. He sniffled and wiped his face with a trembling hand tucked inside the sleeve of his hoody.

"Thank you."

He breathed deep, turned and took a step towards the sea of Redwoods that awaited. He was setting sail into the unknown, and with the right amount of hope and luck, he might just make it to shore.

49

Back at the crime scene, Detective Joe Stines and coroner Cecil Sawyer had arrived via an escort of men arranged by Sheriff Logan.

Warden Phillips, Adam, and Jack stayed with Randy to offer their comfort as they attempted to lighten his heavy heart.

Sheriff Logan, K-9 Officer Chris Breeden, Forensic Specialist Will Swayne and Deputy Jeff Anderson stood next to Stines and Sawyer who were squatted down inside the structure looking over the mangled body. Stines used a stick to probe and poke wherever Sawyer needed as he busied himself with snapping pictures.

"Can you lift his arm for me?"

Stines sighed and reached for the hand which was now a pale bluish color with dark veins snaking about it. It was cold and stiff when he lifted it, the elbow was placed at a weird angle. Likely snapped like a chicken bone.

"Hmm...all right...well let's see what we got under there."

Phillips heard the words and broke from Randy, his curiosity getting the best of him. Randy, Adam, and Jack followed him.

Omah

He reached Stines and Sawyer about the time they uncovered the body's face.

"Whew!" Sawyer said with the help of a whistle.

Stines turned and faced Phillips, blinked his eyes and clearing his throat before returning to the gruesome sight.

"Well...looks like we got ourselves a Grizzly victim," said Logan.

The man's face was barely attached as four large claw marks slashed across it, cutting the nose and lips clean off. An eye was missing along with the entire right side of his face. The left eye stared skyward, the remnants of his mouth hung wide in a mid-scream.

Nothing but absolute terror.

The worst part about it though, was the fact that the man was lying on his stomach, at least that's what Sawyer and Stines were led to believe by the awkward position of his hips and buttocks.

Phillips spread his stance, anchoring himself and crossed his arms with one hand mounted to his face and chin. He swallowed hard.

Randy, Adam, and Jack came to the entrance and peered in. Randy got a glimpse and that was enough. He turned, crossed his arms and buried a fist into his forehead. Adam marched after him and placed an arm across his shoulders. Jack stayed and leaned closer.

Stines returned to the body, "It's our guy isn't it?"

"Looks like it," said Phillips.

"Yeah...that's Al," Sheriff Logan in his gruff voice.

Stines and Swayne removed the rocks and dusted away the leaves. Their first assumption was right. The man was laying on his stomach. His head was twisted around like an Owl. So, if a man did this, he'd have to be an awful big man. Al Frankford was no little guy at six foot-one and two hundred and thirty pounds.

Was the Indian's theory really that far fetched when faced with the evidence?

"Can you roll him over and raise his shirt for me? I need to get to the liver," said Sawyer as he fumbled around in a toolbox full of scalpels and various other assortment of tools one might need while examining a body.

"I need a core body temp," he explained while biting off the cap of a sharpie and glancing to Logan and Phillips. A thermometer like the one you'd use to check a steak was in one hand along with a scalpel.

Stines didn't feel right rolling the man's face into the dirt, so he tried to twist the head around a little, but he was too stiff. Rigor Mortis had done set in. His body was like an overweight mannequin, but Stines and Swayne managed to flip him over to his back, his face now planted in the dirt. Stines sighed and wagged his head as he unbuttoned the man's camo jacket and raised his shirt.

Cecil Sawyer inched closer, sharpie in his right hand, thermometer and scalpel in his left. He stretched forth the sharpie and drew a circle about the diameter of a golf ball, near the upper right side of the abdomen, capped the marker, pocketed it and switched hands with the scalpel.

He made a small incision inside the circle, then retrieved the thermometer and stuck it into the slit, digging his way past the cold flesh and fatty tissue. He reached the liver and counted to sixty.

"Eighty-seven degrees. Current temp is thirty-one, means he's been dead at least ten to twelve hours. If I was a betting man, I'd say sometime between six and seven yesterday evening," Sawyer said, cutting his eyes to Phillips, under thick white brows and behind even thicker glasses.

Phillips nodded and pointed, "Look at his watch."
Sawyer rolled the man's hand over and leaned close.
"Well I'll be. Six-o-two. Not too bad huh?"
"What do think?" asked Stines.
Sawyer took a breath.
"Well...it looks like a Grizzly to me. But the thing I can't explain is...why he's half buried. You all know as good as I do...bears don't bury their dead, they eat it. Could it be a cat? Well, no a cat only buries their scat. I don't understand. The only thing I can think...is maybe it is a Grizzly attack, but a hermit or hunter found the body and was too afraid to call it in, so they tried to do the burying. But that leaves me wondering...what in the world is all this?" he said waving a pointed finger about the graveyard.

"I will have to get him back to the morgue for further examination, but right now...I think the only thing I can put down that'll make any sense, would be a Grizzly. If you think you might have a better explanation...I'm all ears," Cecil Sawyer said in a groan as he stood to his feet. Stines offered a hand, but he refused. Cecil was too proud for that non-sense.

"It's the Omahs," said Jack in a low but steady tone. The men gave him their attention as his eyes remained locked on the body.

"'The hairy men among the Giant Cedars of old, are to be honored and feared, for they are not only charged with guarding us in our walk among the earth, but they take no issue in spreading the prideful among us as a dried weed in a passing breeze. Stay humble and never challenge such authority.' My Grandfather has told me and my brother that since we first learned to walk. It's ingrained in our blood.

"These creatures are real. They are the protectors of the forest and they will not allow harm to Mother Earth. She is a source of life, not just a resource. They will not ignore a poacher and if wronged, they will hold a grudge for years on end until the wrong has been righted. That's why we've been taught to respect them and all of creation."

A beat.

"Well...all I know, is we've found our guy and now we need to find the kid before he ends up like this," said Phillips.

"I don't think he will."

"What do you mean?"

"The creatures are not that vile. I think they took him to get our attention, not to bring him harm. It's like a ransom."

"Why do they need our attention?" asked Logan, his face less than interested.

"So we do not forget the sacredness of life and creation. It's their way of saying, 'Hey...we're real and don't ever forget about us.' It's their way of being sure they have a voice. It's their way of calling out to our spirits and reminding us we were not made for the current world in which we live, with all the technology and commercialization. We were created to live and coexist with Nature and give back to her instead of always taking. Remember, she is a source of life, not just a resource. We can't just take, we must also give.

"The Great Spirit gives life to our spiritual being, but Nature..." Jack turned and waved his arm about the forest. "...gives life to our physical being. We cannot live without one, we must have both. And these creatures are reminding us of that. This is our wakeup call."

Leaves crunched behind them.

It was Randy and Adam.

"He's right...this is our wake-up call and we best not ignore it," said Adam

Омаh

The men remained silent, neither protesting nor agreeing with the words of the Native's. Logan marched off wagging his head.

Within minutes, they had the body of Al Frankford loaded onto a hand-held gurney and toting towards a four by four Gator ATV. Sawyer rode along as Stines drove them out of the woods.

Randy, Adam, and Jack rode on separate ATV's driven by Officer Ortiz and Officer Lindbergh.

Phillips, Breeden, Sheriff Logan, Deputy Anderson and Forensic Specialist Will Swayne stayed behind in the cold and eerie graveyard.

50

The numbness of his hands and feet made it hard to want to keep walking, but he knew he had to. It'd be so nice to have a nice cozy fire to sit by and thaw out a bit. But Tyler knew such thoughts were only wishes, he'd never build a fire out here, he wouldn't know where to start. He knew most every video game character created in the past decade, but he couldn't tell you the first step in making fire. He'd never been taught, because no one thought he'd need to know at such a young age. But boy, if only he knew...it might just save his life.

His knees were stiff and achy, quads and hamstrings tight from the lack of warmth. He could have sworn he saw a snow flake earlier. He'd kept an eye out for one ever since but had yet to see one again.

The fog had lowered and now rested about eye level among the forest. It was thick and cold when he passed through a patch. It reminded him of the cold spots in the lakes and rivers back home in North Carolina. He sped his pace a little each time he came to one.

His teeth began to chatter soon after he started his journey. The muscles in his arms and legs did the same not long after. His gut growled, begging for food, any type would do, it didn't matter.

Omah

He'd noticed a bunch of Mushrooms like the ones from Mario Cart, but he didn't know if he could eat them or not. He kind of thought he could, he'd seen his mom and dad eat plenty, especially when they ordered Japanese food. What's one little mushroom gonna hurt? He might just try one the next time he finds a patch.

Twigs and leaves crunched under him. A squirrel rustled and barked above. A slight breeze tickled the tree limbs.

He was surprised Mother had yet to come look for him, surely by now she knew of his journey. It'd sure be nice to have that warm furry blanket to snuggle up to. But he couldn't go back, not now. He had to keep moving. He had to get home to his family. His real family. Besides, there's no telling what Mother might do to him now that he'd left her. She liable to have him as a meal.

Must keep moving.

Lips dry and cracking more each minute, tongue begging for a drop of something wet, belly howling for something edible, muscles, hands and feet hoping for something warm.

Must keep moving.

Don't stop. Can't stop.

A horrible thrashing and screeching emitted above him, his heart dropped to his bowels and soared its pulse in effort to climb back to its normal position. He could hear its thump as it beat strong under the flesh in his neck.

He shot his eyes above him. A fury tail cracked and waved back at him, the creature still barking and screeching. It was another squirrel and for some reason he acted like he'd never seen a human before. Which being out here in the middle of nowhere, maybe he hasn't.

The joker was mad either way.

Tyler took a deep breath, lowered his head and continued his journey.

He must have taken enough steps to reach second base from homeplate in a straight line, when he noticed an archway in a big Redwood. It looked like it belonged on the front door of a giant's castle. Surely, it'd be warm in there.

He marched on and stole a peak inside. It was so inviting and cozy. Even looked to have a bed made from pine needs and leaves.

Tyler step inside and laid down, forming a fetal position. The pine needles were so warm and comfy. They acted like a magnet, his heavy eyes and tired muscles couldn't withstand their pull. Within minutes, his body felt like it was floating once again.

Everything grew quiet and all went black.

OMAH

51

The Humboldt County Morgue is tucked away deep below Humboldt Memorial Hospital in Eureka, just over an hour drive from Myers Flat. Once there, it demanded an elevator take you down as you'd likely tire from all the steps. The place felt forbidden yet never ceased to welcome new occupants. The temperature dropped ten degrees as you made the decent. There was hardly any need for an A/C unit, the freezers seemed to do the trick. The MD's and women assistants always kept a jacket nearby when they weren't in the middle of an autopsy.

The Mayor had purposed a new spending bill, which included a new morgue, but it never passed. People walking above the dead could never grasp the true need for such a thing.

The elevator whined and jolted on the way down. The iron bar cage was rusted in multiple spots, the light grew weak the farther the caged men descended into the abyss.

Randy couldn't help but wonder if the thing could support four men.

"So how old is this place?"

"Uhh...well...I want to say she was built sometime just before the depression. I reckon that'd be around the mid-twenties or so," said Cecil Sawyer.

"My goodness, so this place is really as old as it looks then."

"Oh yes. She's been around for a while. Seen many a bodies pass through here."

Would she soon see Tyler's? No! Stop it for crying out loud!

"How much longer are you thinking of doing this Cecil?" asked Jack

"Oh, I don't know...I reckon till it's my turn to get poked around on the cold metal slab," he said with his eyes trained to the ribbed iron floor, rubbing his white beard, "Heck I got nothing else to do."

The opening to the morgue rolled into the view as the elevator came to an abrupt halt when it reached its destination. Cecil had to pull the lattice like doors open, they'd lost their power before the whiskers on Cecil's face turned gray. Being around a place like this, could do it to you.

The vibe was eerie, the smell was stale and earthy, but had a faint tint of disinfectant. Like a hospital stored in a dungeon.

"C'mon fellas, follow me," Cecil said with a wave as he crossed to a section of offices around the corner to the right.

Adam leaned close to Randy's ear, "Cecil's a good man, he's just old and set in his ways. He lost his filter years ago, so try not to let his words get to ya. He don't mean nothing by them."

Randy gave a slight grin and nodded. They stopped in front of a stained wooden door, a bronze name stuck to its facing.

M.D. CECIL SAWYER

Omah

Cecil retrieved a set of keys from his pocket and mumbled to them as he searched for the right one.

"Ahh...got cha, you old bat."

He unlocked the door and pushed it in, sliding in a door stop with his foot and motioning for the men to enter his dismal abode.

"Hey, get that lamp would ya?" Cecil pointed next to Randy.

Randy gave the ridged knob of a tall corner lamp two twists. It lit up and exposed a few cobwebs that looked to have been there since the place opened.

"Just let me grab my things and we'll get going," said Cecil as he adjusted his glasses and fumbled through desk drawers.

Randy watched him, curious how a man such as him could still maintain enough sanity to not be deemed fit for a mental ward. Especially after all he'd likely seen through the years.

"How do you do it man?"

"Hmm?"

Jack turned his attention from the framed map of the Cook Islands hung on the wall next to the door. Adam crossed his arms, one hand to his chin, eyes narrowing and awaiting Cecil's reply to Randy's question.

"How do you do what you do and not go crazy?"

The man snickered, "Who's to say I haven't"

"You know what I mean."

"Yes, I reckon I do. Well...it's a job and I have to keep it that way. I can't allow it to become more than that. I have a switch to flick to get me in the zone so to speak."

Randy cut his eyes to lamp he'd just turned on.

"Yeah?"

Retrieving a stack of paperwork that he was quick to tuck away in two large manila envelopes, Cecil answered,

"It's my job to help shed light on the questions and bring justice for the victim and family. If I forget that and allow myself to get caught up in the humanistic side of things...well...I wouldn't be able to do my job now would I? It'd be an injustice to the situation. It took me a long time to figure all that out. But I reckon it all comes with age and experience."

He picked up a clip board with white paper stuck to it.

Randy nodded.

"All right. You fellas sure you want to do this?"

No, Randy wasn't sure, but he needed to know what happened to the man. He needed to know if what the Natives were saying was true.

He took a deep breath and dipped his head.

Cecil grabbed a long white lab coat off the back of his door and said, "All right then...follow me."

52

A dark walnut stained desk sat in the center of a corridor underneath old block walls which were rounded at the top like tunnels. These dismal tunnels met at a crossroads, the information desk in the center, offices along the north and south walls, and cold autopsy and storage rooms along the East and West.

The desk was vacant, but there was a small white jacket hooked upon a swivel chair pushed away from a big box, beige colored computer which wore a dancing Gateway screensaver. It was more than outdated, the darn thing was a dinosaur, but it must've been smart enough to get the job done.

Randy followed Cecil as he cut to the left and retrieved a pen from a deep pocket in his white lab coat, the tail of it fluttered behind. Cecil adjusted his glasses again, bit off the cap of the pen and scribbled a few quick notes on the white piece of paper attached to his clip board.

They passed by numerous doors which were numbered one through twelve, six on each side of the hall. Square white signs were placed on each which read, *Official Personnel Only.*

Randy counted four which wore small cards that dangled from the doorknob, they read, *Autopsy in Progress*. One thing he for sure didn't want to interrupt.

The sound of screeching saws was quite unnerving. The imagination was left to wonder what may lurk beyond the doors. Had Leatherface begun in a place such as this? He'd certainly be aroused by such sights and sounds.

How do these people keep their minds from going sour?

A set of gray double doors waited ahead, a sign above read, MORGUE.

Randy swallowed hard and turned to look at Adam and Jack. Their faces pale. Adam wore tight lips and twisted his head, while Jack sighed out through puffed cheeks and rubbed the back of his neck, head angled low, eyes cutting upward.

Cecil plowed through the doors like a running back splitting the middle, smelling a touchdown. The loud clank of the doors echoed off each wall, resonating throughout the hall.

The temperature dropped once again

The place they'd entered was about the size of the treasury room where you pay your taxes at the DMV. Roughly twenty by twenty at best, fading white tile with black specks, grungy ceiling tile with more leaks than you could count in a quick glance.

To the left was a gray metal vault type structure, that was reminiscent of a bank vault. Cecil took a key that hung around his neck and unlocked the door, then pushed a metal handle down with a grunt. The door hissed and spewed a wave of cold air and fog.

"C'mon on in fellas. Don't be shy," Cecil stood next to the door with an outstretched arm.

Randy rolled his tongue around the back of his bottom row of teeth, took a good long look at the old man, breathed deep and stepped in. Adam and Jack looked to each other, then nodded and followed.

Cecil didn't shut the door behind them, and no one objected. The room was full of what looked like oversized filing cabinets. The top of each drawer labeled with a letter. Twenty-seven columns filled out the room, making it exponentially larger than the one they just came from. Each column had seven blocks. Randy did the math, almost two hundred spaces for those who'd took their last breath. One hundred and eighty-nine to be exact.

In the center of the room was an empty gurney.

Cecil sighed and wagged his head, then glanced at the clipboard.

"Frankford-Frankford-Frankford," he repeated like a chant as he angled to the column containing the F's.

He reached it and scanned top to bottom. Al was second from last, resting about thigh high.

Cecil gripped the metal handle and tugged until it broke free. Could have used some WD-40. It gave away with a pop, sending Cecil stumbling backwards as the only thing keeping him from going down was that handle. The file flung open, revealing a white zip bag containing a rather large form.

Randy steadied Cecil by gripping his elbow.

"You all right?"

"Well there he is," he said ignoring the question.

"I told the boys to have him on a gurney waiting for me. I'll need some help loading him up," Cecil glanced to Randy, Adam, and Jack.

They looked to each other. Neither said a word. Their breath tumbling out in small clouds.

"Oh c'mon...it's not like he bites or something," Cecil said with a smirk. "I'll get the gurney."

Cecil gripped the bar and wheeled it over. The wheels could use some of that WD-40 as well. "Two of you get on one side and me and someone else can get on the other. At least they left us a plank. It'll make it a little easier for us," he said stopping the gurney along side Al and placing a white plank board under his right

side. Randy helped the man slide it under Al's body from the right, Adam and Jack helped to lift and roll him around until he was fully on the plank.

Two hand straps dangled on each side.

"All right, you boys ready?" Cecil sounded strained.

"Yeah," Adam grunted.

"One-two-threeee."

They lifted and hurled the man onto the gurney, his body crashing down causing it to spring and squeak under such pressure.

"All right...time to see what we got," Cecil said raising his brows and wiping his forehead. He gripped the gurney close to where Al's head was and pushed forward.

The men helped him through the vault door. He stopped just outside it and turned to lock it back.

The door hissed again, as the cold air seeped out. The door clanked and creaked as the metal latch slid home.

The warmth of the room was quite inviting.

"All right...back to the hall, second door on the left."

Once they reached it, Cecil unlocked the deadbolt and they stepped in. No lights just pitch black. This time Cecil shut the door behind them. Its latching sent a chill down Randy's spine. Cecil felt along the wall next to the door, his bony fingers scraping the sheet rock.

A click.

The lights shuttered then flashed on. The room illuminated, revealing a large metal table in the center, above it hung a light like that a dentist might use. Wonder if they've ever traded before? If they were such a thing, how many bodies had the light seen that Dr. Salazbo used the last time Randy got his teeth cleaned?

They followed Cecil and Al over to the table.

There were still too many shadows for Randy's liking. The lights above had a twitch and hum to them.

To the left was a counter full of saws, scalpels, masks, shields and long rubber gloves, everything one might imagine a coroner or Leatherface would need. To the right, the wall was lined with refrigerators and
filing cabinets. Why there were refrigerators in a place like this, Randy didn't know, and he didn't care to ask.

Seated atop a small counter beside the last fridge, was a black rotary phone that rested in its cradle. It looked to have been born sometime around the thirties or forties and had likely lived here ever since. No telling what it had seen and heard through the years.

Cecil marched off to the counter where the shield, gloves and saws were.

He came back looking like the real deal.

"All right...let's get him on the table."

They each grabbed a strap and hoisted Al onto the cold metal slab.

Cecil kicked the gurney away, it rolled about ten feet before the squeaky wheels eased to a halt. He had his face shield tilted upward and his glasses pushed tight against his nose.

He unzipped the white bag down to its last tooth. When he stopped at Al's foot, the room was quiet enough to hear their breath. Al's head had been twisted around enough to fit in the bag but was still too crooked for its natural position. His bearded chin rested on the back of his right shoulder. His skin an ashy gray with dark veins zig zagging about it like mini lightning strikes.

His arms were folded awkwardly across his purple and blue chest. It looked like it had taken a blow from a cannonball.

Cecil lowered his shield and gripped the scalpel. He waved the men back and said, "Step back just for a second. Let me make the Y."

They stepped back and Cecil stuck Al just above his right pectoral muscle and slid it down to his sternum, then made a straight line to his navel. He did the same on the left side and connected it to the other cut. As he finished, he tilted his head and glared at Al's throat. Cecil turned and motioned for them.

Randy moved to Cecil's right and Adam and Jack formed around to the left.

Randy craned his head and asked, "What is it?"

"Look," Cecil pointed to the middle of Al's throat with his right and raised the shield with his left.

"Something's stuck in his throat. At first glance I thought it was his Adam's apple, but it's too low. See look here," Cecil lifted Al's beard and revealed it.

"I got to see what that is," he moved in with the scalpel, "Step back a second."

They did but didn't move as far as they did last time.

The flesh opened as the blade slid over it. It scraped against something along the way.

"What in god's name is this?"

Randy stepped closer, Adam and Jack followed.

After some digging, Cecil pried it loose.

He cursed while retrieving it. It was a smooth stone like you'd find near a river. It was stained red and about the size of a golf ball. It clanked on the table when he sat it down. Something else had his attention. Cecil reached back in and pulled it out with a pair of tweezers.

"It's an Eagle feather," said Adam.

Omah

In a slow hushed tone, Jack said, "Tintah—Kiwungxoya'n."

Randy and Cecil turned and looked at him with squinted eyes.

"The Omahs."

53

Floating. Gliding. Bobbing. A slow and steady pace.

Brisk air stung his cheeks. Something was squeezing his waist. Eye lids heavy like weighted blankets, he struggled to raise them. Glimmers of passing forest and light filtered past his eye lashes. Had he been rescued?

Twigs snapped and feet pounded against the earth. Whoever had him, readjusted their grip. Shifting him up, digging a forearm into his gut and bones. His skin rolled around and mashed tight against a rib.

Ow!

No. Not again.

He strained and opened his eyes.

Big hairy feet strode beneath thick fur covered tree trunks.

This wasn't Mother. This one seemed bigger and it didn't run. It took its time.

Maybe it didn't need to run. Maybe this was the one they'd been running from.

54

To avoid any unneeded attention, Cecil Sawyer wrote Al Frankford off as another Grizzly victim. A broke neck, severe lacerations across the face and bruised chest, he translated it into doctor talk and turned the necessary paper work into Sheriff Logan.

But...he told Randy, Adam, and Jack with a low voice, that whatever this was, had squeezed the life out of the man before snapping his neck and cramming the stone and feather down his throat. The claw marks likely came from *it* grasping for the man in *its* pursuit. But *it* definitely squeezed him first, collapsing his chest cavity onto his heart and lungs, then perhaps out of frustration while pushing the objects in the man's throat, thought maybe it'd be easier if his neck was broke.

Cecil never came out and said he believed in the Omahs, but he never denied them either. He did say that Al was not the first victim he'd seen with a crushed chest and broken neck. But he was the first with a stone and feather lodged in his throat.

They'd ascended the holding place of the dead, out the darkness and into the light. The air was chill, and the Sun hid behind darkening clouds. Snowfall was set to begin in the evening with temperatures plummeting as low as nineteen degrees.

Stepping to Jack's Rav4 parked in the adjacent lot to the hospital, a man's voice came from Randy's left. He turned to see a dark-skinned man dressed in black jeans with a black leather jacket and gray wool beanie, racing up the side walk to them.

"Randy Jacobs! Randy!"

Randy looked to Adam and Jack to be sure they were seeing this. They both shrugged.

The man reached them, gasping for his breath, bending at the waist, hands on his knees.

What's this nut want?

The man craned his head to them and extended a hand, taking a few steps closer as he did.

"Curtis Whetstone. Native Cherokee, Wildlife Biologist and Cryptozoologist."

Randy shook his hand with curious eyes.

Adam and Jack did the same.

Curtis stood and placed his hands to his hips.

"I spoke to your wife over the phone. I heard about your story from a friend of mine in Oregon yesterday evening, I was teaching a conference in Idaho when I learned about your situation. I flew in this morning," he said with short bursts, his breath still being fought for through the cold air.

"Yeah? So why are you here?" asked Randy as he crossed his arms.

"I think I can help."

"Yeah? How so?"

A beat.

Curtis took a deep breath.

"Like I said, I'm a Wildlife Biologists and I studied Gorillas in the jungles of the Congo for eight years. I now travel the Country speaking with people who believe they may have encountered something similar here in the states."

"Omah?" asked Jack.

"Well...the Cherokee know him as Tsul 'Kalu, which means the slant-eyed or sloping giant. But yes... Sasquatch."

"What was that you said back there?" Randy turned to Jack.

"Tintah—Kiwungxoya'n?"

Randy nodded.

"It's our elders' word for 'The boss of the mountains' or 'Creek Devil'," said Jack as he glanced about, "But the common name among us Yurok is Omah, which is derived from the sound of their scream. O-o-o-o-o-m-m-m-a-a-h-h," he said in a low tone.

Randy shut his eyes and rubbed his forehead. The scream he'd heard a few nights ago, rang in his mind. The hair on his arms bristled at the memory.

Randy shook it off and cleared his throat.

"So...you think you can help us huh?"

"I know I can."

"How soon can you start?"

"As soon as you want me to. My flight out isn't until Tuesday. So, I'll be around for a few days."

"Can you start now?" asked Adam.

Randy glanced to him, but Adam paid it no attention.

Randy turned back to Curtis.

"Sure."

Randy thought it over, swallowed hard and said, "All right...but listen this is about finding my boy, not about finding your bigfoot. Right?"

"Of course!" Curtis said, his voice hoarse. "But don't be surprised if we find one in the process."

55

In and out of consciousness, he may have been dreaming, it was hard to tell. The sound of cracking branches and crunching leaves were offset by great huffs and grunts. A foul odor stung his nostrils, reminding him of Mother's stench.

His body trembled without his control, his teeth chattered and clanked against one another.

The big arm clung him tight to its fur with a leathery hand gripping the left side of Tyler's ribcage.

Eyes burning and so tired, he forced them open and craned his neck up and to the left.

Through blurred vision, the form of a large hairy creature came into focus. A long gray beard hung past its chest.

Moses?

"Hmm," the creature grunted with a snarled lip.

It was him.

Dried flaky blood streaked across his forehead and cheek. His large black eyes were sunk deeper into its head than Tyler remembered. Steam rolled out its nostrils and gaping mouth.

Omah

His head feeling dizzy and uncontrollable, Tyler blinked his eyes and looked to Moses' left hand which toted something silver.

Tyler squinted and through the jarring, was able to make it out.

Salmon.

A big one at that.

Tyler jolted forward when Moses stopped.

What was it?

Moses tilted his rounded head back, snarled his flat nose and sniffed.

After smelling the air for a few minutes, he lowered his head and dropped Tyler to the ground.

Almost knocking the breath out of him when he landed. That was a long drop, longer than Moses likely realized.

Tyler winced and grabbed his knee as it had banged into a rock. The Salmon lay next to him. Tyler twisted his head, a tear running down his face. Moses was angling to a tree with a big stick in his right hand.

KnockKnockKnock

He waited.

Tyler glanced about the woods.

He got that eerie feeling of being watched again.

KnockKnock, in the distance straight ahead.

Moses dropped the stick and returned to Tyler and the Salmon. He scooped them up and marched off in the direction of the knocks.

The bobbing pulled harder on his tired little body. His eyes got heavy again. He was cold, hungry, thirsty, and all alone. Would they ever find him? Would he ever see his family again? He couldn't survive out here much longer could he?

Was he dreaming? Surely, he'd wake up any second.

Half of his vision began to fill with blackness, the other half showed passing leaves, stones, sticks, and those big hairy, ugly feet.

His body felt light again. Blackness filled his vision.

OMAH

56

Tyler awoke with a start as his body bounced off something prickly but with a squish to it. His eyes flashed open. A bed of green pine needles. Trees. Gray sky. Hairy beasts. Bigfoot.

Tyler scrambled from his back and planted his hands in the ground next to him. He scanned his surroundings.

Moses', Andy, and Jenny glared back at him, seated on their haunches a few feet in front of him.

Humongous Redwoods lined around them and in the center were a stack of stones which grew smaller the higher they ascended.

Looked like stones from the river.

His breath in short gasps, his body shivering to preserve heat.

The creatures glare gave him the creeps. It went deeper than just his flesh, as if they were peering into his soul. He could feel it in his heart. They sat there emotionless, just staring at him as if they'd never seen him before.

The roar from behind, stopped his heart as he had to search his gut to get it beating again.

He jerked around to see Mother standing over him, glaring down with tight lips, bearing her big teeth.

Hairs straight as a Porcupine. She looked like she was ready to deliver a good spanking.

She fell to all fours quicker than he could blink. She slapped the ground with both of her hands. Long thick arms slinging up and down like loose ropes.

Growling and grunting, she tossed her head back and let out a roar so deep, he felt it vibrate within his chest. He covered his ears to keep his drums from rupturing.

Mother stopped, nostrils flaring, eyes drilling him deeper than a twelve-inch blade. She dropped her head and took long deep breaths; her hairs went limp and fluttered with the breeze.

Satisfied, she stood slowly to her feet then turned and walked a few feet behind her, bent down and scooped up a pile of berries and returned.

The Salmon slapped the ground and slid across the dirt towards him.

Mother lowered herself next to him, cradling the berries like precious currency.

Once on her haunches, she released the berries, allowing them to tumble to the ground at her feet.

Moses and the kids crawled closer.

Mother picked up a handful of the berries and tossed them down her throat.

Andy and Jenny crept near and reached with slow hands towards the pile.

Looked like a mixture of blackberries and something round and red. It was smooth and without the dimples like the blackberry.

Moses took hold of the fish again, raising it to his mouth and snapping out a big bite.

"Hmm," Mother nudged his side. Tyler turned and a handful of berries smooshed into his mouth and chin. He swallowed two or three whole ones before he could start chewing.

Smacking and eating sounds filled the air.

Tyler turned again to Moses who still held the Salmon to his face, taking another bite. Red meat and silver skin pulled away like taffy.

Moses tossed it next to Tyler's leg. Andy and Jenny bolted for it, diving atop one another, but Mother snatched it up and growled.

She took a bite, then nudged Tyler, holding the raw meat to his face and grunted. A strong fishy smell fumed up his nose.

His stomach turned and almost tossed up the berries. His cheeks filled with puffs of air as a growing lump tried crawling up his throat. He fought it off, but Mother insisted. Much like his real Mother did when it was time to eat his veggies.

He swallowed hard and stole a good look at the fish. His stomach was screaming for it, but his mind and senses rebuked it.

"Just shut your eyes and imagine it's a double cheeseburger from McDonalds," he kept mumbling to himself.

Mother nudged and grunted once more as she inched the fish closer to his face.

He squinted his eyes, took a gulp, opened his mouth...and dug in.

Cold. Wet. Fishy.

He chewed the big bite, imagining the ketchup and mustard, the warm beef and cheese. But no matter of imagination could block the reality of what he'd just done.

Pugh. Ahh.

He spit and sputtered, wiping his face of scales and raw meat.

Moses entered a whooping, chimpanzee like chuckle. His shoulders jolting up and down, the corners of his mouth rising to reveal big teeth.

Andy and Jenny joined.

It was like he'd been dropped in the middle of a zoo.

Mother didn't say a word.

Cold leathery knuckles rubbed the side of his cheek.

He turned his attention from the mocking apes, a handful of berries crammed into his mouth once again. A welcomed relief from the fishiness.

Now these he could eat.

A mixture of sweetness, tart, and slight bitterness rid the foul taste.

He chewed and swallowed.

His vision blurred as his mind wandered.

These things really weren't that bad, underneath all that hair and muscle. Sure, they can be a bit scary at times, but really beneath the first impression you get, they're not that much different than his real family.

Another handful of berries filled his mouth, Mother's hairy knuckles tickling his chin.

He blinked.

What is that?

Something round, bulged from the ground a good distance in front of him.

He blinked again, this time rubbing his eyes.

A camo jacket...an arm...a boot...a body.

57

Mother followed his glare, looked to the body, then turned back to Tyler with her head low. She grunted and avoided eye contacted, looking to the side.

Tyler stood, his legs cold and stiff. He took a step towards the body. He stopped and squinted his eyes, waiting to be scooped up and yelled at.

Nothing.
Another step.
Nothing.

None of them said a word, but he could feel their eyes drilling into his back. More so out of curiosity than anger. At least he assumed it that way.

Seven steps later and he was within kick's reach of the body. A man lay on his stomach, right cheek in the dirt, right arm twisted at an awkward angle behind him. His leg was bent backwards at the knee cap, toes pointing to his gut. An orange and white hat laid next to him with the letters S.T.I.H.L across the front. It looked familiar, Tyler thought he'd seen it on his dad's chainsaws before but wasn't sure.

Without him even noticing, his breath had quickened, he swallowed a large lump in his throat and had to gasp to catch his next breath. His whole body began to tremble. His heart knocked against its cage, goosebumps spreading across his skin.

His teeth began to clatter and with a quivering hand he rubbed his face.

He shut his eyes and turned around.

It's not real. It's not real.

He's just imagining it.

He took two steps, his eyes still shut, but the image of the man's body was still there in his mind.

He took another step and a wall of hair and muscle flash in front of him. He stumbled backward and crashed on his rump.

He opened his eyes to see Mother and the others standing over him...expressionless.

He swallowed hard again and blinked his eyes.

In an instant Mother had done yanked him to his feet and was prodding him back to the body. As they edged closer, Tyler clung tighter to Mother's leg and tucked his face away from the dead man. He'd seen enough and whatever they were about to do, he could do without. And if they start eating on him...well...he'd just have to take his chances at fleeing the beast, however stupid that might seem. He wasn't about to start chewing on a dead man.

They stopped, likely within just a few feet of the man. Tyler had his eyes clinched as cold tears began to snake down his cheeks, the tip of his nose stung when he sniffled. At least he could still feel it, better than it falling off from frostbite.

He did his best to force his mind some place else, but no matter how hard he tried, he still found himself clinging to a Sasquatch only a few feet form a dead man.

Mother grunted and peeled him from her leg.

He stood there without any cover. He gripped each elbow and pulled them tight against his body. He'd turned his back to the body as soon as Mother pulled him from her

Омаh

leg, but he was quickly nudged and grunted at by Moses. His stubby fingers were even
bigger than Mothers and they forced him to turn around.

When he peaked open his eyes, he was all alone. Just him and the dead man. He jerked his head around searching for Mother and the others. There. Mother was to his right squatted down upon her calves. She had an arm full of sticks with the other raking across the ground.

To her right was Andy, doing the same. But where was Moses and Jenny. He snapped his head to the left where he thought he heard some rummaging in the leaves.

There they were. Moses had an arm load of rocks and Jenny had a load of twigs and leaves like Mother and Andy.

What are they doing? Are they going to bury him?

Tyler standing there in amazement watched as the creatures returned to the body and dropped their gatherings next to him. Then one by one, they lowered to all fours and placed their objects upon him. Within seconds, he was just a big clump of leaves, sticks, and rocks. You'd never know he was under all that unless you looked for him.

Satisfied with their burial, they stood and admired what they'd done. But a solemn vibe was among them. After a moment of eerie silence, in which none of earth's creatures or critters said a word, Mother tilted her head toward the Heavens, pursed her lips and let out that high pitch whistle Tyler heard her do when they were down by the river.

When she finished, Moses found a piece of wood that suited him and crossed to a pine to their left. He too looked to the Heaven's, lowered his eye lids, took a breath, then fixed his gaze upon the tree, pulled back and gave it three good knocks.

The cracks ringing out into the forest, echoing, echoing, echoing.

58

Before launching into the forest, Randy and the men returned to the Giant Redwoods RV Park, just as he had promised Bev over the phone.

Curtis Whetstone followed behind them in a black Ford truck.

Passing the check-in cabin, the old man with a smoking pipe drooping out his mouth, glasses hanging on the tip of his nose, gave a reluctant nod from his rocker as they went by.

"Mr. Crawford...boy does he got a story to tell...if only he'd tell it," said Jack.

Randy craned his neck over the back seat as the man grew smaller through the foggy back windshield.

Gravel crunched beneath the tires of Jack's Rav4, pebbles tinging against the metal underneath,

Jack made a left turn, the old man and the cabin hiding and peaking behind a row of pines.

Randy turned around, there were now even less campers and RV's than before. His and Bev's were visible toward the back, as it was the only one left on the row. In its driveway, was their Jeep Wrangler, Adam and Brenda's black Ford Sport Trac, and behind that was a gold Dodge Ram pick-up truck.

Оман

Who's that?

"Y'all know that truck?"

Jack and Adam wagged their heads.

"Huh. Your wife and grandpa are still here aren't they?"

"Yeah. She said they were," said Adam.

Jack pulls off on the grass as the driveway was too full. Curtis Whetstone parks behind him. They get out and head for the door.

Randy could hear chatter from inside, so he gave two quick knocks before opening it.

Inside were Bev and the kids, Kosumi and Brenda, and seated on the couch next to each other were an older white man and woman. Randy nodded then looked to Bev with raised brows. Bev stood from the couch next to the woman and said, "Honey, this is Jimmy and Suzanne Davis. He's the hunter from Hoopa."

AFTER BURYING the body, Mother scooped Tyler up in her arms and along with the others, they marched off into the forest. That's when Tyler noticed the first snow flake, then another and another. Now it was coming down faster than he could count. Mother's and the others fur looked like it'd been sprinkled with powdered sugar, the ground did as well.

He still couldn't get that man out of his mind. What happened to him? Had they done that to him? Did Moses kill him while he was gone? If they could do that to a full-grown man, he didn't even want to know what they could do to hi—wait...what was that?

Mother heard it too. She stopped dead in her tracks and snapped her head side to side. It sounded like someone talking. It was. And they were coming closer.

They were in the middle of an abundance of pine trees, the Redwoods had faded soon after they left the body. In a flash Mother bolted to a pine and scurried up it. Twigs sticking and slapping Tyler as she squeezed him close to her side with her right arm and pulled them upward with her left.

 Moses, Andy, and Jenny did the same with three other pines nearby. They climbed almost to the top, hidden by an array of branches and pine needles.

Mother reached a point where it suited her, clung to the tree with her left and covered Tyler's mouth with a black leathery right.

Leaves crunched, twigs snapped, and men spoke. It sounded like they were coming from the left, which would've been behind them as they walked. Gosh, they were almost caught.

The woods were so thick here, Tyler couldn't see more than the length between first and second base into them. The men sounded like they were still a good ways off, so hopefully they didn't hear them climbing the trees.

Wait...why would he hope they didn't hear them? He wanted to be rescued right? What if his dad was with these men?

The second he flinched his mouth, Mother tightened her grip. A bitter salty taste filled his mouth, must be sweat from her palms. He snarled his nose, clinched his eyes and twisted his head. Mother shook him and gave a soft grunt. Her way of saying, "Enough, be quiet."

He opened his eyes and tried to find Moses, Andy, and Jenny in the adjacent trees, but they must've blended in too good with the limbs, because his eyes weren't good enough to pick them up.

"What do you say the chances are this Randy dude knocked the boy off because he never wanted a third kid?"

Tyler's eyes widened, those words hurt worse than a bee sting, his heart pounded with a dull ache.

Omah

"Mack...you're terrible man."

"Hey, I'm just saying. Stuff like that happens more than you'd think."

Tyler could feel Mother's heartbeat as it knocked stronger and harder against her chest. Her breathing had quickened as well.

The men still weren't visible, but by the closeness of their voice, they should be any second.

"Man...it'd take a truly heartless person to do something like that."

"Oh yeah, but I've seen it on those crime sho—"

"Will you two shut up!?" a deep gravelly, third voice roared. The sound of their steps stopped.

"I've heard about all I'm going to hear. That's enough. Now in case you've forgotten, we got a job to do and I'd appreciate it if you two joined us."

Silence.

The footsteps picked up again.

"John...what you got?"

There. There's movement. That's them.

There's three of the—no four—no...five? Yeah five of them. Dressed in black pants and black jackets with silver stars on their chest, except for the one in front, he was wearing a camo jacket. The one behind him had a gold star on the right side of his black jacket. He also had a thick white mustache too.

"Well, it's hard to say, the snow is thinner here, so can't get a good track. Let's keep going, see if I can pick it up again."

The men passed directly under the tree him and Mother were in. If the men only knew what was above them.

Tyler wanted to scream, but after seeing the rifles strapped across the back of their shoulders, he was afraid of what they might do. He wanted to be rescued, but he also didn't want them harming Mother or the others.

Mother began a low grumble just loud enough for Tyler to hear. He jerked his head to see her with slanted and searing eyes, quivering lips pulled tight against her big yellow teeth.

She and Tyler watched as the men continued on into the forest, disappearing beyond its thickness. Their voices and steps gently ebbing away.

Minutes passed and so did the sound of the men. No voices, no foot falls, just the sound of the woods. Rustling leaves tickled with the breeze, gossiping sparrows and barking squirrels.

The loud click gave Tyler's heart a start. He looked to Mother in time to watch her give another. Her front teeth poked out, her big cow like tongue rolling across the roof of her mouth, smacking against the back of her teeth.

She did it three times.

A beat.

About five trees over, three clicks returned her call.

With that, Mother with Tyler still squeezed in her right, began the descent.

Bark fell to the earth as Mother's claws and toenails raked along the tree on the way down, much like a blade raking off the scales of a fish.

The same sound could be heard where the other click came from. It was Moses working his way down. Coming down the tree next to him, was Jenny and Andy.

Mother dropped from the tree and landed with a thump on all fours, jarring Tyler's head and heart. Moses and the kids did the same.

Mother angled to them and entered a low chatter which sounded like another language. Maybe Chinese or something. It was weird whatever it was. Lot's of clicks and grunts mixed in with it too.

They finished the gibberish and returned to their march through the woods. Going a different direction than the men.

Once again Tyler found himself tucked tight to a Sasquatches side, gliding through the woods, watching trees, limbs, and leaves pass beneath, much like riding in a car and watching the passing trees and mailboxes.

The snow continued to fall as small flakes mixed with others the size of cotton balls glided to the earth. He'd have to be sure to sleep close to Mother tonight, because boy it sure was getting cold.

Who were those men though? Was that the cops? What about what that one said about his dad? He was wrong, wasn't he? His dad would never do something like that.

Oh, how much longer before they find him? Tears streaked down his cheeks, his body began to quake against Mother's side.

How could they rescue him and not harm the others? Someone would get hurt or even worse. He can't let them find him with the Sasquatches. But he can't wander off again, especially now. He would never survive the night without the warmth of Mother's fur. What should he do? Wait for his dad to find him? But what if Mother got mad and did what one of them did to the dead man back there?

Oh gosh.

Tears streaked down his cold cheeks.

Mother stopped as his crying and jolting body got her attention. She sat him down and hunched over like a Gorilla to look him in the eye. She poked him with a stubby finger in the chest. He winced.

Tears continued to snake down his face, she caught them with the back of her hairy knuckles.

She grunted then looked to the ground.

Tyler lowered his eyes as well, sniffling and gasping through quivering lips.

Mother raised her head. Her eyes were glassy too. Tyler watched in amazement as a tear grew in the corner of one of her big black eyes, before rolling to the edge and dropping to the earth.

"I have to get back to my family," Tyler said in a soft voice. "I can't live out here with you. I have my own family."

Mother cocked her head and squinted her eyes.

"I'm worried about you though. I don't won't nothing bad to happen to you," Tyler glanced to Moses, Andy, and Jenny as he said it.

Tyler shut his eyes, forcing out more tears and sniffles. His shoulders jolted up and down. His heart feeling heavy as a wave of fear and sadness at what may be coming, overtook him.

He couldn't contain his sobs.

That's when he felt Mother's cold hand take him by the arm and pull him in close. She was hugging him, comforting him, just like his real Mother would do. She began to purr like a cat. The warmth of her embrace was exactly what he needed. His heart grew lighter. For the first time since being out here, he kind of felt some hope.

He pulled back and looked Mother in the eye, "I promise I won't let nothing happen to you. But you have to promise me you won't hurt my dad and the men when they find me."

Tyler looked at her with a downward gaze for effect. She glared back, then snuffed, twisted her head to the sky and oohed and ahhed soft and deep like a chimp. She lowered her gaze back to Tyler and gave two clicks, then rose to her feet and scooped him up against her ribs. They returned to their journey, crunching over snow covered

Omah

twigs and leaves, swatting away the branches that attempted to slow them down.

Tyler craned his neck around to see Jenny, Andy, and Moses following behind. Moses continued to glance about the area, keeping a good watch as his head twisted like an owl over each shoulder.

"Please don't let nothing happen to these creatures."

Tyler thought as Mother took one thudding step after another. Where they were going, who knows? But hopefully his dad would find them, and they could all meet on good terms. And hopefully Mother will be willing to give him back to his real family. He hoped and prayed she wouldn't give much of a fight

59

"So, you really saw one of these things?" asked Randy.

"You dang right I did. I'm telling ya..." Jimmy Davis took a breath and said while sighing it out through puffed cheeks and wagging his head, "...its something I'll never forget."

Jimmy had done showed Randy, Adam, and Jack the marks on his back. Looked like he'd passed through a giant cheese grater and lived to tell about it.

"How ethical of a hunter are you?" asked Adam.

Jimmy looked at him with squinted brows.

"You know, like, do you follow the regulations and do things the right way when you're out there?"

Jimmy nodded, "Can't say I've ever done something I shouldn't've. Yeah...I'd say I'm a pretty ethical hunter, and fisherman for that matter."

"Good. That's good, we need more men like you up here. Honestly, I think that's the only reason you're still here. I think this was more of a scare tactic than anything. If they wanted you dead...you'd be in the morgue like Al Frankford."

"Well, I really feel like something stopped it from doing more than it did. I think there were more out there and they may have saved me from the one that attacked me."

"Hmm. Well, yeah there are good ones and bad ones. Just like with us humans. There is good and evil everywhere, even in nature. Maybe the good ones knew your heart and felt your spirit, so they protected you from the one that got you."

Jimmy nodded, his wide eyes trained to the floor, his mind tossing and turning over an array of thoughts.

"You know, I've heard stories about these things all my life and I've heard their screams more times than I can count over the years, but I never would have thought something like this was really out there. I mean to think of all the times I've been out in the woods, whether in the early mornings or evenings and to now know what is really out there...my goodness..." his eyes lifted to Adam, then went to Randy, "...I may never hunt again. I just don't know if I could ever go back into those woods."

Suzanne patted his knee and encouraged him with soft words.

"Boys...I've spent my whole life in these woods, either hunting or fishing, I've seen bear, heck I've been face to face before with a Grizzly," he wagged his head, "this wasn't no bear. The way it was crouched down, spread out on all fours like a spider and the way it craned its head at me..." Jimmy shuddered in effort to shake the sight from his mind, but it was no use, something like that will always be there.

"It looked so human yet wild and animal like too. That scream...I tell ya, you'll think you've fallen into the pits of hell. It's just so unnerving, like it's from another world."

Randy sighed and rubbed the back of his neck.

"I'm sorry, I shouldn't be talking like this. I just want you to know what you're dealing with, I don't want you people thinking it's just a bear out there. I wanted you to know the truth, I wanted you to know what I saw."

"No, I needed to hear this. I have to say after everything I've seen and heard over the past few days, I'm becoming a believer. Because honestly, I don't have any other explanations," said Randy.

Bev sat at the end of the couch dabbing her eyes with a Kleenex, "If something like this is really out there, why would they take Tyler?"

A beat.

"To get your attention. Its their way of saying, 'Hey, we're out here, we're really out here and don't you ever doubt it,'" said Curtis Whetstone.

Jack nodded and added, "He's exactly right. And it's also to have us remember our obligation to protect and enrich Mother Earth."

Kosumi cleared his throat and said, "Like my grandfather always said, 'The hairy men among the Giant Cedars of old, are to be honored and feared, for they are not only charged with guarding us in our walk among the earth, but they take no issue in spreading the prideful among us as dried weed in a passing breeze. They will not tolerate those ever taking and never giving to Mother Earth, for she is not just a resource, she is a source of life and one must only take what they need. One should also seek to give back to her, whether it be in protecting the ecosystem or sowing seed for future generations, we are to always seek to give more than we take. The Tintah—Kiwungxoya'n will see to it that this is carried out. Stay humble and never challenge such authority.'"

"So, I guess with all the people that have been killed and abducted through the years, they've yet to get our attention?" asked Randy.

"Us humans can be quite stubborn at times," said Adam.

"So how do we end this?" asked Bev.

"Like my mother told Mr. Stone, when the Omahs ravaged the village...I need hair," Kosumi looked to

Randy, Adam, Jack, and Curtis. "You get me hair, and all of this will end."

"And just how do you expect us to do that?" Randy asked.

"With the Creator's blessing...nothing is impossible."

60

A half hour later, after having planned their expedition, Randy found himself standing at the hood of Jack's Rav4 looking at a map of Humboldt County. Bev stood close to his side, clinging to an arm, while the kids were next to Bev standing on their tip toes trying to peak at the map. Jimmy and Suzanne Davis had left moments ago. Adam and Jack took turns pointing out the lay of the land: mountains, valleys, Redwood forests, thickets, rivers, creeks and what have you. While Kosumi added his knowledge of the land with a pointed finger. Randy marked each point with a black sharpie. A black triangle for big hills and mountains, two squiggly lines for a river, one line for a creek, one tree for a pocket of Redwoods, and three for a thicket.

Curtis Whetstone stood with a foot propped on the driver side tire, chin cradled in his right palm. Brenda whispered to Adam as Randy was busy circling the place of pick up, Curtis noticed, but pretended he didn't.

"So, if we launch here, it should be about what? Say eight miles to the northwest till we reach government land?" Randy asked as he traced the map with his finger.

Adam nodded and said while snaking his finger over the paper, "Yeah, we can zig zag our way up there. Being sure we cover enough ground. Lot of land between here and there. Considering the terrain and current

Omah

conditions, we should be able to make it to Grasshopper Road before night fall, then if we need to, set out at dawn to cover the rest."

"Yeah and remember there's a creek that meanders along through there too, it'd make for good place to set up camp for the night," said Jack.

Bev squeezed Randy's arm, "Oh, honey be careful." Her irises hazel in color but strained in appearance, her cheeks moist beneath her white beanie, her black hair slipping out in straight strands.

Randy dropped the marker on the hood, pulled her close and held her. The marker rolled off and hit the ground. Bev, with grace and gentleness, allowed her tears to flow.

"Ssshhh...it's okay. We will be safe. I'm going to bring our boy home. You have to trust me."

She didn't say anything, but he felt her nod against his chest.

Curtis picked up the marker and positioned it above the map in a way so that it wouldn't roll off again.

A gentle breeze whisked by, tickling the pines adjacent to them. Kosumi looked to the swaying trees, his eyes lowered, and his lips moved, but no words formed.

He breathed deep, his palms now dangling open by his side.

He looked to Randy and Bev, "The Great Spirit is with you. The Tintah—Kiwungxoya'n will see. It is hair you must bring. I await your return."

61

With the snow becoming heavier, Randy put on an extra layer under his jacket before heading out. The forecast called for two inches by midnight. The storm would move on up the coast after that. But not without sending temperatures to the mid-teens.

Channel 14 news had pulled in the campground as Randy was busy rolling the map into a scroll. Bobby Thatcher along with his cameraman rushed to Randy and the men as they made their way down to the river where Tyler had vanished.

Randy waved them off as they edged closer.

"Mr. Jacobs-Mr. Jacobs! What can you tell us about your son's di—"

Randy was walking away, mumbling while holding up a palm behind him. He bit into Thatcher's question with one of his own as he spun around with the reporter's last few words. Marching to Thatcher, with a red face and bulging neck veins.

"Don't you fellas have something better to do?"

Thatcher swallowed hard and took a step back. He motioned to Dale, his cameraman. Dale lowered the camera from his shoulder, Thatcher lowered the mic.

"I'm sorry. I'm just trying to do my job."

"Well go find the Sheriff or the Warden to question. Don't come racing down here, shoving a mic and camera in my face trying to pull something from me."

Adam placed a hand on Randy's arm and said softly, "C'mon Randy."

Jack and Curtis waited halfway down the trail leading to the River.

"Besides...not like you people would believe it anyhow," Randy turned and angled down the slope.

"Believe what?"

Randy and the men down by the top of the riverbank now. Their heads peaking just above the dead grass and weeds where Thatcher and Dale stood.

"The bear story, Thatcher. Go with the bear. At least people will believe that," his voice echoing but ebbing away.

Thatcher looked to Dale with scrunched brows. Dale shrugged his shoulders and spit his chewing gum.

"You don't think those Indians have him talked into believing their stories, do you?"

"Who's to say. These woods have always been a mystery to me man and with all the things that's happened over the years, heck they'd probably make me a believer too," said Dale.

"Well...I just hope they know what they're getting into. I don't want to be reporting a story with him on a gurney behind me."

CRUNCHING OF loose pebble and course sand, the rustling of the river, and sound of snow fall, would have made for a relaxing moment any other time but now. Randy and the men angled alongside the river, heading for the patch of brush around the bend. Twenty yards from where Randy and Andrew found the footprints beneath the water. A fallen tree stretched to the other side. It is here that Sheriff Logan and countless others, clam Tyler must have crossed. But Randy felt otherwise.

When adding up the collection of evidence he'd been presented with...he was starting to believe. Though it'd take a face to face encounter to remove the last ounce of doubt that was till present, however sparse it might be, he found himself leaning more and more to the side of *it* being a possibility.

With that said, he did his best to reign back the images of something big and hairy toting his son across the river. Big enough to not need a fallen tree for footing.

Afterall...what else could do something like that to Frankford? What would shove a stone and feather done his throat like that?

Randy shut his eyes, breathed deep and shook off the images of Frankford and his killer jolting through the waters with Tyler. His skin tingling with gooseflesh, whether from the cold or the thoughts visiting his mind, he didn't know.

He glanced across the river. Pines, mountains, and the wailing woman awaited. He adjusted the positioning of his back pack, tightened the straps and looked once again up the river, where the prints were left in the sand.

A gentle hand touched his elbow, "You ready to do this, Randy?" Adam asked.

Randy nodded and lowered his gaze to the log in front of his feet. He swallowed hard, may have said a silent prayer, then planted his size twelve Rocky boot onto the tree, then the other. Adam, Jack, and Curtis filed in behind. Their backpacks loaded with food, canteens, tents, and sleeping bags, they crossed the river.

Omah

62

Having passed between Redwoods and Pines, swatting away any branches that crossed their paths, the sudden stop in their journey caused Tyler to wonder what had gotten their attention.

Mother stood with her snarled nose high in the air, lips stretched tight to her gums, still toting Tyler like a football.

Andy and Jenny made a few monkey sounds before being hushed by Mother with a grunt and poke.

Moses had already found a decent sized stick and was just looking for a tree to beat it with. Tyler watched from his sideways point of view squashed against Mother's side. It may not have been all that comfortable, but it kept him warm and beat having to walk.

Whap! Whap! Whap!

They waited.

With the snow lighting to his fur, Moses now reminded Tyler of the Abominable Snowman from Rudolph. Not quite as white, but close.

Nothing.

Mother continued to sniff the air, her black eyes darting every which way.

Moses glared with squinted eyes, his head twitchy like a crow.

He reared back and beat the tree twice more. He waited, catching his breath as it escaped in quick clouds.

Nothin—

Knock...knock...knock.

There!

It sounded far off as it traveled in echoes to reach them. Mother snapped her head to Moses and grunted. He huffed back. Mother tilted her head and let out that high pitched whistle, that could have easily been mistaken for a tea kettle.

It trailed on long and high before tapering off, emptying Mother's lungs.

They waited.

Nothing.

Moses dropped the stick, clicked thrice, Mother crossed to him and they headed in the direction of the knocks.

They'd travelled long enough for Tyler to begin to doze once again, before Mother stopped with such abruptness, he thought he'd get slung across the forest. He lurched forward, then his legs swung around to the right. Moses continued, halted by Mother's tongue clicks. He came scrolling back with his long, powerful strides, arms swinging past his knees.

Tyler fought for the angle to see what held Mother's attention. She was standing in front of what looked to be a Redwood, judging by its size. Hard to tell from his angle, and besides that, he could only see half of it, as the rest was hidden by Mother's thick body.

He heard her sniff.

Omah

    He could see Moses and the kids in his peripheral edging closer, backs hunched, heads lowered, faces stoic. A look of curiosity he supposed.
    Mother jerked away from the tree, holding something in her hand. Andy and Jenny grasped and yapped for it, as if she held their favorite bone. Mother jerked away with a hiss. They eased off. Moses just
stood by, eyeing her with pouty looking lips and scrunched brows.
    She lowered to the ground, her back against a pine, allowing Tyler to ease down beside her. For the first time he saw what it was.
    A feather.
    She stroked it with gentle rubs from the back of her knuckles. Her breathing quickened as her eyes became moist. She looked to Tyler and took a hard swallow.

63

After three o'clock now, and an hour after Randy and the men set foot into the wilderness. The clouds were darker with snow falling slowly in big flakes. The ground covered in about an inch or two of white. The little birds enjoyed such a sight, for some it may have been their first snow. At least judging by the looks of it. They hopped and chirped among the limbs, embracing the rare occurrence. High above the low snow clouds, an Eagle screeched in search of another meal. A squirrel or rabbit would be sure to calm its gut and silence its call for feeding.

"Ahh...the Great Spirit has shown us favor," said Adam with his head tilted to the sky, flakes lighting upon his chiseled, copper toned face. "Hear that? That's the Great Spirit's messenger. It's a sign that His presence is with us in our journey and efforts. A reminder to trust His wisdom."

Randy looked to Adam, then glanced toward the heavens.

Jack nodded with a grin.

Curtis looked to have said a prayer.

The cry of the Eagle trickled down among the forest with the snow. It cried again, then five more times before it finished. Adam and Jack counting each one.

"Seven?" asked Jack.

Adam nodded.

"The number of completion and inner wisdom," said Curtis, his eyes now open and trained to the clouds.

"So, its like good luck or something?"

Adam lowered his gaze to Randy and smiled, "Even better."

Randy unbuttoned the chest pocket on his jacket and retrieved the map.

"We're about here...right?"

Jack standing closes to him, took a few steps and fixed his attention to the map, pointing at it as he spoke, "Yeah...roughly three miles to Bull Creek. With a zig zag pattern...and with the snow...should be about another three hours. And that's giving us time to break when we need to."

The rustle of branches and quick crunching of snow caused the men to yank around to their left, just in time to catch glimpse of something big and hairy charging at them like a raged bull.

A deep throated roar pounded their ear drums. It happened so quick, neither Jack nor Adam had time to draw their weapons. The hair covered blur swatted and knocked Jack to the earth, before tackling Randy.

The breath was squeezed out of him as the ginormous beast sat atop his chest, growling and digging its dagger like claws into his jacket. Shredding it like ribbons. Randy had his hands and forearms up to cover his face when a powerful set of jowls cinched down on his right forearm.

Randy yelped. The teeth tore through his layer of clothes, scrapping his flesh and squashing his arm as if it were in a vice grip. It could break any second. But better a broken arm than a crushed skull.

The beast shook violently like a K-9 training for the academy, slinging Randy about the snow-covered earth as if he were a stuffed animal.

It's one of the creatures, my god it's going to kill him! He's the next Al Frankford.

It's going to snap his neck any second.

Randy tucked his head tight between his arms, like a turtle shying from predators. Still screaming from the agony, he used his left arm to search for his pocketknife.

Boom! Boom! Boom!

Randy opened his eyes just in time to see past his flailing arms, a humongous head, big black nose, with mouth full of crocodile like teeth.

A bear.

It jolted from Randy's chest and charged toward the sound of the gun.

BoomBoom!

The thing grunted and crashed to the ground.

Boom!

Huffs and gasps for air were in abundance.

Randy could feel his heart beat in his arm. He sucked in a lung worth of air as if he'd just surfaced from the deep. His chest felt like it had caved under such weight, he touched it to be sure it hadn't.

Curtis rushed over and plopped in the snow next to him, he was saying something as he scanned over Randy with darting eyes. Jack moaned and squirmed a few yards beside them.

Randy's vision began to blur as sound ebbed away. His eye lids could have been made from concreate, he didn't have the strength to keep the open.

He felt a cold hand smack his numb cheek. It didn't sting, but he felt the pressure.

Omah

His sight was now just below his eyes, his lids were coming to a close and he couldn't do anything to stop them. The voices sounded a million miles away. Everything went black. Then turned to a dark red. The back of his eye lids.

Silence.

THE SIX SHOTS in quick succession was enough to stop Warden Phillips in his tracks. He reached for the radio on his shoulder and called out to Sheriff Logan, who may have been trying to reach him to ask the same question, "Was that you?"

Phillips and him both learned it wasn't, which meant it must've been Randy and the Indians.

"Where are you at?" asked Phillips.

"In the thicket, between the campground and Rossi Ranch Lane. What about you?"

"A mile east of the loop in Bull Creek Road."

A static hiss.

Logan's slow, gravelly voice crackled back, "Was it close to you, or did they seem distant?"

"It wasn't close. If it hadn't of been so close together, we might not would have paid it much attention. We bout didn't hear it."

"Okay. It sounded closer for us. Still a ways off, but I'd say we're closer."

Static.

"10-4."

TYLER FIRST thought it was more knocks and Mother and Moses seemed to think that way too at first, as they once again stopped to listen and wait. Mother and Moses went back in forth in their coded language, while Andy and Jenny toyed around in the snow, acting spunky. Andy's attempt at trying to catch a snow flake with his bare hands, was enough to give Tyler a chuckle, something he forgotten how to do recently.

Jenny shoved her brother and fought for a few flakes herself.

The discussion between Mother and Moses seemed a little heated, there were beginning to be more grunts and hisses than yapping.

Moses gave a deep, gut bellowing grunt that was followed by Mother's searing eyes and low grumble.

With that they marched off in another direction than that in which they were going. Andy and Jenny were still occupied with the snow and at Mother's click, had to rush to catch up.

Being from the North Carolina Coast, it wasn't every day you got to witness snow fall and by the looks of it with Andy and Jenny, the California Coast must not have been that much different.

He could relate to their jovial welcome of such a sight. If he wasn't in his predicament, he'd be doing the same with his brother and sister. His real brother and sister.

The thought of them stung his heart. He swallowed hard to keep the emotions in his gut from rising to his eyes.

He pressed into Mother's fur. His nose and cheeks numb and stinging, his fingers and toes felt the same.

A nice cup of cocoa by a warm fire would sure be nice right about now.

If he tried hard enough, he could taste the smooth richness of the hot chocolate against his tongue, soft marsh mellows squishing between his teeth. All while snuggled up close to Mama as she read a story.

Gliding, bobbing, thrashing through the forest, while nestled close to Mother's fur was the closest thing he get to such fine memories. And it was the closest he could get to comfort. It wasn't long before his memories of home, faded into dreams. His body numb and weightless, his eyes closed without his consent, and before he knew it, he was at home, next to Mama in her chair, sipping cocoa and listening to a story, next to a fire and under a warm blanket.

KOSUMI AND BRENDA had left moments ago to get food for Bev and the kids and to swing by Kosumi and Jack's place to grab a few things they'd be needing.
    Bev sat at the edge of the couch, holding a damp Kleenex while Jennifer and Andrew sat on either side of her. Though on the inside she was nothing but a mess, she had to be strong for the kids. As much as her heart was drowning in the fear of never seeing her son again, she couldn't let them see her doubt. She knew the chances of finding him alive were diminishing with every passing second, but she had to keep faith that they would find him. If she couldn't do it for herself, then she would have to do it for her kids.
    "Now I want y'all to listen to me," Bev said with sniffles as she glanced to the two of them, her voice strained, "No matter what happens in the next few days...we're going to get through this...and we will get through it together. Understood?"
    Jennifer and Andrew nodded.
    "Your dad and the Lightfoots along with the police and game wardens are doing all they can do. They're going to find Tyler and they're going to bring him back to us." She wiped the tears that blurred her vision and swallowed the lump that choked her voice.
    "Mom...do you think what Kosumi is telling us is the truth? You really believe there could be something like that out there?" asked Jennifer.

"You know they're really out there. Have you seen all the stuff on YouTube? And what about your book?" said Andrew.

Jennifer looked to him, but didn't have the strength to counter, she fixed her legs in an Indian style and watched as she picked at a thumbnail.

Bev took a breath and said, "I don't know honey. It makes sense what they're saying, but honestly, I don't know that I could believe in something like that. It's kind of silly if you ask me."

Jennifer took a breath and glanced out the window for a moment then returned her eyes to Bev, "But what if a bigfoot really did take him? What if its true?"

"Oh goodness you too?" Bev said with a half chuckle as she dabbed her eye.

"Listen...Kosumi and Brenda will be back in about an hour, how about we try and get us a nap while we have the chance? Hmm?"

Jennifer and Andrew nodded.

"Mom...I really think Tyler was taken by one of them. I can't see him running off in the woods all by himself. You know he's a scary cat when it comes to stuff like that," said Jennifer.

"Yeah, he wouldn't have just walked off like that."

Bev rubbed her face with both palms and said with a gentle smile, "Well...we'll just have to ask him when he comes back."

LESS THAN half an hour later, Bev and the kids were sound asleep in the back bed of the RV. Bev was on her back with Andrew and Jennifer snuggled up to her on each side.

Out of this world, but passing into another, Bev found herself seated in a rocking chair next to a warm fireplace,

Omah

like the one at the cabin in Maggy Valley they oftentimes visit in the North Carolina Mountains. A soft throw blanket rested across her waist and knees, her right arm and hand nestled around her youngest son as she held a book with her left hand. Most likely a Dr. Seuss book, it was too blurry to tell. On the table next to her were two cups of warm cocoa.

She glanced down at Tyler, he looked back at her with those big blue eyes, half hidden by his croppy blonde hair. He gave a snaggletooth grin, then squeezed her tight.

Her heart filled to the brim as her eyes couldn't contain it. But these weren't tears of fear or sorrow, these were happy tears, good tears.

He pulled back and said, "I'm okay, they're taking good care of me. Believe—"

Before she could form a reply, everything turned to a blur. She jolted awake and sprung up from the bed, her spine straight, her breath gasping. Her heart full of hope and joy.

She had to tell Randy.

64

Riding along Highway 101 south towards his and Jack's place in Miranda, Kosumi grabbed at his gut and took a hard swallow. Something wasn't right. His heart began to palpitate, knocking strong against its cage.

"Brenda, pull over for a second."

"Huh?"

"Pull over. Hurry pull over."

She waited till they made it around the curve they were in and pulled off the road along the straight away.

Kosumi fumbled for the door handle, already beginning to heave, he got the door open just in time to spew onto the dirt.

Brenda leaned over and patted him on the back, "Are you okay?"

Nothing.

He hacked and spit the last of it out.

Brenda searched the center console for a napkin of some sorts.

She found one and nudged his arm with it. He took it and put it to use.

He breathed deep, sat back in his seat, head tight against the head rest and dabbed his mouth, "Brenda...we have to talk to Randy and the men, something's wrong. Something's happened."

Omah

65

The crackle of a flame, sour and hot to his lips, pressure on his arm, the savory smell of something roasted, pulled his mind back to earth and gave his eyes reason to open.

Through the black blur, he saw the fire, he was closer to it than he thought. Adam pulled back a steamy tin cup which he grasped between two gloved hands. He sat next to him and placed the cup of what must've been a type of tea to the ground.

Randy found his left arm tucked inside a sleeping bag along with the rest of his body, but his right arm was rested across his chest, wrapped tightly in a thick bandage.

His mind dazed and his vision coming and going, he blinked and wagged his head. There was Jack by the fire, holding a stick over it, that's where the smell came from. He was cooking something.

Curtis sat behind Jack, looking over a map.

"How you feeling?"

Randy craned his head which felt like a bowling ball, to Adam and focused his sight. Adam's face cleared.

Randy nodded.

"What happened?"

Adam turned and looked to Jack and Curtis, then looked back to Randy, "We crossed a Grizzly. A mother at that. You're fortunate my friend, heck we all are." Adam lowered his gaze, tightened his lips and wagged his head.

"Is everyone all right?"

Adam raised his glazed eyes to Randy and said,

"Yeah...we're all good."

Adam threw a thumb to his brother and said, "He took a gut punch, but he'll live."

Randy nodded, "How's my arm?"

"It's still there, if that helps ease your mind."

"Seriously...how is it?"

A beat.

"I've got it wrapped with Tobacco and Sage right now. She got you good, but it would have been a lot worse if not for all the layers you were wearing.

"You'll be sore for a while, but as long as we keep an eye out for infection, I think you'll be fine. Jacks roasting some chanterelles now. Mushrooms. They'll help with the pain and give you strength. Same for the serviceberry tea. It'll ward off infections and inflammation. You'll be fine brother," Adam said as he patted him on the leg and offered a slight grin.

"What about the bear?"

Adam took a breath, "If it wasn't for our situation, I'd took her home and harvested the meat and hide...but...we all agreed, we couldn't do it. It'd only slow us down. I'd like to try and go back and get her before we head in. I hate to let her waste like that."

"Keech chey-po-rey-gehl-leykw," Jack mumbled just loud enough for all to hear.

"What'd he say?"

"See, its cold weather outside," said Adam, "Being as cold as it is, we will have at least two days before the meat and hide ruin.

Randy took a breath, "So, she's the one that's been causing so much trouble."

Adam looked at Randy with scrunched brows,

Jack retrieved the mushrooms from the flame and craned to look at Curtis, who was now peaking up from the map, looking over his glasses.

"Yeah...she's the one that killed Al, tried to kill Jimmy and now tried to kill me."

Adam dropped his eyes and shook his head.

"It's obvious isn't it?" Randy asked with wide eyes.

"Your mistaken my friend. You think the bear shoved a stone and feather down Frankford's throat? Then slung a rock the size of a bowling ball through the windshield of Les and Sam's truck?" Adam wagged his head and looked off to the woods.

Randy followed his gaze. The sun beginning its descent. The snow had stopped, as a cold fog rose quietly from the morgue like forest. Cecil Sawyer would be right at home in a place like this.

"How close are we to Bull Creek?"

Curtis cleared his throat, "Half a mile maybe."

Randy nodded.

"We think it'd be best to stay here for the night. Then rise at dawn to finish our journey," said Adam.

Randy grimaced.

"It's in everyone's best interest," added Jack.

Curtis bobbed his head.

"I don't know how much longer my boy can survive out here," Randy said with tears stinging his eyes and cheeks. His heart may have just taken a sledge hammer swung by one of the creatures themselves. It ached with a pain he'd never felt before. He did his best to withhold his emotions, but when they're this strong, no human on earth could stop the pressure of such a river, no matter how big you try and build the dam. Randy's broke.

He choked and covered his face with his left, his whole body jolting, his breath escaping in short gasps and sucking in through clogged nostrils.

Adam moved in to hug him. Randy gripped Adam's back, hanging on for dear life.

"Randy...you have my word...we're going to find your boy."

Omah

66

The sudden array of clicking and snorting, pulled Tyler from his slumber. Mother sounded like an idle engine as she began her low grumble once again. Tyler opened his eye lids to see Moses and the kids standing around something big and hairy stretched out across the frosted earth. Still being toted by Mother, his vision was distorted at an angle. He blinked and wiped the sand from his eye. Mother stepped closer. At first, he thought it may have been another Bigfoot, judging by the size and thick brown fur, but when he located the head, he knew. A bear.

Moses' nostrils flared as he had an intense continence about him, enough to cause Tyler's spine to shudder. Moses huffed and stomped around in circles, his fist balled and dangling at his sides. Andy and Jenny clicked and made chimp like oohs and ahhs, not sure what else to do.

Mother dropped Tyler from her waist, sending him to the cold earth like a skydiver who'd forgot to deploy the chute. Something she had yet to learn was how frail his body can be. He wasn't like the other two she'd raised. They could probably withstand such an impact, but for Tyler, it was taking its toll.

This time he landed on his tail bone, never a good thing. He writhed in what may have been mortal agony, squirming and groaning on the ground. Mother gave him a glance but continued to the dead bear.
    After taking in some deep breaths, moaning them out and wiping away some tears, Tyler sat up, forced himself to his feet and hobbled over to Mother and the others. Clutching his lower back as if he'd aged eighty years with the drop.
    Moses was still huffy, mumbling something in that awful chatter like they do. Talk about something that will give you the chills. Tyler shook away his initial reaction. He edged to Mother and clung to her leg. To his surprise, she lacked emotion. With the way Moses and the kids were acting, he figured Mother would be upset as well, but she was rather stoic, almost as if she was in deep thought. Her eyes narrowed, she sank atop her calves, then moved to all fours, eying the bear, poking at it with those painful stubby fingers of hers. She leaned in close and sniffed the bear's head, then poked at its mouth. Not satisfied, she took both hands this time and placed them on either side of its jaws and like opening a book, she pried them open. She gasped when she did. Moses stopped and glared at her as if knowing the sound and its implications. She reached with her lunch box sized hand into the back of the bears mouth, took hold of something, then retrieved her hand. What was it?
    Tyler tried to move around to her right a little bit to see it. Andy barked and dropped to all fours, Jenny made some odd click sounds, he'd yet to hear. Moses stepped closer then lowered to the earth next to Mother, his eyes wide, his breath heavy.
    What is it? Tyler's view now blocked by an

Omah

assortment of hairy bodies. He finally brushed through between Andy and Moses as if he were passing through a clothing rack of fur coats. Now in plain sight was Mother's hand holding and twirling a large feather, just like the one she'd found stuck to the tree earlier.

67

Having spoken with Bev, Kosumi, and Brenda via the black Motorola walkie talkies Curtis Whetstone had brought along with him, Randy did his best to ease Bev's worry. Something he'd yet to learn how to fully do even after a combined twenty years of marriage and courtship. If she had one flaw, it was the fact that she was a professional worry wart. In which case she could just as quickly point out Randy's OCD and label him a control freak. Not that he controlled her in anyway, just that he did his best to control everything else.

When Randy was at his worse was when things seemed out of his control, when Bev was at her worse was when things seemed worse than they sometimes were. She had a habit of cranking up her worry, like turning the speed dial on a treadmill, sure it gave her something to do, but it never took her anywhere. Randy did his best to soothe her over the static crackle and hiss of the Motorola, wishing he could reach through it and hold her in his arms. His words would have to do for now. Through tears and sniffles, they did their best to keep it together.

Randy promised her he was all right and once again promised to bring Tyler home. He was determined, she had to give him that much.

Omah

They finished and gave Adam and Brenda a turn.

Randy settled back into his sleeping bag, head and upper back propped up by his backpack. His chest still ached as each breath felt like it came from bruised lungs. That was a big bear and how he still has his life and arm, he couldn't say. Orange and yellow danced in his eyes as he stared at the crackling flame in a daze. His mind all over the place, bolting from one thing to another with rapid succession. First, Adam's warning at the store, then the creepy filling at the hallowed-out Redwood the day they got their picture taken...one day before Tyler's disappearance. The old man at the check-in cabin. Then the howl he and Bev heard that night from high on the mountain, the next day when Tyler vanished...the footprints jutting across the river. The thing that rushed passed them after it attacked and terrorized Al and the hunters. That chatter they heard the first night they set out on the hunt. Jimmy telling of his encounter. Al's body at the morgue. What the heck is this thing? Are the woods haunted? Is it ghost or something? Indian burial grounds? The bear has to be the one doing the physical attacks right? But what's with everything else?

A faint voice calling his name.

Randy? Randy?

"Huh? What?" Randy answered wagging his head and searching for the source. Across the flame from him at his ten o'clock sat Jack with a slight grin and a moving mouth.

"I'm sorry. What?"

"I was asking how your arm was holding up? Can you tell the wrap and tea are working?'

"Oh...yeah, it still hurts, but whatever y'all did seems to be working. How deep did she get me?"

Adam clutched the Motorola to his ear and moved a few feet to get a better grasp on what Brenda was saying.

Jack leaned close and said, "I'd say maybe an eighth of an inch. Not too bad, but enough to hurt like a devil."

Randy nodded while looking to his arm rested atop his abdomen.

"Your lucky man," said Curtis from Randy's right as he poked at the fire, "They could be hauling you out in a body bag right now. The Creator was watching over you, that's for sure."

"I don't know...I don't think He was or I wouldn't have gotten attacked. Wasn't the Eagle supposed to bring us good luck or something?"

"If the Creator wasn't with you, you'd be dead right now. And not luck...favor. And yes, the Eagle confirmed the Great Spirit's favor upon our journey. In case you forgot, we all just survived encountering a mother Grizzly. If you can't see the divine with that...well...I'm afraid you may need new sight my friend."

With raised brows and twisted lips, Randy craned his head as he continued to glare at his bandaged arm.

"The Creator is with us, something good will come out of all this. You'll see...just trust Him Randy," said Jack.

Adam finished his static filled conversation with Brenda and was now making his way back to the flame.

Jack looked to his brother and asked, "How'd she take it?"

Adam bobbed his head, "Well...not too bad I don't guess. She's worried a bit, but she and grandpa have sought the Creator for His blessing and asked for His protection over us. You know Brenda, she's a strong woman."

Jack nodded.

"You're lucky to have her man," said Curtis.

Adam dipped his head, "Well, thank you."

"So is your real names Adam and Jack or are they short for something?"

"Adahy. Kajika," Adam said patting his chest and pointing a thumb to his brother, "My name means 'Lives in the woods.' And his means, 'Walks without sound.' We just started calling each other Adam and Jack to make it easier."

Curtis and Randy nodded slowly.

"So, tell me something I don't know about the Yurok Tribe. Give me something else to think about for a bit," said Randy with a slight wince as he readjusted, being careful with his arm.

"Oh boy, where do I start?" Adam snickered, "Well, our tribe has lived on the south end of the Klamath River since the early fourteenth century. We've thrived by being close to three main ecosystems. The river, ocean, and the forest. With the Klamath River, we had plenty of Salmon and Trout and with the proximity to the Pacific, we had plenty of clams and rockfish. And of course, we hunted elk and deer along with taking only what we needed from the forest, such as the Chanterelle that you ate earlier," Adam said looking to Randy.

"Us Yurok are strong believers in sustainability, so we never take more than we need, and we make use of everything we take, being sure nothing goes to waste. The Dentalia Shell, which could pass for the rib bones of a small varmint, comes from a mollusk shell. It served as our main source of currency back in the day. We would use the giant Redwoods for timber to build our plank houses and any other structures we might need."

Adam drew a breath.

Jack nodded and added, "We always respect the Giants though, they are the guardians of our sacred places. They protect us from evil spirits and curses, while the hairy men protect us and our environment from physical harm," Jack said as he looked up a towering Redwood some twenty yards from the campfire.

"Yeah, everything was going well until around 1849, when the white man moved in. We first had productive trades and commerce with them, but once they found gold in the mountains...it was a whole other story.

"More and more people began invading our land. They treated us harshly. By the early 1850's we had lost 75% of our members due to mass murders by the gold rushers and diseases they brought with them. Other tribes in the area lost 95% of their people to the same things.

"Then in 1855, the Red Cap Indians began a revolt against the settlers, in what would eventually cause a war between the two. The Red Cap's had almost driven out the miners when the government stepped in and took control of the upper Yurok reservation. We were outnumbered and out gunned. We were forced to surrender to avoid losing more of our population as it had dwindled to only a few hundred members.

"The government set strict rules and such over us to try and squeeze us out, but no matter how hard they tried and how harshly they treated us, we persevered. You fast forward to today and we are strong as ever with around 5,000 members," Adam said with a half-smile.

"Wow, y'all really know your history don't you?" Randy said.

"Yeah, we sure do. Our parents and elders always made sure we knew our background, it's something they've instilled in us since we were young," said Jack as Adam nodded

"Do you have your Pau-Waus during the fall and spring harvest? Because some people back home say y'all do it different than us," said Curtis.

"No, we have ours during fall and spring. Usually, the first weekend of November and first weekend of April."

"Okay, well I'll have to tell that to my Cherokee folks back east."

"So, how do you say hello in Yurok?" Randy asked.

"Aiy-yu-kwee," Adam said with a big grin.

"A-u-key."

Adam looked to Jack as they both chuckled.

"Yeah, close enough, we'll figure it out."

Randy bobbed his head with a grin.

A beat.

"I tell ya...I don't mean no disrespect...but I'm just having a hard time believing in the hairy men. I'm torn to be honest. Half of me wants to believe, simply because I can't otherwise explain everything I've witness these past few days. But the other half of me, says there's no way something like that could live out there. If it did, how come we haven't already found one alive? Or found a body for that matter?"

Another beat.

"Randy...have you ever seen the wind?" asked Adam.

Randy craned his head like a dog when it hears an unfamiliar sound.

"Well...I mean...no. But I guess I've seen its effects if that's what you're asking."

"Exactly. You've never actually seen the wind. Yet you know it's there, because you see, feel, and hear its presence or effects. Correct?"

Randy bobbed.

"So, just as it takes faith to believe in the wind, though you've never actually seen it physically, so to speak, yet you know it's real, so does it take Faith to believe in the hairy men. The same can be said for our Creator as well. We may not see Him physically, but that doesn't mean He isn't real.

Because if you look hard enough, you will see the effects of His presence all around you. Just take a look at how beautiful creation is. Breathe in the fresh air wafting down from the jagged peaks of the majestic mountains, listen to the sounds of nature, smell the fresh earthy aroma after a good rain. That's the effects of our Creators presence. It takes faith my friend, but if you allow your spirit to embrace what's around you...you realize it doesn't require a lot of faith to see what I'm talking about. I'm telling you now...the hairy men are real...and so is the Creator."

"Whew. That's some Native wisdom right there man," said Curtis with a soft whistle as he wagged his head.

Randy allowed his gaze to linger skyward passed the pine limbs towards the heavens. The snow clouds were easing their way northeastward, revealing a jet-black sky filled with a million burning lights, the moon about half its size, burned with a radiant glow.

Randy breathed deep and lowered his eye lids.

"He counts the stars and knows the each by name," a faint voice echoed in the far corners of Randy's mind. A voice he'd heard speak those words more than once when he just a youngster and a voice he'd do anything to hear once more. He loved his grandpa Herman and he loved sitting out on his and grandma's porch, star gazing as grandpa pointed out the Milky Way, Orion, the dippers and if they were lucky, perhaps the tropic of Cancer.

Randy could hear his soft, yet raspy voice as he said to Randy and his cousins, "And He knows the number of hairs on your head. Your Heavenly Father up there, knows everything there is to know about ya and He loves you more than anyone on earth. He's your father and you are his children. Just the very thought of you brings a smile to His face. He loves you kids...never forget that, you hear me now...He loves you."

Randy sighed and wiped a tear trickling down his cheek with a cold knuckle. He swallowed hard and said under his breath, "God...please watch over my boy and please help us find him."

A log shifted in the flame, sending embers skyward. Rising. Rising. Now at the tops of the pines, Randy and the men like ants around the glowing flame below. An owl cries in the distance. The orange embers dance their way to the heavens, going this way and that. High above the pines and Giant's of the forest, a fog lingers,
the embers pass through it, almost burning out from its coldness, yet they press on and continue their journey skyward, before finally disappearing into the star lit night.

A red colored star blinked out and fell to earth, as it did so, a soft rumble of thunder from a snow cloud emitted.

68

Birds sang, crickets chirped, cicadas screeched, squirrels barked, and the wind howled. But it all sounded so distant. As if he were at the bottom of a glass bottle while the sounds rolled across the opening with someone's breath.

The air was damp and chilled, but much warmer than before. A loud, raspy breath reminded him of when he and Andrew used a baseball card to get the flap effect on their bike as it swatted against the spokes. Brought to that place between dream and reality, Tyler wasn't sure which state he was in. Visually he was in his neighborhood running alongside Andrew on the bike as they laughed at their new amusement, but audibly, he felt he was in the presence of a sleeping Sasquatch. Something cold, prickly and wet, soaking through his pants, caused the vision of his brother to slowly fade like a dissipating fog.

His sight turned to a sudden sea of black and red. The chatter from the creatures of the earth grew louder, as did the clogged windpipes of the raspy breather. It had to be Moses.

Tyler opened one eye lid at a time, hoping against hope he was dreaming and would awake in his bed back home or in the rocking chair next to his Mama.

Omah

It was dark. Darker than dark. A constant drip echoed and raked at his psyche. The sounds were so different. Was something wrong with his hearing? Why did everything sound so weird? Distant. Hollow. Echoey. Weird.

He raised up, sitting on his haunches, hands beside him. Something pricked his hands. It could have been a porcupine.

Ow!

He jerked a hand to his mouth and sucked on a finger that felt like it'd just been checked for his sugar. Something he'd seen his grandma do more than once.

He felt with his other hand, groping about, careful and slow as if feeling for a soft rabbit among a pit of vipers.

It was needles. Damp needles. Pine needles. He snaked his hand through the brush and stopped when he hit something solid. It felt like rock.

The drip, plooping, plopping, pinging in a puddle somewhere.

The critters still gossiping, the wind still howling at the moon, or sun. Whether it was daylight or dark, he couldn't tell. Heck, he couldn't even tell if his eyes were open or not.

But the cold slab of rock and the constant drip, suggested his worst fear. A cave?

Please no. Anywhere but a dark cave filled with Sasquatches. The raspy breath fluttered again.

Had he been taken from Mother and Moses? Was this the den of the one Mother fought off that time?

His heart thumped hard, so hard he could hear and feel its cry, causing him to grasp his chest to ease the pain. A thick thump forming in his throat. He swallowed hard. He felt his fingers begin to tremble. Tears stung his eyes.

"Mama? Mama?" he mumbled with quivering lips.

Remembering how they'd slept in that den and Moses covered the opening with the branches, Tyler twisted his head in quick jolts, searching for any glimmer of light.

What if the raspy breather was a bad one like the one that came into their den? Could Sasquatches see in the dark? Is that why they liked it in places like this? Were they like a cat? What if the bad one was looking at him right now? He'd never know it.

His heart knocked harder, like how the police knock on those crime shows his dad watches. He felt his own breath quicken. His throat tightened.

Wait…what was that? Is that light? Yeah…look there's a ray of light. Like a flashlight peering into the dark. His heart eased its knocking, but only for a moment. The feeling of cold leathery and hairy fingers grasping at his arm, caused his heart to leap from his chest and bolt for the light. It was like getting struck by lightning. A jolt of energy passed through him so quick, his bowels couldn't withstand such force. A warm sensation covered his inner thighs. It stung when he tried to stop.

His breath now in a pant like a sun baked dog, his whimpers were silenced by a familiar clicking sound, followed by two grunts.

He relaxed a bit, though still on edge, it was more than unnerving being in total darkness with something big, hairy, and capable eating your head in one bite.

The gentle strokes moved from his arm to his cheek. The grunts seized, but the clicks continued and so did the raspy breather, which must've been Moses as he first expected.

Though his sight failed him, he knew by the touch and voice…it was Mother. He just knew. He didn't need to see her…he could feel her.

Omah

Those cold fingers pulled him close, bringing him into her bosom. Her fur so warm, erasing any chill that may have tried to tingle his spine and crawl along his flesh. She entered that purr he'd heard her make one time before. He could feel it vibrate within his chest.
She held him tight and began a slow rock, back and forth, back and forth.

The warm embrace and cat like purr, soothed him back to his neighborhood, playing with Andrew.

THE SMELL OF SMOKE, the sizzle of a dying flame, and the clanking of pots were only side notes compared to the vast symphony of natures own composers. The wind controlled the violins, rustling leaves the snare drum, rummaging fowls the choir, and the lone squirrel that seemed to have a voice equal to a dozen, acted as the lead vocalist.

Randy awoke and was welcomed with a creak in his neck. Not to mention the ache and burning he felt with his arm. His chest still felt like it may have been ran over by a steam roller.

He scooted up, using his one good hand, keeping his right tucked tight to his navel. He winced as he did so.

Adam was busy rolling up his sleeping bag, as Jack gathered the pots and cooking utensils, with Curtis taking care of the fire, being sure no embers were left to cause destruction.

The sun was beginning to rise. From what Randy could see through the limbs, the sky seemed clearer than days past and the air wasn't as chill either. Snow dripped from the trees and was slow to dissolve among the earth, but with clear skies and a warm sun, it'd soon be gone. They'd likely gotten two, maybe three inches with the storm, thank goodness it wasn't any worse.

RANDALL LANE

Now on the third day of Tyler's disappearance, Randy was determined this would be the day to end it. One way or another, he wasn't coming out of the woods till he had Tyler in his arms. They just couldn't risk leaving him to survive another day. The three-minute rule playing through his mind on repeat since he fell asleep the night before: Three minutes without
oxygen, three days without water, three weeks without food.

Today would be the day. It had to be.

"How you feeling?" asked Jack.

Randy nodded and said with a grunt, "I'm all right. Sore, but I'm good. How about you?"

"Sore, but I'll live. Just thankful it wasn't any worse."

"We need to get you a new bandage before we head out," Adam said finishing the roll of his bag and strapping the strings around it.

"Man, I'm sure glad that storm moved along," said Curtis.

Randy nodded with wide eyes, "Me too."

Using his left hand, he unzipped from his cocoon and crawled out. He pushed himself up with a grimace. Adam tried to reach him in time to help, but Randy was already to his feet. Wobbly, but stable. A fire scattered through his ankle. All the walking he'd done the past few days had sure taken its toll. The pain would ebb once they set out in search of his son. Adrenaline and anxiety is a good pain reliever when needed.

Randy hobbled a step or two to his right, easing his weight on the ankle, testing the waters to see how bad it'd bark when it met the earth.

He winced. Rough, but manageable. To steal Jack's words, "Sore, but he'd live."

Omah

He bent and grabbed his sleeping bag and rose to roll it up. Keeping it tight to him with his mauled arm and wrapping the bag like a fruit roll up with his good one.

It's brighter now and when he glanced to the rising sun, he noticed for the first time, a jagged set of snowcapped mountains in the distance. Such a beautiful sight. What he'd do to have Bev and *all* the kids here to see it with him.

Randy tightened his lips and eyes, sighed and wagged his head.

"Nice view isn't it? Grasshopper peak," said Adam, "Because people like us look like grasshoppers from up there?"

"Or people like us are like grasshoppers compared to those that live up there," said Curtis with a grin.

Jack cut his eyes to him.

A beat.

"How about we get you a new bandage, huh?" asked Adam.

Jack and Curtis finished cleaning the campsite while Randy and Adam sat next to one another by the smoldering embers. Adam toted his backpack and retrieved from it, a purple, black, and blue seashell and a bag of herbs.

"What's that?"

"This is an Abalone shell I'll use to grind the herbs in. Its beautiful colors remind us of the creativity of our Creator. This here is tobacco, sage, clove, and rosemary. I'll grind it into a paste then rub it over the wounds and wrap it."

Randy watched as he grinded the herbs with a smooth river stone.

He finished and was now ready to remove the old bandage. Adam was careful and removed it at a pace that was sure to cause the least amount of pain.

But there wasn't much he could do once he got to the last of it. It was stuck to Randy's arm and hair and would take a quick yank to separate it. Adam raised his eyes and looked to Randy.

"This might hurt just a bit, but I'll—"

He didn't finish. He snapped his hand back, yanking the wrap off.

Randy griped through clinched teeth.

"What the heck was that about?" he growled.

"Like a band aid, its best to do it quick."

For the first time, Randy saw his wounds. Looked like he'd been attacked by a jagged hole puncher. He had about half a dozen teeth marks, the biggest the diameter of a dime, that left gaping holes packed with yesterday's paste.

Randy gulped, "You think it'll heal quick with all of that?"

Adam nodded and applied more paste, before wrapping it with gauze.

"We're about half a mile to Bull Creek and another two miles to the National Forest, I say we fill our canteens down there by the river before getting started," said Jack as he and Curtis now stood next to Adam with loaded back packs. Jack gripping the rifle strap with a thumb and forefinger. Curtis scratched his black chin strap of a beard that ran into a goatee.

"Sounds good," Adam finished and gave Randy a few pats on the leg. He helped him to his feet. Adam checked the cylinder on his revolver, after yesterday's shots, he had enough for two more reloads.

With that, they headed for the river.

The orchestra of forest critters seemed to dim, must be taking a break. The forest fell silent. Other than the men's own footsteps and the howling wind, which if heard at the

Omah

right angle, may have passed for the wailing woman, it was quiet.

    Eerily quiet.

69

Noticing the silence among them, Adam stopped to listen, the others halting behind him. They were only a few paces from the top of a ridge that would look over the river below. They would have to take their time going down it, it could be quite steep in some places, and rocky in others.

The men were motionless like statues, listening to the dead and snow melting forest. Other than the wind whispering in the trees, there wasn't much chatter among them. Something had the critters in a hush and Randy didn't like it when even the birds and squirrels got quiet. He scanned the woods, glancing up the trees, around the trees, behind the trees, trees, trees, trees.

The bark and screech of a squirrel was enough to give them each a start. They yanked their heads above them to see the fury thing snapping its tail like a whip. With that the rest of the forest came back to life. A woodpecker in the distance returned to its search for a grub, as other birds returned to their giddy chatter.

Randy lowered his head, breathed deep and took a step forward. Adam was still standing in place, now wearing a slight grin with his eyes shut and angled to the heavens, black hair hanging off the back of his shoulders.

"What is it?" Randy asked.

Adam didn't open an eye or move his head, but said in a soft tone, "They're near."

Randy looked to Jack and Curtis who both nodded with blank faces. He turned back to Adam and asked in a whisper, "What do we do?"

"I say we continue to make our way to the river. Just keep your head on a swivel and be quiet."

Randy bobbed his head as Adam moved with caution toward the ridge. The sound of the river grew with each step.

Careful not to snap too many twigs, and pushing away the pine branches and fern leaves, they reached the ridge.

Beyond the branches, was the river. It was big, more like a creek than anything, but it did have the same blueish green tint that the South Fork Eel had where Tyler disappeared.

"Does the South Fork run into this?" Randy whispered.

Adam nodded and said low enough, that Randy had to lean close. "Kind of. Yeah this is a run off creek that feeds into the ocean. We call it Salmon Run, because it's the Salmon's road to get back and forth from the river to the Pacific. The South Fork continues north for about 37 miles towards Loleta before cutting west to drain into the sea. So, down this way, Salmon Run branches west and actually joins Bull Creek at one point before emptying into the ocean."

Randy nodded. He took in the view, careful to store it in his memory. The rushing water below, a rocky river bank, jagged mountains capped with frosted tops, surrounded by forest and nature. If not for having to peak through the branches directly in front of him, this could have made for a nice postcard.

"All right...watch your step and take your time going down," said Adam.

Easing each foot softly into the soil, grasping onto roots and small trees, the men make their way to the bottom. The rush of the river now a constant roar. It wasn't big, but it was fast.

Randy breathing through his mouth, doing his best to ignore the pain in his arm, chest, and ankle. They continue their stealth like moves and pass through a small thicket at the bottom of the ravine. Protruding out the other side like a ship through a patch of fog, the river and mountains now in full view.

Jack retrieved his canteen and marched to the waters edge, about twenty yards away. Adam and Curtis followed. Randy was too awestruck at the moment. The view was like something out of a movie. He wanted to be sure to take it in.

The sun rising over Grasshopper Peak, its warm rays shining from his feet to his knees. A cool breeze caressed his face. The sound of the rushing water, a soft, tranquil tone. He shut his eyes and took one last deep breath before allowing the moment to pass. He opened his eyes, there was Adam, Jack, and Curtis by the river, squatted upon their calves which a canteen dipped into the water.

But it was the object in his peripheral to the left that felt out of place. He couldn't remember seeing something that big before. He craned his head around in a slow sweeping motion. Who is that? Someone else is down here. A tourist maybe? No. No.

His heart dropped to the earth, his lungs failed to muster another breath, his skin crawled at such a sight.

His lips and hands began to tremble. He couldn't move. It was like those times he'd experienced sleep paralysis. Inside, he wanted so bad to scream and alert the others, but it was as if his brain had short circuited and forgotten how to function.

Omah

    This creature stood head and shoulders above any man he'd ever met, its gray hair was thick and matted and twitched like a bull shrugging off a fly. It was full of muscle, built like a Gorilla, but standing on two legs. Its long arms dangled down past its knees. A long gray beard hung past its barrel like chest. The eyes were blacker than night and seemed as big as a baseball and sunken deep into its boney face. The eyes were locked on him with such an intense glare, it was as if it were looking into his soul to discern his motives. His heart palpitated even faster than before, banging against his ribcage, begging for mercy.
    His mind a fog thicker than what they saw in San Francisco that morning, thoughts just wouldn't form. It was as if seconds turned to minutes and minutes into hours. He kept his head on the animal, only cutting his eyes toward the river, hoping against all hope, they saw this thing too.
    As he did so, he heard the thing grunt. He shot his eyes back to it, its head now turned to the men.
    Randy swallowed and heard a faint voice, "Randy..." it was Adam. He saw it too, he could tell by the tone.
    "...don't move. Stay calm."
    The hair and muscles on the thing still twitching. By god it was massive. Must've weighed six hundred pounds easily, maybe more. The thing's snake like lips pulled tight, revealing its square yellow teeth. It hissed like a cat ready to strike, but barely opened its mouth. Randy heard and felt movement from the river. Adam and the others were coming to him. The thing watched them with a searing glare.
    Clack-Clack-Clack!
    Randy cut his eyes to the left, up the hill. Sounded like two rocks clacking together. The creature never moved, keeping its attention focused on the soon to be prey.

Clack-Clack-Clack!

The creature, still starring at Adam, Jack, and Curtis, tilted its head back at a slight angle before letting out two grunt like whoops.

It lowered its head, its eyes moving within its skull like a haunted picture. The eyes moving closer to Randy now. Footsteps crunching over pebbles and twigs stopped just to his right.

"Stay calm and do exactly as I say," Adam whispered as he, Jack, and Curtis were now next to Randy.

The sound of scraping bark came from the place the rocks clacked. It sounded like something with claws scurrying down a tree. Two loud thuds followed it. Then came a gentle rustle through the brush, that could have easily passed for deer.

The men and creature stood motionless in an eerie stare down. Randy's thoughts now cleared from the fog, he wondered if Tyler may be with whatever was coming through the thicket. They couldn't have been that far from them when they came down the hill, if he was here, why didn't Tyler yell for them?

That's when he heard it. The sound of a muffled cry. For heaven's sake! It was true! They had his boy!

Randy lurched forward toward the sounds of clambering feet and obstructed whimpers, only to be grasped around his right arm, just above the wounds. He winced and snapped his head around. Adam shook his head and said quietly, "Not yet."

The creature grunted again. The woods wouldn't conceal the others much longer as they edged closer to its boundary.

Randy grinded his teeth and jerked away, taking a step closer. The gray beast, dropped to all fours, its long muscular arms propping it up, it thrust its head back, sucking in an atmosphere worth of air, then came back down with such a roar, you'd have thought a nuclear plant just erupted. Randy's heart knocked hard enough to send a sharp dagger to his head that may have been an aneurism. His whole body vibrated from the ordeal, as the creatures blast continued, deep and raspy, until it began to pierce the men's ears, forcing them to squint their eyes and close their ear flaps.

When it finally finished and the men were able to open their eyes again and remove the fingers from their ears, the creature was low to the earth, craning its head at them with an eerie angle. But now, it was joined by four others.

Two little ones clung tight to a big one which was obviously a female. These were a dark reddish color, much different looking than the gray colored male. The female held what looked like a baby under its burly arm, gripping it like a football with the other hand tight to its mouth.

Randy must've blinked a hundred times after wiping his face. His lips moved, but the words just didn't want to form, "Ty-Ty-Tyler-Tyler...Tyler!" Without realizing it, he found himself in mid stride, before once again being tugged back by a firm hand.

Randy stopped, his heart pounding, his breath escaping faster than he could gather it.

Tyler's eyes were glazed and locked directly on his. He was dirty and scared, but he was alive!

"Randy...we have to be smart and think this through. You've trusted me this far...I need you to trust me again."

Randy nodded absently, his eyes filled with tears and focused on his son.

"Tyler...it's okay buddy...we're going to get you home," Randy wiped his cheeks.

"Put the rifle down. Put it down slow," Adam said out the corner of his mouth toward his brother who was a few paces over his right shoulder.

Adam eased his hand to his hip and unsnapped the holster containing the weapon responsible for taking the life of the Grizzly.

The two bigger creatures furrowed their brows and emitted a low grumble, their muscles tensing and twitching. The female stopped her grumble and did two loud clicks that could have passed for two finger snaps.

Randy heard the sound of the rifle planting to the dirt and saw out the corner of his eye, Adam lowering to the ground with his revolver. While down there, he carefully rummaged through his backpack, the creatures eyeing, looking like they could twist the men's necks like Al Frankford any second. Adam crinkled some wrappers and stood with a granola bar, a baggy of Chanterelles and...an Eagle feather.

The beasts were taken back by the sight. As even the smaller ones gasped and began to sound like two chimps. The big gray male, stood to its feet, reminding the men just how big it really was. It and the female leaned their heads toward the men and sniffed with their flat nostrils that looked like a man's leather wallet spread open with two big holes in it. They craned their heads, sniffing and huffing, but their eyes seemed to be locked on the feather in Adam's right hand.

Adam placed the granola bar to the ground and emptied out the bag of Chanterelles next to it, took the feather and waved it above them, then with his eyes locked on the female's, lowered the feather atop the mushroom and bar.

Adam stood to his feet and took a step back with an arm stretched across Randy.

"We need hair," Adam whispered.

Right.

"Tyler...we need you to get some hair buddy. Can you do that for us?" Randy said with his head tilted downward for effect.

Tyler looked to have gulped, then gently nodded his head.

Randy and Adam now standing just in front of Jack and Curtis. The big male took two quick strides forward, its arms swinging by its side, its gait hunched at the back, the creature was just another step from the goods. The female took a step forward as the younger ones moved with it.

Adam gave a grunt of his own.

The creature stopped and looked at him as if he'd just insulted his mother.

Adam raised his hand and pointed to Tyler, then returned his finger and pointed it to his chest.

70

Moses looked to Mother then back to Adam, his lips stretched tight, his teeth clinched, he snarled his nose and gave Adam a death stare.

Mother huffed, then lowered Tyler to the ground, dropping him feet first this time. Of course, she'd learn how to by now. Without her rubbery fingers across his mouth, he belted out, "Daddy-Daddy-Daddy!" and took a step forward but was quickly snatched by Mother.

Now firm to her leg, Tyler whimpered and looked to Randy, eyes and cheeks glistening.

"Tyler...hang on buddy. Stay calm, we're going to get you, just hang on. Okay?"

Tyler wiped a cheek and nodded.

"Hair...remember? We need hair."

Tyler gulped and looked to his hand gripped to Mother's tree stump of a leg.

Adam grunted once again and pointed to Tyler then to himself.

Moses looked to the goods, then to Mother and Tyler. Mother with squinted eyes did the same. Then they looked to each other and began their hair-raising chatter that could have passed for two demon possessed Japanese soldiers conducting an interrogation. Mother finished it with two clicks. Then she nudged Tyler forward, causing him to stumble a few feet. He gained his footing, looked to Randy, his heart pounding, his throat tightening, he turned and looked to Mother. As intimidating as she was trying to appear, he could see the tenderness in her eyes, he could have sworn he saw a tear tumble down her cheek. He looked back to Randy then snapped his head back to Mother and without giving it another thought bolted to her.

"Tyler! No! What are y—"

Randy's words were cut short at the sound of a deep grunt as Tyler crashed into her, attempting to wrap his arms around her leg, though he could only reach half of the way around. Much like the way he tried to hug that Redwood tree a few days ago.

Tyler squeezed, then looked up at her. With tears staining her eyes, her lip quivered as a low barely audible purr emitted deep within her. She raised her big hand and brushed his cheek with the back of her knuckles, drying some tears in the process. She clicked and pointed with her chin towards Randy and the men.

Tyler swallowed hard and nodded, "Thank you."

He lowered his gaze to Andy and Jenny. They each looked at him with those big wild eyes, their mouths forming O shapes and uttering O sounds.

Tyler smiled, then gave two soft grunts of his own. They each looked to Mother and clicked, she quieted them with clicks of her own.

Tyler took a step back, breathing deep, then spun on his heels towards his daddy.

Moses was squatted on his calves and groping at the granola bar and mushrooms. Tyler passed him, smiled and grunted, dabbing his face with the sleeve of his hoodie.

Moses picked up the feather, twirled it in his hand, craned his head toward Tyler and snapped it upward in two quick arcs while clicking his tongue.
    Only a few more feet to Randy. In the clear, Tyler turned his attention to his daddy and made a bolt for it. Crashing into his arms, Randy locked him in and vowed to never let go. Picking him up, his hand over Tyler's head, his cheek flush against the side of his head. Randy could barely speak, the lump in his throat was just too big.
    "My God! I love you buddy! I'm so sor—" was all Randy could get out before his voice left him. Gripping Tyler in his arms, he pulled back and kissed the crown of his head. Tyler snorted through stuffed nostrils, a soft grin crossed his lips, his hand raised to eye level. In it...was a clump of hair.
    Randy smiled, then pulled him back into a good squeeze.
    The clicking sound could have passed for the creatures, but Randy knew better. His heart skipped a beat, his eyes flashed wide, his pupils dilating, he knew that sound and he knew it wasn't the creatures.
    It was someone chambering a round in a rifle.

Omah

71

"Don't any of you even think of moving. You're going to stay right there, unless I say otherwise. Ya hear?" it was a deep, gravelly voice, a bit shaky, but one Randy knew instantly.

It came from behind and just inside the wood line, close enough to hear the clatter of the rife over the sound of the rushing water.

A rustle in the brush. There were more than one.

Moses bolted once again from his squat, standing to his feet and squaring his shoulders. His gray beard swinging past his chest, burly arms ready to rip a head from its neck. Mother hissed, her lips tight to her gums and with protruding teeth she stepped backward, her arms in front of Andy and Jenny.

"Well my word, you engines weren't lying were ya? So, this is what's responsible for taking all those lives over the years? Filthy savages," his last words were cold and emitted from clinched teeth. "I'm afraid I don't have cuffs big enough for your friends...but I do have bullets that might fit."

Randy looked over his shoulder to see Sheriff Logan, Deputy Anderson and three other officers he'd yet to properly meet. They each had rifles but Logan, he'd chose a Magnum .357, which suited him well. With weapons aimed to the chest of Moses, Mother, and the kids, Randy dropped Tyler next to him and bolted forward. He spun in the dirt, his back to Moses and the others, with outstretched arms, he wagged his head with narrow eyes.

"You'll have to take me with them. You don't want a murder charge, do you?"

"Randy! What are you doing?" belted Adam as he took hold of Tyler's arm.

Moses craned his head to him and gave a soft grunt.

Randy backed up closer to Mother and the kids, Moses moving with them, eyeing him curiously.

"For heaven's sake Randy...have you lost your mind. The hell you thinking? You're protecting murderers for crying out loud! Besides...you know the kind of money you could get for these things?" Logan growled.

Tyler looked to Adam standing next to him, then looked to his dad. Tyler yanked from Adam's grip and bolted to Randy, crashing into his waist in front of Mother and the others.

"Randy...this is ridiculous. Getoutdaway!" Logan waving his hand as he hissed through gritted teeth.

Randy wagged his head in slow defiant waves, his hands now resting on Tyler's shoulders.

A beat.

"All right then. Suit yourself. Take aim fellas."

Logan raised his revolver, the others gave it some thought, but did the same.

"Headshots. Go for the softest part. The triangle between the nose and eyes."

Randy's jaw firm, his breath pulsing, his heart pounding, "God protect us," he uttered in a faint whisper as he heard Logan cock back the hammer.

OMAH

72

"Hold it right there!" the voice and sight of movement came in a simultaneous flash. Stepping out of the wood line was a man dressed in dark green slacks, a thick black jacket and a black beanie with a gold signet on it, Warden Phillips. His rifle trained to Logan's back.

"You kill those animals...and I'll book you all for poaching a newly discovered species which is likely endangered. Not to mention the fact you did while shooting past a man and his young son. You wouldn't want that on your records, now would you?"

Silence.

"He's right Sheriff. We best be smart about this," said Deputy Anderson as he lowered his rifle.

Logan didn't say a word, he just stood there steaming.

Phillips took a breath for the first time in what seemed like ten minutes since having watched this whole ordeal form the cover of the woods.

He lowered his rifle with his exhaling lungs, he entered a sigh and was attempting to scratch the back of his head, when at the top of his eye, he saw Logan rotating in place, revolver rising upward. It all seemed to move in slow motion. Before Phillips could recover and take aim, a flash of fire exploded from Logan's barrel, followed by the deafening blast.

He clinched his gut and crumbled to the ground.

Logan standing there with a wry smirk, satisfied the warden was finished, jolted around and aimed back at Randy and the creatures.

Randy's eyes wide, he crouched down and covered Tyler.

Boom!

Randy flinched.

Silence.

He peered out a squinted eye.

Logan's eyes were wide and distant, his breath gone, he lowered his gaze to his chest, blood ooze out of his mouth. He crashed face first into the dirt.

Standing behind him, gripping his rifle...Deputy Anderson.

Anderson cursed. "Why Sheriff? Why?"

Adam and Jack rushed to Phillips, writhing in the dirt, holding his gut.

Adam popped the buttons and yanked the zipper loose on Phillips' jacket. His green pressed shirt now wearing a growing red stain on his lower right side.

"Aggghhh!" Phillips growled through gritted teeth, his face flushing, his veins protruding along his neck.

"Hang on...you're all right. You're going to be fine," Adam said as he and Jack began packing the wound with dirt, doing their best to stop the bleeding.

Anderson stood over Logan's lifeless body, wagging his head. Officer Mack Duggar got on his walkie talkie and made a 10-24 call to the station as he and the dispatcher went back and forth over the crackling radio.

"Hey...what's going on down there?" a voice came from up the hill. Sounded like officer Breeden.

Omah

Randy scanned the hill and spotted him, officer Ortiz and Lindbergh standing at the edge of the ridge peering down.

Anderson waved them down.

Here comes Curtis Whetstone with a half grin, "You believe us now?"

Randy blinked, then turned to look over his shoulder at the creatures. All he saw was the river meandering its way through the mountains.

They were gone.

73

After making their way out of the woods, toting the injured Warden Phillips, Randy, Tyler, Adam, Jack, Curtis, Officer Ortiz and Lindbergh were met with an array of news reporters as the RV park had never seen so much traffic. News vans, police cruisers, ambulances, fire trucks, the whole deal. All of Humboldt County offered whatever they could.

An ambulance rushed Phillips to the hospital where he'd be taken into emergency surgery. Luckily, with Adam and Jack's packing, he was able to maintain enough blood to save his life. He'd be sore, but he'd live.

The other men stayed back at the sight of the accident. At least that's what it'll all go down as. A tragic accident while shooting at the charging Grizzly. The truth would only cause more issues. And besides, the creatures had enough money chasers as it was, no need to add to the numbers.

After getting Phillips on the ambulance and being sure Randy and Tyler were situated with the rest of the family, along with Tyler's help, Adam, Jack, and Curtis sat out to find the bear. They couldn't let it go to waste. With the cold air and remnants of snow left on the ground, the meat should still be good and so should the hide. It could make

Omah

for a nice rug, or if possible, Adam might just have it stuffed and placed in the Legends and Tales gift shop.

After doing some back tracking, they were able to find it exactly as Tyler had told them, buried by the Omahs.

They field dressed it there, to make for an easier transportation. Adam left an Eagle feather by the burial site.

RANDY AND BEV declined to speak with the reporters, not like they'd believe the story anyhow, it'd only make matters worse, so just like countless others who've crossed path with the creatures...they kept it to themselves.

The Jacobs spent the day together...as a family. Thankful for Tyler's return and cherishing every second of each other's presence. The Lightfoot's, Kosumi and Curtis Whetstone allowed them their personal time for the day. The following day, Brenda planned for a big meal and get together over at her and Adam's place in Garberville, while Kosumi had plans for the hair Tyler had managed to take.

THE NEXT DAY with the sun setting and darkness crawling out from its crevices, the Jacobs' found themselves with full bellies from Brenda's traditional cooking, which included Buffalo stew over rice and rabbit bites. Seated around a fire in the backyard of Adam and Brenda's home, they watched as Brenda adorned herself in full Indian regalia, head dress and all. Adam played a hand carved flute made from Redwood bark, while his brother Jack played a drum made from Elk hide. He kept a steady beat as it mimicked a thumping heart.

"I am now going to perform the Nay-Dosh. It's a traditional dance, which is usually performed near the Winter Solstice in December. We do this to give thanks to the Creator for blessing us with our many food sources, our special ancestors, our sweet little children, and for His beautiful creation. As I perform this dance, let's all give thanks to our wonderful Creator," with that Brenda entered a rhythmic sway with steady thumps of her feet to the beat of the drum. She twirled as her head dress full of beads, ribbons, and feathers floated and sang along with Kosumi who begin to sing in Native Yurok.

"Heyaahhh....heyyahhhhh."

Brenda had an Eagle feather in her right hand that she waved about, her eyes watching as she did so.

She danced and moved about in a circle around the fire, doing so in a clockwise manner. The crackle of the flame, the rising embers, the jingle of Brenda's regalia, the beating drum, the flute, and Kosumi continuing with his Native singing seamed to brighten the stars above as they could only look on with a smile. A few even seemed to wink.

Nature came to life as the crickets and night bugs sang louder. Kosumi chanting louder and faster with his mix of vowel sounds, A-A-A-O-O-OHHH-E-E-A-A-Y-O-O-OM-OM-AH-AH. The drum gaining speed, Brenda twirling faster, her head and arms now angled toward the heavens, she stepped backwards then forwards, repeating the movement three times.

Then as quickly as it all began, it ended.

Silence.

Even nature seized.

Brenda breathing hard, she looked to the stars, shut her eyes and said, "Thank you Great Creator for your many blessings upon us. Thank you for your loving kindness you have showed us in bringing Tyler home to his family and for guiding and protecting his father, Adam, Jack, Curtis and the officers during their search efforts. We thank you

Omah

Grandfather for what you have done. I pray this dance has brought you great honor. Amen."

Everyone repeated her last word.

"Now...as for the hair...there's something we must do and we must do it tonight," said Kosumi looking to Randy and Bev, then to Tyler. "We will need a hollowed-out Redwood."

THE JACOBS' loaded into their Jeep Wrangler along with Curtis Whetstone, as Jack toted Kosumi, Adam, and Brenda in his Rav4. They found themselves pulling into a small gravel parking lot along Highway 101 in the Avenue of the Giants, the same pull off, Randy had taken the family to before Tyler went missing. The place they had their last pictures taken.

Climbing out of their vehicles, the night darker than dark during this moonless night, they angled for a foot beaten path leading to an abundance of Redwoods. A handful of them with open entries.

"This is it. This is where it ends," said Kosumi being helped along with the aid of his cane and Jack's steady arm.

Tyler gripped the hair between his hands, now secured in a zip lock baggy. He swallowed hard and clung tight to Bev's hand. She gave it a good squeeze, then bent down and kissed the top of his head.

Randy breathed deep and cracked his neck to both sides.

Moments later after finding a tree that suited them and getting a small fire going in the center of it, they sat around it with crossed legs. Kosumi placed a head dress made from Buffalo hide onto his head. Its mouth wide with polished white teeth, black fur and black ivory spikes sticking out the sides. Kosumi rubbed charcoal over his brown chiseled cheeks. He closed his eyes, rested his open palms upon the inner parts of his knees and looked upward. The smoke and embers rising through the tree.

Adam played a soft tune on the flute.

Kosumi swayed side to side for a solid five minutes or so.

Satisfied, he stopped his movement. Adam followed and eased to a halt with the flute, dragging out the last note.

Kosumi lowered his head and looked to Tyler. He stretched forth his hand and said, "Let me see it son."

Tyler passed him the bag of hair, then clung tightly to his Mother.

Careful while removing it, Kosumi retrieved the hair as if it were a scroll of the Ten Commandments written by Moses himself.

He sat the bag next to him, then held forth the hair in both hands, palms up, eyes closed, lips muttering a silent chant or prayer.

He took a deep breath and sighed it out. Then, a little bit at a time, he began to sprinkle the hair onto the fire. It turned orange as it caught flame and took flight with the rising embers. The smell of burnt hair filled the air.

Kosumi continued, slow and steady, keeping the sacredness of the ritual.

Again, and again, the hair caught flame, emitting its stench, and rose heavenward with its orange glow.

Diminished of the hair, Kosumi returned his palms to his knees, rolled them open, and looked once more to the heavens.

Silence.

Every critter had been silenced.

Then, in the distance, a faint scream emitted. The wailing woman belted out, "O-o-o-o-o-m-m-m-m-a-a-a-a-h-h-h-h-h!"

Omah

Four tent goers a mile north of Myers Flat seated around a campfire, went silent as they looked to one another, their faces asking the question, "What the heck was that?"

Standing at the base of Grasshopper Peak, among a sea of Redwoods, listening to the forest, their noses in the air sniffing for a scent, Mother and Moses looked to one another and began their chatter. Andy and Jenny tight to Mother's side.
 They finished.
 Moses found two rocks and clacked them together.
 They waited and waited, but the wailing woman never responded.
 Mother grunted and clicked twice. Moses dropped the stones and returned to Mother and the kids. He breathed deep, looked to the stars, then continued his gait deeper into the woods. His sights on Grasshopper Peak.
 Mother twirling an Eagle Feather in her fingers and Andy and Jenny tight to her leg, filed in behind him. Together they passed through the rows of trees, dodging punches from their boney branches.

The wailing woman had done it three times before going silent.
 The wind howled back when she'd finished, signaling the crickets, cicadas, and a lonely owl it was okay to return to their order of business.
 A wide grin crossed Kosumi's face as he opened his eyes and lowered his head.
 "It is finished."

Epilogue

The next morning, with the RV and Jeep packed and ready to hit the road, Randy was checking the tail lights on the Jeep as he called to Jennifer in the driver seat of the RV.

"All right, now do the left one...bingo!"

Randy angled around the back of the Jeep, heading up the side of the RV, when he caught glimpse of Tyler seated on the pick-nick table, elbows on his knees, chin in his hands, looking to the mountains and vast wilderness.

Randy stopped and watched his son, then raised his vision to the mountains.

"They took care of you, didn't they?" Randy asked in a slow steady tone as he walked up behind Tyler, his gaze still fixed to the forest ahead.

Tyler nodded his head, sniffled and turned to reach for his dad. His eyes strained and moist.

Randy hugged and lifted him up, Tyler wrapping his arms around the back of his neck.

Through his tears, he said, "Dad...I don't want nothing to happen to them."

"Oh son...they'll be fine. That's their home. They know what they're doing, and they know where to hide. Ain't that right?"

Tyler nodded on Randy's shoulder.

Omah

"Going to have to keep an eye on you, you know? Make sure you don't start getting hairy all of a sudden.
Your feet start popping out of your shoes, we'll know you caught their cooties."

Tyler chuckled past his sniffles.

"C'mon...let's get you in the RV, before they come looking for you."

Situated and ready to begin the journey home, Randy turned the ignition, shifted into gear, causing the RV to lurch forward. He pulled out of the space, site number thirty-one, over the gravel and toward the check-in cabin on the left.

Seated in his rocking chair, wearing a black and red flannel shirt beneath a pair of overalls, cradling a tobacco pipe to his mouth, the old man raised his hand in a slow mechanical like fashion, two fingers and a thumb pointed upward with the ring and pinky pointing to the ground. His hardened face solemn, dark eyes squinted behind those thick glasses.

Randy nodded with a slight grin and raised his hand.

By the time they reach Highway 101, Tyler had already begun his stories. Enough to quicken the forty-hour ride back to North Carolina.

Fifteen minutes in, and passing Legend and Tales gift shop, Bev had Randy to stop, said she needed to grab something.

She wasn't gone for more than five minutes when she came back toting something about three-foot-long beneath her arm. Much the same way Mother had carried Tyler over the last few days.

Adam and Brenda waved to Randy from the window. He waved back and tapped the horn. They had already said their good byes, exchanged numbers, emails, and addresses, and promised to visit again when time allowed.

Bev opened the door and climbed up in the passenger seat. The souvenir concealed in wrapping paper. She sat it between the seats and wore a big grin.

"What is it?" asked Andrew.

"You and Jennifer help your brother open it."

Jennifer tilted her head and smiled with curiosity. Tyler bit his lip, his eyes big and gleeful.

"Well go on...see what it is."

Randy looked to Bev and scrunched his brows, she returned his look, her smile and sparkle in those big brown eyes caused his heart to skip a beat. It never failed. She snickered covering her mouth as she watched the kids unwrap it. Randy followed her gaze.

The kids gasped.

"No way!" Tyler said with a toothy mile wide smile.

"Wow!" Andrew and Jennifer marveled.

It was a hand carved statue of bigfoot, much like the eight-foot-tall one outside Adam and Brenda's store.

"Oh, my goodness," said Randy.

Tyler stared into its beady black eyes.

"You should name it," said Jennifer.

"Yeah-yeah...good idea. What do you think Tyler? What are you going to name him?" said Andrew.

Tyler still staring into those eyes, "Omah."

Omah

Myself at the Legend of Bigfoot gift shop in Garberville, which was the inspiration for Adam and Brenda's store.

RANDALL LANE

The wooden carving that Bev buys for the kids

"Omah"

Omah

San Francisco Bay and the Giant's baseball stadium

Randall Lane

Snowstorm just outside Giant Redwood RV Park, that we almost got stuck in on the way back to the Carolina's

🌲 OMAH 🌲

Thank you for reading *Omah!* I hope you enjoyed it as much as I did writing it! If so, I would be grateful if you'd be kind enough to leave a review on Amazon as reviews truly are the life blood of any Author's career.

About the Author

I am a former college baseball player turned writer who thoroughly enjoys the outdoors, whether it be fishing, kayaking, hiking, and exploring new places, or watching a game of America's greatest pastime. I'm an old soul at heart, so I love old music (especially classic rock from CCR, Bob Seger, Bruce Springsteen, or vintage rock and roll from Chuck Berry, Muddy Water's, Elvis, etc) old movies and antique items. I own a Victrola Turntable in case you're not getting the picture yet. I'm an avid reader and writer of Mystery, Horror, and Suspense. I enjoy reading Stephen King, Ted Dekker, Frank Peretti, Thomas Harris, Steven James, C.J. Box, and James Lee Burke to name a few. I also enjoy a fun/inspiring Southern Story as well such as Where the Crawdads Sing. I was a top ten finalist in Inkshares 2018 Mystery/Thriller contest. I am a member of the Horror Writers Association. I hold an MBA from Coastal Carolina University and am currently practicing real estate in Myrtle

Beach. You can find me on Instagram, Facebook, and YouTube to stay up to date with my latest work.

You can find me on Instagram, Facebook, and YouTube to stay up to date with my latest work.

     Instagram: randall_lane31
     Facebook: Randall Lane Fiction
     YouTube: Randall Lane Fiction
     Amazon: Randall Lane Fiction

Other Books Available

If you enjoyed *Omah* then you'll likely enjoy my latest novel *The Reaping* as well. Available on Amazon! The book trailer is posted to my YouTube channel.

Synopsis: Something strange is happening in New England. Over the past 17 years, numerous children have disappeared after each of their parents were discovered brutally murdered and left with taunting notes. With rumors of the man in a black hood who roams the woods at night, to an escaped mental patient from Cushing Island, and a snake handling church with a dark past, veteran Homicide Detective, Laurie Daniels must work through this high stakes enigma to learn who the ghost-like killer really is. The deeper she goes the more she begins to believe the killer may be connected to her past. And a new, horrifying clue emerges... Daniels isn't closing in on the killer, but he's closing in on her. Can she catch him before he catches her?

Devil's Den is also available on Amazon. You can check out the book trailer for all my stories on the YouTube Channel.

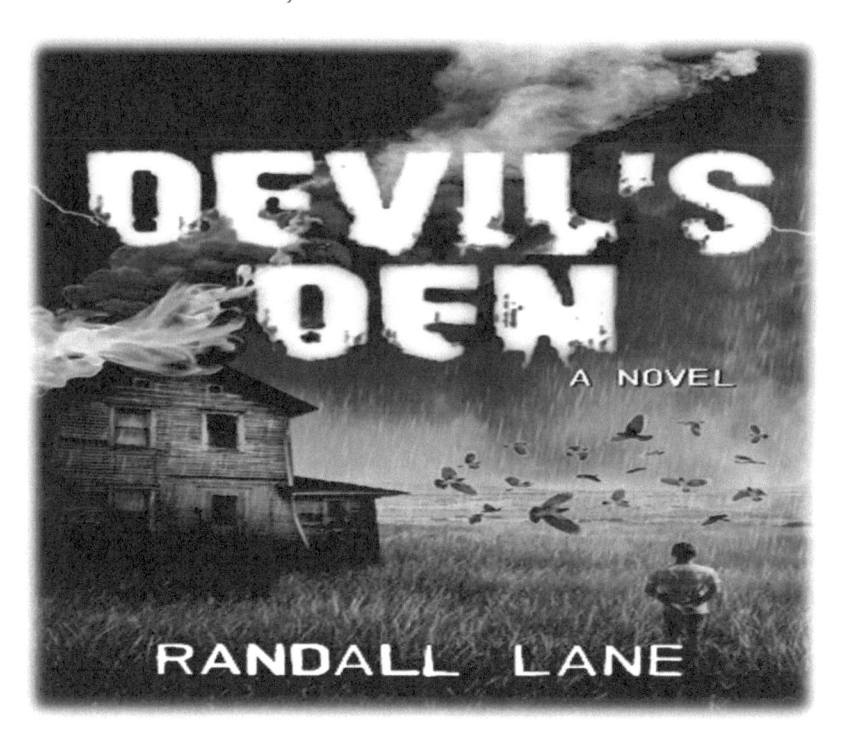

Synopsis. The year is 1989 and as Detectives search for a local serial killer, James and Rebecca Randolph can't help but wonder if it may be Ethan, the new co-worker of James. After causing a horrendous accident at the Georgetown International Paper Mill, Ethan vanishes before further questioning. Locals are quick to term him the GTK or Georgetown Killer. 25 years later, after relocating to Holden Beach, James and Rebecca find themselves once again in the cross hairs of the GTK. As they consult the spiritual guidance of Native American Friends, they soon learn there is a lot more going on than meets the eye. Embarking on a Journey from Darkness to Light, passing through the Devil's Den along the way, they gain a whole new perspective of the saying, "Good vs Evil."

Be sure to check out my collection of short stories titled, *Night Terrors!*

INCLUDES EVERYTHING FROM GHOSTS, ALIENS, BIGFOOT, WEREWOLVES, SKINWALKERS, STRANGE DISAPPEARANCES, AND MANY OTHER CREEPY MYSTERIES.

RANDALL LANE

Inside Look at Chapter 1

of Randall's next Novel

OLD GHOSTS OF THE VALLEY

A NOVEL

RANDALL LANE

OMAH

1

Chapel Valley, NC

October 2023

3:33 p.m.

Carol Gore is a fifty-nine-year-old divorced mother of two, who lives alone up in the backcountry of the Blue Ridge Mountains. She has lived in the same house since the early nineties. She and her husband, Steve, moved to the area after he'd picked up a mining job in the town of Chapel Valley. It was also around this time that Carol learned of the Abbott cult. A co-worker from Piggly Wiggly wouldn't shut up about the sweet little Abbott family and its parishioners, so Carol finally relented and accompanied her to an event at the compound. That was all it took for Carol to become hooked.

As Carol thinks back to the moment she first stepped foot on the Abbott compound, she subconsciously rinses off a few glass plates from previous days meals. Skylar, her white Himalayan cat, is busy weaving in and out between her feet. The tickle brings her back just in time to hear the strange noise. Carol thought she'd heard something earlier but only brushed it off as a play upon her ears. Must be the house settling or something, she'd said to herself. Isn't that what we always say? Or at least what we always hope for, right? What if we're wrong though? What if we're not alone during all the times we think we are? What if someone or something . . . lurks within the shadows and watches without our knowing?

As Carol asks herself these questions, she hears it again. The sound is unmistakable this time. The creaking of a floorboard beneath a sturdy, unwelcomed foot. All day she had fought the eerie feeling of being watched. It seems a presence had been hovering just over her shoulder. She's being too paranoid, she'd thought. Things are different now. To think she's still being watched . . . well it'll just end up driving her crazy. She can't allow herself to go on thinking this way. They would end up throwing her away to the place where people drift along in white gowns, while being force fed medicine and whipped into submission. She'll never go back there. She'd made a promise to herself, and she's determined within her heart to keep it.

No amount of self-encouragement can eat away the growing feeling she has of being watched. It is stronger now than ever before. The home is quiet other than the running of the faucet, and the black and white film playing in the living room. Carol stands frozen with her back to the rest of the kitchen. She looks down to find Skylar staring behind her. Together they listen.

Creeeaaak!

Skylar hisses and enters in a low crouch, his ears flare backward, his hair stands straight. Carol feels someone in the room. She turns just enough, so she can scan the room with her peripheral. She goes over the China cabinet full of Grandma's dishes and scans over the kitchen table. Her heart leaps at the big shadow of a man standing in the kitchen's door frame. She gasps and drops a dish. The crash of the shattering glass fills the room. She fights the urge to look directly at the man, knowing that the chance of her survival will quickly diminish should she see his face.

Skylar emits a low growl and backs up to be between Carol and the sink cabinet.

"What do you want?" Carol asks with her words sticking to her throat.

A moment passes.

"You."

Creeeeaaaaak!

The dark man takes a step.

"Stop. Don't come any closer."

He stops.

She grips the sinks hard enough to hurt her fingers.

"Look at me."

She shakes her head.

"Carol."

Her heart sinks at the knowledge of this mystery man knowing her name.

"Carol. You have to look at me. It's very important."

She clamps her eyes shut and shakes her head again.

She hears him breathe deep. He holds it, then sighs.

"I don't want to do this Carol, but I'm afraid I have to. You're leaving me no—"

Carol snatches Skylar up and bolts through the side door of the kitchen for her bedroom. Heavy thuds pound towards her. She slams the door shut and engages the lock. She rushes to move a chest of drawers against the door.

The dark man slams against the door as soon as Carol slides the furniture into place. The door rattles hard on its hinges. She stumbles backwards with one hand to her mouth, and the other reaching blindly for the bed.

Her heart will surely explode any moment as adrenaline courses through her veins in an icy rush. Her legs meet the edge of the bed, and she bruises a heel against the metal railing below. She winces and bends to tend to the pain.

The door rattles hard once more. Skylar growls again before going into a frantic search for cover. Another hard thud pounds against the door.

As Carol rubs her heel, she begins to hear a faint but hoarse whisper coming from under the bed. The scratchy voice stalls her racing heart and sends her body freezing in place. Movement comes from beneath the bed. It sounds like something crawling across the hardwood floor. Carol jerks herself up and looks toward the window. A sudden thought hits her. What an idiot. Last week she'd nailed the windows shut after fearing someone was secretly entering in the night. In her efforts to keep someone out, she ends up trapping herself in. She must break it. She races over to a nightstand and begins to search for something to break the glass.

The whisper under the bed becomes more audible now. Between the thuds against the door, she can make out the words. It's saying, "Come near my dear."

Carol yanks open a drawer to her nightstand and pulls out a hammer she's used for hanging pictures. She tucks her face into the crevice of her elbow and takes a swing. The window shatters. She rakes away the shards along the seal and rushes over to the nightstand. As she begins to swipe away the clutter, lamp and all, the thing beneath the bed growls loudly. Carol catches a glimpse in her peripheral of a long, bony hand reaching out from beneath the bed, aiming for Carol's ankle. She screams and jumps backwards. The thing continues to growl. Its pale fingers fall limp to the hardwood. Its nails make a loud tapping sound.

Omah

Carol hurries and places the nightstand beneath the broken window. The door thuds again as she climbs upon the nightstand.

She wiggles through the window and falls to the ground. Her hip barks in protest. She grunts and manages to get to her feet. She hears her bedroom door burst open. She doesn't turn back to look but makes a break for the grove of pines.

Running and stumbling her way into the tree line, she pushes away the swipes of bony branches. Her tender feet scream with every poke and jab from the sticks and pine needles. Her lungs burn like they've been doused with gasoline and lit to a flame. Her breath steams into the frigid air. Running between the pines, she retrieves her cell. Moments later she finds the contact she's looking for and places the call.

Panting and glancing over her shoulder, she waits for her son to answer.

RANDALL LANE

Coming in 2024!

Tales from Uncle Joe

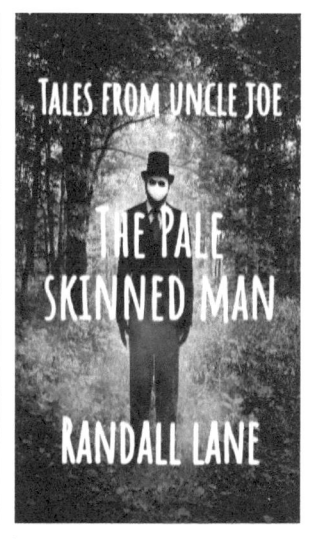

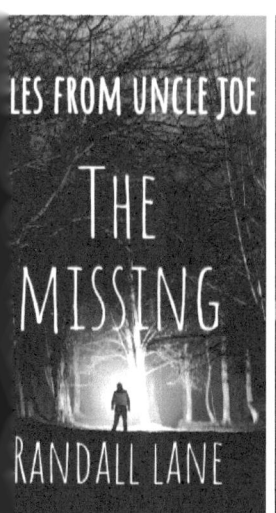

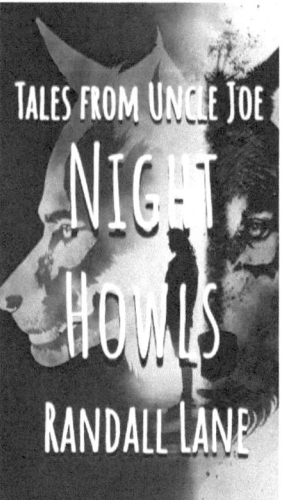

- Blood in the Swamp
- When the Bayou Sings
- The Pale Skinned Man
- The Missing
- Night Howls
- Native Son

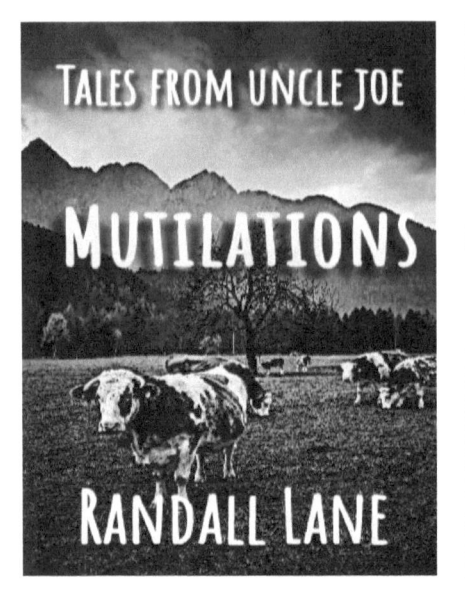

Omah

Tales from Uncle Joe: Mutilations — Randall Lane

Tales from Uncle Joe: It Roams at Night — Randall Lane

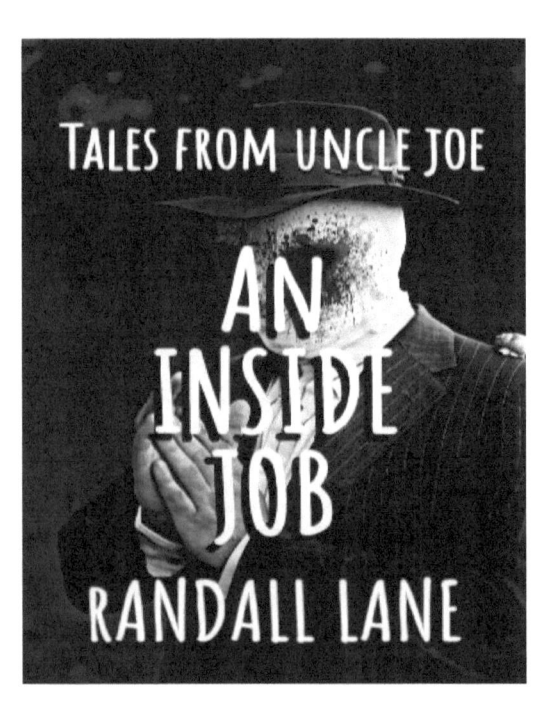

Tales from Uncle Joe: An Inside Job — Randall Lane

RANDALL LANE

Thank you once again for joining me on this journey through story. It was such a joy crafting the Jacob's adventurous tale. From one reader to another, may we all continue to find ourselves as we escape into the written word.

                                Till next time!

                                All the best,

Randall Lane

Made in United States
Troutdale, OR
03/10/2024